Murder in A Minor: Paris

Laurie Stewart and Julie Stewart

Murder in A Minor: Paris

Copyright © 2024 Laurie Stewart and Julie Stewart

All rights reserved.

ISBN: 97 9 8323 916634

The Orchidea Rose Hotel, Paris

September 1996

Monday Evening

CHAPTER ONE

The lights in Le Salon Jazz slowly dimmed until the only light in the large room was the small spotlight on her face as she began to sing, unaccompanied and *rubato* - out of time. The strong, clear voice cut through the darkness with the powerfully emotional, sweet but mournful melody of *"Autumn Leaves"*: *"C'est une chanson ... qui nous ressemble ..."* The level of conversation dropped to silence as Andie sang the original French lyrics, *"Toi qui m'aimais ... et je t'aimais ..."*

The room was full, and as the song continued, the crowd was drawn into the poignant lyrics; the feeling of rapt attention was palpable in the dark. The song was about bittersweet love affairs that leave regret as well as gratitude when remembered years later. The song was requested tonight by a group of friends gathering for a funeral for one of their own, a young filmmaker.

Andie continued to sing, still a lone voice wistfully reminiscing about the disappearance of someone dear as well as the enduring deep affection over time: *"Nous vivions tous ... les deux ensemble ... Toi qui m'aimais ... Moi qui t'aimais."*

She had an ache in her voice as she began a crescendo summing up the nostalgia for a lost love, *"Mais la vie sépare ... ceux qui s'aiment ... Tout doucement ... ans faire de bruit ... Et la mer efface sur le sable ... les pas des amants désunis."*

As the last line ended, Bernard, the drummer, began a soft, slow shuffle with his brushes; Benoit - his twin - played his bass quietly with him; Adrien joined in on piano, and Max started his saxophone solo, which showed the influence of Lester Young while retaining his own original voice. The full band – sax, piano, bass and drums –

accompanied Andie as she sang the song in English for its last chorus.

The crowd erupted in warm applause when the tune ended, led by the long table of mourners who had requested it. Andie bowed to the audience in general then turned to the long table and nodded to the group as she bowed again. They responded with a renewed burst of applause.

She turned to Max and said quietly, "Well, that was a bit of a downer. All I could think of was the dead man. It's already a sad song but that was really …" and she shook her head.

Max nodded and called "*Lullaby of Birdland*"- an uptempo tune they played quick and bright - and gave a look and nod to Bernard who kicked it off with Andie.

When he took his solos, the spotlight switched from Andie to Max, and she had a chance to look at the audience, in particular the table of mourners. There were maybe a dozen of them, all well-dressed and, naturally, quite subdued. They had only been seated for a short time, however, and given the number of wine bottles she saw at the table, Andie expected they would loosen up sooner rather than later.

At the end of the table and appearing to be the head of the group was a portly man with greying temples who appeared to be a doctor or lawyer – serious, thoughtful but with a keen, appraising eye on his guests. His face indicated he was younger than his serious demeanor suggested. He was someone whose precocious maturity had always made him seem older than he was.

On his right was a distracted light-haired woman who could have been in her thirties or forties; she held her companion's hand firmly. He looked North African – perhaps Algerian - and was the same age as the woman and as beautifully dressed. They were both wearing trouser suits of soft wool and silk in shades of charcoal and black - they matched perfectly; Andie thought they must be a couple, perhaps married.

Next to them was an actress Andie was excited to recognize. She was Danielle Dufault, a long-time star of French cinema and a fashion plate; she wore St. Laurent and was frequently photographed with the designer for the tabloids. Andie noted that the star was as stunning as ever and had aged naturally without plastic surgery. She was heavier than in the past, and her blonde hair had gray streaks in it but her face – still lovely - reflected a soulfulness born of experience. She retained her grace and elegance which only enhanced her advanced years; she was a timeless beauty.

Andie was surprised to see the actress's ex-husband, Jean-Paul Toussaint, at her side. He, too, was as handsome as he ever was, and the sight of the reunited couple reminded Andie of their passionate marriage long ago. Back in the day, they were as famous as Liz and Dick in the '60s - too hot not to cool down. A cliché, yes, but this love affair was very French; Marie and Jean-Paul were stylish, chic, and very romantic.

And they were together now, Andie thought. The rumors of his infidelity and their subsequent fights, reconciliations and – finally - divorce seemed meaningless now that they were older and, presumably, wiser. They looked close and affectionate; they seemed to have retained a friendship long after the intense love affair ended.

On the left of the host were an elderly man and woman. Andie guessed they were relatives of the deceased. Aristocratic and reserved to the point of being comatose, they had the good manners to be there and to be there inconspicuously. Next to them were two younger, livelier versions of the elders. More relatives thought Andie. The female of the duo was animatedly chatting across the table to the movie star, M. Toussaint. She was plain-faced and overweight but sparkling, and Jean-Paul found himself enjoying her vivacity.

The young man next to her resembled her too strongly to be anyone else but her brother. Like her, he was a blue eyed, pug-nosed and freckle-faced plump blonde, and right now he was lost in thought, as silent as his sister was charmingly verbose.

Sitting alongside Toussaint was a striking, forty-ish woman. She had curves where she shouldn't with stocky legs and ankles; but she also had beautiful, expressive hands, and she used them profusely to accentuate her words when she spoke. The sight of her bright red nails flashing in the air was mesmerizing, and the extravagance of her gestures matched the overdone makeup on her face which attempted but failed to disguise a slightly sneering mouth and crooked nose. Her coiffure most closely resembled a cement bouffant - large and heavily lacquered - balanced on an unusually small head. A pinhead thought Andie who then chastised herself for being mean.

Across the table from the pinhead sat another couple: a tanned playboy of indeterminate age but closer to forty than fifty, and a striking woman whose face was unlined but whose features added twenty years or more to her appearance: her nose was too large for her face and her eyes were old and jaded - they had seen it all, and it appeared to be carried in the bags under her eyes impossible to disguise with make-up. She wore a beautifully cut vintage St Laurent pantsuit - le Smoking – and it was topped off by her thick, long, bright red waves of hair. Even seated, she was tall and very thin.

The man, who was too handsome with thick, dark hair which was brushed off his forehead in flattering waves, wore the navy blazer and flannel trousers that served as a uniform among his peers because it was almost always appropriate for any occasion. This 'tennis, anyone?' fashion coupled with his deep tan and soft, manicured hands, made him look effeminate and ineffectual compared to the redhead, who appeared strong and capable. Andie sensed they were not a couple, but only seated together as singles at the table.

As the evening progressed, Andie's eye was caught by another figure in Le Salon. A few tables behind the group, a woman was sitting, dividing her attention between the band and the table of mourners. She wore a big lavender hat and a jacket with a high collar and lace ruff; the combination was stylish and *au courant* but also served to cover her face and hair. Andie thought it was a bit like the emperor's new clothes in reverse.

Then the woman motioned to a nearby waiter who came to her immediately. She spoke to him, pointing slightly at Andie, and he wrote something down, left her table and walked straight to Andie.

At first, she was mortified at being caught staring, but when she read the note the waiter handed to her, she was relieved to see it was another request. When Max's solo ended, Andie passed the note to him as she started singing the last verse of the song they were playing.

"*Windmills of My Mind*," he said to the rest of the band: the twins, Benoit and Bernard Moulin and the pianist, Adrien Dubois.

"By special request, we're going to play a Michel Legrand tune," Andie announced to the crowd.

When the song began, Andie could feel the shock of the table of mourners, even if she couldn't see them in the dark. It seemed the entire group gasped. How strange, she thought. What a queer reaction to the tune. By the end of the song, the table had resumed their previous *sang froid* and clapped loudly, while all of them searched the room for the guest who'd made the request. Andie looked for her, too, but the table was empty – she had gone. Even stranger, Andie thought.

******

Tuesday

The next morning dawned with an autumnal bite in the air. Although the previous days had been seasonally sunny and warm, the day of François Desenfants' funeral was a preview of the coming winter with cooler temperatures and a crisp breeze blowing fallen leaves along the ground. The sky was bright blue, however, and the sun leavened the heavy mood of the mourners. Eddie Bancroft, the personable maître d' of Le Salon, had left voice mails on everyone's hotel phone to meet in front of the hotel where he had arranged luxury town cars for everyone going to the cemetery. When they were all accounted for, a limousine pulled up in front of the waiting cars, and a flamboyant figure emerged.

"Darlings!" she called out with her arms spread out in a welcoming greeting, "I'm here!"

She was a colorful, glamorous woman of about sixty years, but she seemed ageless. She wore loose black silk trousers with a matching black silk blouse and a beautifully embroidered purple open Japanese kimono that reached to her calves. The surface of the coat was stitched in gold and silver thread that portrayed a dragon. Around her neck she wore a chunky necklace made of antique Chinese temple bells, and her hair was a thick white bob, the bangs highlighting her big grey eyes.

Danielle greeted her with air kisses, "Celeste, my pet."

Morgana gave her the same air-kiss greeting as the rest of the group nodded their greetings. Eddie heard Bella say, "It's C.C."

He approached Celeste and put his hand out, "I'm Eddie Bancroft."

She put both her hands on his and said, "I'm Celeste, but you can call me C.C. - everyone else does."

He fell in love with her at first sight. She was everything he would want to be if he were a woman. Such style! Such zest!

They all entered the cars Eddie had ordered and made their way to Père Lachaise cemetery, the world-famous burial ground where the Desenfants mausoleum was built shortly after Napoleon oversaw the creation of the world's first landscaped cemetery in 1804.

Père Lachaise had the appearance of a garden that happened to have graves – seventy thousand of them – crowded under the trees and along the narrow streets and walkways in the cemetery. Père Lachaise was a surprisingly romantic cemetery, not only due to the beauty of the lush gardens, but also to the aura of the immortal celebrated artists buried there. The tombs and mausoleums looked like little houses – grey concrete and white marble, highly decorated yet solemn, crowded side by side on the named streets spread over one hundred and ten acres. The monuments reflected very different design aspirations which gave them a disparate, but unique style generic to Père Lachaise. The Desenfants mausoleum was a plain, conservative marble structure housing generations of the aristocratic family. The small group of the late François Desenfants' friends and relations gathered at the tomb to memorialize the man who'd died too young.

He had been fatally burned when his jeep went off the road in Mumbai, India, turning into a ball of fire as it tumbled down a cliff. As a result, there were only charred remains left which his lawyer, Mark Redmond, who was also in Mumbai, identified as François. According to François' last wishes, le Maître cremated the remains in India and had the ashes spread in Kashmir, the site of his last film and a country he had come to love.

The group of mourners here today had all waved him off as he drove down the road after the sumptuous banquet held to celebrate the completion of his latest documentary. As they watched him go around a curve and out of their view, they couldn't have known that within the hour, their cheerful farewell would be their final goodbye to François.

In Père Lachaise, his name was engraved onto the face of a small bronze cenotaph erected just in front of the mausoleum. The design was not ornate, but a simple marble plinth topped by a bronze plaque. With or without his body, not to reference his death on the Desenfants mausoleum was unthinkable, and the elderly man and woman who were clearly relatives of the young man looked satisfied that he was commemorated in proper fashion where they themselves would join him in the not-too-distant future.

The younger versions of the Desenfants elders were carefree with no thoughts of their own mortality; but respectful of the sanctity and honor of their ancestors, they managed to assume the proper expressions of gravitas appropriate to the occasion.

The rest of the bereaved reacted in different ways to the symbolic burial of François - some with tears, some with frustrated shaking of heads – but all of them exhibited some degree of anxiety. The car accident had been sudden and shocking and yet incomplete without a body to bury. Nobody questioned his death, but the memorial gathering at the mausoleum seemed to be an empty gesture.

"It might have been easier if we'd waited longer to do this," his sister Marie-Claude suggested to her husband in a low voice. "This gathering seems surreal, and his death seems unfinished …" she put her head on Hassim's shoulder.

He responded by putting his arm around her, holding her close, and saying to her, "I understand. It was so unexpected – how could we be prepared? We must get through this, and then we can grieve for him in private, by ourselves. It will be fine when we put this -" he waved his arm towards the cold marble block of death, "- behind us."

The two of them walked slowly away from the monument, accompanied by the fiery leaves skittering around their feet.

Celeste was walking with Danielle and Jean-Paul and told them how happy she was not to miss this ceremony. "I had such trouble coming in and going through customs! I was just about to abandon my wardrobe to the officials when they waved me through. Who is speaking today?"

"I don't think anyone is going to say anything," Danielle said disapprovingly.

Jean-Paul added, "I think we're just supposed to observe the mausoleum and say silent messages of farewell."

"Really? Well, that's strange. I don't understand," Celeste commented, shaking her head, "although I suppose if the lawyer set it up, that explains it. Lawyers are not to be trusted with ceremony – they are like accountants: they hardly look up from their papers to notice life is passing by. Well, maybe we can all speak later at a gathering, n'est-ce pas?"

"Yes, and it might be more personal if we are all seated together. We are going to have a bit of a reception at the hotel after we leave here." Jean-Paul said as they approached the mausoleum.

The woman standing in front of the cenotaph was taller than anyone else, and her long, bright red hair – a color that matched the bright maroon maple leaves - contrasting against the all-black ensembles of the others made Morgana Standish stand out, and she said to them in an authoritative voice, "Shall we go now? I'm cold. I believe the hotel is providing us with a high tea in the lounge. Let's reconvene there. We can eulogize François with a highball. That would certainly be the best way to remember him."

She gave a harsh laugh as she spoke the last line. She was an ugly woman, and her abrupt and brutal words only served to emphasize her grim and bitter presence. Everyone else winced as she spoke but started to move away from the small cenotaph, all that remained of their friend. Carter Philip shared their chagrin, but then he sighed with good humor. She just needed a man like Carter to show her how to behave, emphasizing her good features and minimizing the bad. And he knew she had the money to fund a major changeover – it was his business to know. She just needed to relax, and Carter could teach a master class in relaxation techniques.

At the moment, though, Carter Beauregarde Philip, in a black cashmere suit with a merino scarf the color of cantaloupe, focused his attention on Chantal De Caqueray who stood with her back to him, facing the mausoleum. He couldn't see her face and the slight smirk – indicating both humor and mean satisfaction. Instead, Carter marveled at her hat, a shocking pink felt oversize fedora wrapped in a lace veil of the same shocking pink. Her dress was a black wrap-around with shocking pink lapels that was quite flattering to her figure, he noted when she turned around. But the four-inch stiletto sandals in the same color were, well, *de trop*. And the ribbon ties on the espadrille-inspired shoes only accentuated her heavy ankles. In addition to her whippet thin figure, Morgana Standish had style, unlike this lumpy gargoyle.

Some distance away from the group stood a lone figure, a woman wrapped in black including a veil that covered her facial features. She was there for the unveiling of the monument but was not a part of the group. She was rather tall but looked fragile and delicate. But when she moved, it was with purpose. She stood firmly in the background, unwavering and not giving an inch – she radiated power. When the mourners moved down the streets of the cemetery, she shadowed them, following them back to the hotel.

******

Andie and Max slept late in their room at the Orchidea Rose. There was a coffeemaker in the room, and as they slowly woke up with cups of strong, black coffee, they lazily reviewed their performance the night before.

"I thought it went very well," Max offered. "I especially liked the way you sang *Autumn Leaves* - it was powerful."

"Thank you – what a nice thing to say. I enjoyed singing it. But I couldn't shake the emotions I had for the dead man. The request used the term 'young friend' and it was hard not to think of him. Normally I enjoy the philosophical point of view, but to have it expressly dedicated to someone who died too soon, well, …" and she shook her head sadly.

"It can be rough emotionally, I agree, especially if it's personal. But, to tell the truth, I think your feelings of sorrow and regret enhanced the lyrics. Oh, and I meant to tell you, your French was wonderful. No American accent at all."

"Ah, yes, well. I did feel more French than American when I was singing. The lyrics are best sung in French. The English lyrics are insipid compared to the original French." Then she cheered up, "They do have a way with words; this tune is so poetic – it conveys the complicated nature of love lost incredibly well. The French have always produced sensitive and psychologically intelligent writers, don't you think?"

"I agree about the song - not all love affairs end in anger. And I always think of it as a song sung for dead soldiers after a war. It was written in 1945. And you're right - the lyrics *were* written by a poet."

"Pretyman for the win. You are just full of all kinds of esoteric knowledge, aren't you?" she teased him and then shuddered a little, "It seems morbid to me now. Or am I just reacting to this one performance?"

Max nodded reassuringly, "I think that's it. You've never mentioned this before, and we've performed the tune hundreds of times."

He smiled when he spoke, and Andie agreed, "That's true – and I like singing that song. It can be dramatic."

"How about I go out and get us some pastries for breakfast?"

"And a paper?"

Max smiled as he stood up, "Of course, and no, I won't even open it until I get back here."

Andie laughed, "You know, I don't think you've ever started the crossword without me. I don't know why I always tell you not to – you never have."

"Probably projection – it's something you would do."

"Max! I would never."

"Hmmmm. I'll be back soon – there's a patisserie across the street, and it will take just a moment. Don't drink all the coffee."

"Speaking of projection," she smiled.

******

Later that day, they went down to the lounge off to the side of the lobby for tea before a late lunch and then a trip to thrift shops. They were talking to a good friend of theirs, the superb maître d' of Le Salon Jazz, Eddie Bancroft, when the group from Père Lachaise began to straggle into the large, comfortable room. Eddie stood up quickly to greet them, telling Max and Andie he'd come back after he'd seated the others.

The lounge was thickly carpeted and paneled in old walnut with small tables here and there, surrounded by leather club chairs, worn and deeply seated – you don't sit in them, you sink in them, Andie once pointed out to Max. Aged brass sconces lit the room, and a full bouquet of chrysanthemums sat on a grand piano in the corner. The pianist, a young woman, played arrangements based on well-known classical pieces, the lighter works of composers such as Debussy, Chopin and Eric Satie. She played on soft pedal, and her performance was as warm and welcoming as the room.

Eddie had arranged with the hotel staff to reserve tables for the group in the lounge with waiters ready to receive them. He was so charming as the maître d' in Le Salon Jazz that he often performed services usually reserved for the concierge. Guests who met him considered him a friend and preferred asking him for advice and aid when they visited Paris. He had lived there a long time and knew the city well. More importantly, Eddie was both engaging and thoughtful - with a wicked sense of humor.

Eddie Bancroft was born in New York City and spent the first twenty-five years of his life in a privileged home; he attended Dalton, then Putney and finally Columbia College, but his WASP exterior disguised a true bohemian. His mother had wanted to be an actress when she was young, but her status-conscious family refused to underwrite the notorious occupation and pushed her into marriage with a socially acceptable friend of her brother's. When her son expressed interest in an acting career, she was delighted, encouraging and supportive and paid for his extended trip to California.

When Eddie's father found out she had been subsidizing his acting career —or lack thereof — and cut him off, he found work as a maître d' at the very popular restaurant Spago in Beverly Hills. His natural charm and upper-class social skills combined to make him the best maître d' in Hollywood. The owner of the Orchidea Rose was visiting Los Angeles, and when his host took him to Spago, he was so impressed by the stellar maître d' that he poached him from that restaurant, after promising him the world if Eddie would come to the Hotel Rose and work his magic in Paris.

The money was excellent, and the chance to live in the City of Light was too good to refuse so Eddie crossed the pond and embarked upon the best role of his career. His superior education, his ease in society and his genuine desire to make people happy combined to make his new job effortless for him. Most of all, Eddie felt as if he had finally come to his true home in Paris. Although many people assumed he was English due to his clothes and good manners, he felt French to his bones.

Before Eddie reached the group, Andie saw a woman in a shocking pink hat walk from the lobby into the lounge and towards the mourners looking bewildered. When she reached their table, she said to the group at large, "Sasha hasn't even checked in -- he should be here."

At first, nobody responded, but then she repeated, "Sasha isn't here. Where could he be? He hasn't checked in yet."

As the woman slowly took her seat at the table, Danielle asked her, "Wasn't he going to Bali, Chantal? Maybe he decided to stay there a while."

"No, no – he would never miss a memorial for François. Never – *jamais!*" switching to French for emphasis.

"Perhaps he missed a connecting flight?" Bella suggested.

"There are direct flights from Tahiti, and Bali can't be too far from Tahiti," Morgana argued, enjoying Chantal's obvious distress.

"Still," Bella offered, "It's a long trip and who knows how many different things can hold you up? Customs can be awful."

"Perhaps," Chantal murmured.

Eddie reached the table then, interrupting them as he said "Please let me know if there's anything I can do for you. I understand from le Maître," he nodded at Mark Redmond, "that you will be here a few more days, in memory of your late friend. We understand how difficult things can be at this time, so please don't hesitate to let me know how I may help you." As he finished speaking, he nodded and then turned and walked away.

Eddie came back to Andie and Max and took the third chair which went 'oooff' as he sank into it.

"I know you're curious about those guests. Well, it's an interesting story – tragic and a little strange. Do you have time?"

Andie spoke first, "Nothing but. Tell, tell."

"Well, as you may know, they," he nodded at the entire room where the mourners were scattered about, "are here to attend a funeral, of sorts."

"'Of sorts?'" Max asked.

"There is no actual body, so I guess you would just call it a memorial service. And in truth, it was just a visit to the cemetery. But, let me explain," he paused for effect. "A long time ago, in a galaxy far, far away …"

"Eddie!" Max and Andie chorused.

"O.k., o.k., well, first of all, I should say I got all this from the bubbly little blond who's with a young man who looks just like her. They're cousins of the deceased. Her name is Bella, Bella Jardine; she's a chatterbox and told me the tale.

"A few weeks ago, her cousin, François Desenfants, who is an award-winning filmmaker, had finished his documentary about the conflict in Kashmir between Pakistan and India, and he was in Mumbai to celebrate with his investors and friends at a special dinner at the best restaurant in Mumbai. He came from a very wealthy family in France, members of the *ancien régime*, and his investors were similarly wealthy, if perhaps a bit more *nouveau riche*. These people," he gestured toward the others in the room, "were all there. Towards the end of the evening, François excused himself, saying he had to return to his makeshift studio to make sure he had packed all he needed for the final editing in Paris. They all accompanied him outside and waved at him as he drove off."

Eddie took a sip of water and a breath.

"And then he died." Andie deadpanned.

"Well, yes, he did," Eddie retorted.

"How did he die? And why did they 'just visit the cemetery'?" Max asked, steering the conversation back to the specifics of the unfortunate demise of François Desenfants.

"One answer for both: he was killed when his jeep ran off a cliff moments after he left the restaurant and exploded into a fireball as it crashed and rolled down the hillside. He was to die from the burns. His lawyer was there – he had attended the dinner - and he identified the remains. What was left was cremated and the ashes spread in Kashmir. Hence, no body, no burial. But the strange thing is that they all went to the cemetery - Père Lachaise – to the cenotaph installed at his family's mausoleum, but nobody eulogized him. They just stood around and then came back here. I can't imagine why, but nobody spoke a word!" Eddie was offended.

"Well, why do you suppose they all got together if no one was moved enough to speak?" Andie asked.

Eddie shook his head, "Well, that's just as odd. These people were all invited by the lawyer, le Maître - his executer. When the man with the will calls, you answer. He's the distinguished looking man at the end of the table," Eddie gestured to Mark Redmond across the room.

He added, "It all seems *très bizarre* to me – and a little tacky, if I'm honest. I only got involved because his sister," Eddie pointed discreetly towards the woman in question, "came to me as they were leaving the Salon last night. She seemed distraught and when I asked her if I could help, she told me they needed to go Père Lachaise in the morning, and nobody had made any arrangements to get there or where to go. Naturally, I offered to arrange everything the way I thought was appropriate. But I fear my efforts were lost on that bunch. They seem like strangers to each other and to the deceased!"

"Nonsense," Andie replied. "They're probably in shock. You know what everyone says about people grieving differently. And I'm sure you eased the whole process for the family. This is a lovely space for a reception. Really, Eddie, think what a mess it would have been if you hadn't stepped in. The sister seems to be truly sad, and so is her husband. Is that her husband?"

"Yes, he is. He's Algerian and was her brother's cinematographer. Apparently, they were an award-winning duo. So, yes, it must be very difficult for them without him."

"So far," he continued, "I haven't been able to identify all the others. Bella is the cousin who's filled me in thus far. She and her brother grew up in England. Her mother moved there from France when she married a London financier. Her brother's name is Wei Fan" he said waiting for Andie's response.

He didn't have to wait long, "No, it isn't," she deadpanned and shook her head. "That's absurd, and it just isn't true."

Eddie laughed and she joined in.

Just then, Celeste walked into the room after going to her room to unpack before joining the others. Andie gasped a little at the sight of her. "Oh, she's wonderful, Eddie. Who is she?"

"I agree, she is fabulous. Her name is Celeste Colewood, and she was an 'It' girl in the 1960s. She traveled with all the big music acts – the Beatles, the Stones – as well as the most *au courant* painters and writers – Andy Warhol, Norman Mailer – like that. She is legendary. I knew her name, of course, but I have never had the opportunity to meet her before. She is everything I ever imagined and more. What a woman."

"Indeed," Andie concurred. "I hope I get a chance to meet her. I've heard about her too. She looks too good to have gone through the '60s, though." She laughed.

"She never did drugs or drank to excess." Eddie explained. "She would participate, but you never heard horrible stories about her, unlike so many from that time. It could be because of her background - her mother was old money from Connecticut who worked in Manhattan in fashion and media, and her father was an English baron. Not to say that the upper class doesn't have drug casualties, but Celeste wasn't one of them." He stood up, "Well, I'd better check in on the sad sister and her oblivious friends once more. Then I need to run some errands." He adopted a sarcastic tone, "Such grief!" He rolled his eyes. "These people don't seem to have any experience with proper mourning."

"Well, treat them like celebrants," Max suggested. "Maybe that's what they are."

"Hmmm," Eddie and Andie nodded slowly in agreement.

"Ciao, kids," Eddie said as he walked away. He headed straight towards the cousin, Bella, who was waving at him.

"Yes, Bella. How may I help you?" Eddie asked as he reached the table.

"Well, I was thinking about things we could do in Paris while we're waiting to hear the final disposition of the estate, and I realized I have always wanted to see the catacombs. Would you give us directions for a visit?"

"I would be happy to do so."

Bella spoke to the group, "Have any of you been to the catacombs? They're incredible. There are tunnels underneath this city with over six million bodies – an ossuary. They moved the bodies from a cemetery – reburied them - at the end of the eighteenth century, so the bones were already very old when they were stacked up. Part of it is open to the public. I've always wanted to see it - we should all go tomorrow...". Her explanation was rambling due to Bella's excitement, but the others already knew about the catacombs.

Morgana spoke up, "Considering we just came from a funeral, don't you think that's in poor taste?"

"Nonsense - one has nothing to do with the other," Chantal retorted.

Mark Redmond, speaking in his usual serious attorney voice, nodded and said, "I've always wanted to go, too. When you live in a city, you rarely see what the tourist sees. You take it for granted and miss out on the experience."

Carter said, "Well I'm all for it; I've been meaning to visit the catacombs for a long time. Let's go."

"Eddie? What do we need to know?" Bella turned to him.

"I tell you what – I have the day off and would be delighted to take you. I think I know someone else who'd like to go, too. How about we meet here at 8:30? It's cold down there, so bring a sweater. Oh, and be sure and wear strong walking shoes – it's dirty, wet and the ground is uneven. We don't want to have to leave you there if you fall down in the dark," he directed the last sentence to Bella.

Bella's eyes were huge and gleeful when she laughed, "Oh, Eddie!"

Everyone else at the table agreed to meet him the next morning, and Eddie walked away to invite Andie and Max. He knew Andie would jump at the chance to see a cellar full of skeletons.

******

Meanwhile, the mourners were finally relaxing and were ready to reminisce about their late friend, François.

Mark Redmond addressed the table, "Please excuse me, I have other appointments I must keep. I will see you all in the morning, but if you need anything before then, please call my office. My secretary will be able to reach me." He stood up and gave the group a short bow after he spoke and then put his hat on and started to leave the room.

"Mark! Wait a minute!" C.C. called to him. He stopped to wait for her, and she told the others, "I've got to check in with Mark before he leaves. Darlings, I'm exhausted - absolutely fanned out – from getting here this morning, and I need a nap. I'll see you in the music room – can't remember the name – tonight, I expect. Until then, my loves, au revoir." And she joined Mark in leaving the lounge.

Everyone murmured farewells to C.C., and then Bella started the ball rolling, "His parents were our guardians after Mother and Father died, and when his parents died, he was available to help us when we needed him. But we were fine on our own, and we only met Cousin François a few times – my brother Wei Fan and I. We knew he was famous, and we did admire him from afar. We saw his documentaries. Brilliant, just brilliant." Her brother nodded in agreement whenever she spoke but added nothing himself.

"Of course. I never had the opportunity to visit my English cousins. I was always at school when François went. It's nice to finally meet my English relatives," Marie-Claude smiled.

"Oh," she continued, "I'm sorry, how rude; this is my husband, Hassim, Hassim Barkat. He is François's cinematographer." Her face fell suddenly, and she said sadly, "He *was*; I have to remind myself François is gone. Hassim *was* the cinematographer," her voice broke.

Hassim put his arm around her shoulders, and she leaned on him.

Bella spoke, "It must be very difficult. If something like that happened to Fan – especially so suddenly! I don't know what I would do."

Morgana's harsh voice broke a moment of silence, "I must know - why in God's name are you named Wei Fan? You're not Chinese – are you?"

"Oh no. No, no." Fan's voice was quiet. "It's actually an old family name, dating back to the China troubles, you know – the First China War?"

"You mean the Opium War?" Carter Philip asked.

"We don't care for that name," Bella spoke up in a pleasant tone, "the war - for lack of a better word - was about opening China, not drugs," she argued agreeably. "Our family had a direct interest in China at that time. We owned merchant ships. And our ancestor's life was saved by a loyal Chinese man who worked for him. He hid him from an attacking Chinese ship, and our great-great-whoever promised to name his first-born son after his rescuer. Well, he survived, and the first-born son of each generation is named after that man: Wei Fan."

"Extraordinary," Morgana drawled, "Really, I never." She gave a quick toss of her head, and the bright red hair flew back from her forehead.

"It's a bit of a cross to bear," Bella turned to her brother with an approving smile, "but Fan has risen to the occasion."

Fan smiled gratefully back at his sister, "Well, I hardly have a choice, do I? Besides, many of our friends have absurd nicknames anyway, so it doesn't matter as much as you'd think. I'd rather be a Fan than a Nobs or a Poosh."

"Surely no one is named Poosh," Chantal De Caqueray said dryly, "is there?"

"Oh yes there is!" Bella exclaimed gleefully, then added, "And I've been meaning to tell you, that's quite a hat. So … pink!"

"Thank you. It's quite bright, but I think François would have enjoyed the joke."

"Do you?" Danielle turned to ask her.

"What do you mean? Of course, he would have laughed. He had a great sense of humor," Chantal retorted.

"He also had great taste," Danielle said quietly.

"François was many things, and to many people, surely?" Jean-Paul smoothly interjected. "Everyone here must have a story to tell, eh?"

Hassim laughed at the thought, "Well, of course I have many such stories. We had so many adventures when we filmed," he shook his head. "François was special. He was brave and funny, smart and foolish – oh, he was a good friend."

Marie-Claude put her hand on Hassim's arm, "He was a good brother, too. We lost our parents, and he was the only one left. I don't know what will happen now."

Carter Philip asked them both, "What will you do with the film? Can you finish it, Hassim?"

Hassim nodded slowly, "I will have to. François worked with a woman when he edited, and she can help me. I know she will have an eye for what he wanted."

"You don't have to worry, you'll get your money back," Marie-Claude said with some sharpness.

"I didn't mean --"

"It's all right, Carter. Your nest egg is safe," Chantal said, the sneer she tried to hide unmistakable.

"That's uncalled for, Chantal," Danielle rebuked her. "He asked a legitimate question. And I feel as Carter does, Marie-Claude - we just want to see the film. It was almost an obsession with François. He fell in love with Kashmir; the fate of his film meant everything to him. We all want to see it finished, for his sake."

"I'm sorry, Carter. I know you loved François. My nerves are -" Marie-Claude shrugged her shoulders at the same time her eyes filled with tears. "I can't seem to control my emotions."

"Of course, we understand, darling," Morgana assured her. "It's a big shock; it's not something anyone can prepare for – it was so sudden!"

"That's what everyone keeps telling me – I don't know what that means! I cannot -" she dropped her head and shook it, "No. I am fine. It's just the finality – that's what takes the longest to accept." She made a shrug and gave a small smile as she picked up her wine glass.

"I'm not surprised – how painful it must be for you," Bella said. "For all of you. It seems everyone here had love for François."

"Oh, I somehow doubt that's the case for everyone." Morgana said as she sipped her wine. "I mean, we're all only here because Mark Redmond told us to be here."

"Le maître would naturally invite everyone – he is the man François trusted with his last wishes," Danielle spoke up. "And if François wanted us to gather in Paris, then, naturally, we are happy to be here."

"I'm just saying, maybe not everybody is happy to be here. And I have reason to believe François was not as well-loved as everyone is claiming," Morgana replied.

"What are you talking about, Morgana? Or is this just another ploy to be the center of attention? Really, you never stop, do you?" Chantal said to her.

Morgana laughed, "I'm not the one taking center stage. I'm just saying I know --- all right, answer me this, don't you think it's awfully strange that a man whose livelihood depends on a working vehicle would let it fall into such serious disrepair? François drove across the Sudan, through the Burmese jungle, up into the Himalaya foothills – don't you find it peculiar he couldn't manage a curve in the road in a city like Mumbai?" She looked around the table and then added, "And don't tell me I'm the only person with these thoughts," in a lower voice because she noticed Andie was close to the table as she walked towards the ladies' room.

In fact, Andie did hear Morgana's declaration that François's death was probably not an accident, but the result of deadly sabotage. Eddie's right, she thought as she continued walking towards the ladies' room, these people are odd, and they don't seem to know how to grieve. Moreover, her hypersensitive nose for mystery picked up a scent.

At the table, Bella attempted, per usual, to defuse the situation, "Mumbai? Oh, how lovely. We've visited relatives there; they had a really stunning home, remember Fan?"

He cleared his throat and said, "Yes. I recall going to someone's palace, hmm?"

Bella nodded. "It had a lovely park in front – with beautiful flowering trees – brilliant, it was brilliant."

Carter Philip - Carter Beauregarde Philip – thought not for the first time that the English will always throw in 'it's brilliant' when they're at a loss for words. He wondered briefly about Bella. She did have an abundance of energy, but she was also charming and inviting. He enjoyed her company, she seemed genuine, authentic. And if she was in François's family, she must be very rich. He bit his tongue – wealthy, she must be wealthy. He mustn't slip up.

Bella was young. But maybe that was a good thing, he thought. It would be a refreshing change. He might even have children! Then, frowning, he rejected the idea. He could fulfill many occupations, he could satisfy many desires, but he was not a family man. A bridge too far, he smiled.

"What makes you smile?" Danielle asked him.

He regarded a woman he never thought he could meet, much less speak to, "Oh, nothing. Maybe fate, I suppose."

"Ah, fate," Jean-Paul smiled. "So mysterious and yet we recognize it all the time." He looked at Danielle.

She scoffed, "You are too romantic. Destiny is a fairy tale, something you tell children. Fate? It's not real."

"No, you are too cynical," he smiled at her when he said it.

"That's because she's a woman – we have learned more than men not to believe in fairy tales, n'est-ce pas?" Chantal challenged him.

"Ah, here it comes, the suffering female. And a man is the villain, no? Come on, Chantal, you can do better than that."

Both Chantal and Danielle broke into a derisive laugh.

"We are not victims, Jean-Paul. We are the victors – hah!" Danielle spoke with animation and affection.

Jean-Paul smiled in admiration, "That's a good one, Dany. You are a clever girl," and as soon as he said it, he groaned. "I mean to say --"

Chantal laughed, "We know what you mean to say, mon petit. We know before you say it; you are not as surprising a fellow as you think." she continued, smiling triumphantly.

Bella was enjoying the Frenchwomen teasing one of her favorite movie stars. Jean-Paul Toussaint was a long-held crush of hers. He was so handsome, she sighed. And so amicable and mellow, smiling at the ladies and letting them mock him. He was confident, a man who enjoyed being a man.

Jean-Paul threw up his hands in defeat. "I surrender, I confess, I am a man and I think like a man," he said, standing up from the table. "And now I am a hungry man. I must say au revoir. Dany?"

"Yes, I find I'm very hungry, too; let's go eat an enormous meal." Danielle stood up and Jean-Paul helped her into her coat. "A tout à l'heure", she addressed the group, and they walked away.

Chantal also stood up, without a word, prompting Bella to get up from the table, too. First Fan and then Carter followed Bella's cue - like dominos falling in reverse.

******

When Eddie returned to Max and Andie, he asked if they'd be interested in joining his trip to the catacombs. Andie was as excited as Eddie had expected.

"Oh, I'd love to go!" she exclaimed. "I've always wanted to see the catacombs. Yes, we will definitely be there – when do we meet?"

"Here - at 8:15 tomorrow morning – on the dot!" Eddie was pleased at her reaction. It was as if he'd given her a priceless gift.

"We'll be there," she said happily and looked at Max.

"Yes, I'll join your little group of morbid tourists," he assented with a smile.

Eddie laughed at his response and nodded, "I know – I share your feelings, but it is a wonderfully macabre experience. After all, the French invented the guillotine, and they seem to be very comfortable with dead people."

"The Brits were just as savage," Andie interjected, "they were chopping heads off at the slightest provocation."

"Well, I wouldn't say 'the slightest provocation'," Max countered, "There were many plots against the king. It was too dangerous to let treasonous aristocrats live and attract like-minded conspirators."

"Like Lady Jane Grey?" Andie pointed out. "That was one dangerous teenager."

Eddie stepped in to defuse the argument, "I think we can all agree that in the sixteenth century many people overreacted to the politics of the time with lethal results."

"And who came up with drawing and quartering a person? That's just hideous!" Andie was still attacking England, oblivious to Eddie's attempt at peacemaking.

Max shuddered and looked at his wife, "I have to agree with you about that —it's always frightened me how diabolically ingenious capital punishment can be." He shook his head, "I mean, imagine the mind of the person who came up with that; what a monstrous form of execution. Beheading was preferred and requested by those convicted of treason and was considered a favor for those who still had influence with the King – or Queen."

Eddie sighed dramatically as Andie took a breath in readiness for her next argument, "Excuse me, you two. Are we still on for tomorrow?"

"Yes," Andie and Max chorused happily.

Eddie shook his head in amusement, "You must wear strong walking shoes. It's a dirt floor and it's wet and dark down there. Oh, and it's a constant 57 degrees down there – the cold feels colder in the dark and damp. O.k., I've gotta go; ciao, kids. See you tomorrow."

Max turned to Andie, "All this talk of death and dying has strangely made me very hungry. Let's go eat something wonderful."

"Wonderful idea, Max. Let's eat and then go to second-hand shops."

"Works for me," and he put his arm around her as they started to leave.

"Oh, damn! I left my purse upstairs. I'm going to go get it - I don't want to have to talk you into financing my purchases."

"I'll come with you. I may need more money myself for when you 'don't talk me into financing your purchases'. Somehow that always costs me."

They entered a waiting elevator and just before the doors closed, a loud voice called out, "Hold the doors!"

They complied as a tall thin woman with a mass of very red hair ducked into the elevator.

"Merci," she said breathlessly and then looked at them and added, "Thank you."

"Pas du tout," Andie responded.

"De nada," Max chimed in.

Morgana gave a short bark of a laugh, and Max and Andie joined in.

"How did you know we're not French?" Andie asked her.

Morgana lowered her chin and raised an eyebrow very high on her unusually smooth, very white forehead.

Max and Andie laughed again, and Andie put out her hand and said, "Andie Kirkness and this is my husband, Max Pretyman."

Morgana took her hand and said, "Morgana Standish." Then she turned to Max and said, "I think I know your parents – the Pretymans of Sussex?"

Max nodded, "Yes."

"Your mother is quite a gardener – positively famous for it. And I see your father at all the important races; his horses are magnificent, just brilliant."

"I'll be sure to let them know they're not laboring meaninglessly but are appreciated."

"Oh, please do," she replied, fussing with her hat. "Damn thing," she muttered.

Andie wanted to hear more from her since she knew the woman was a gossip.

"Are you here for the funeral?" she asked.

"Funeral? Hah!" she barked again. "I wouldn't say that was much of a funeral, would you? I mean, no body, no burial, no one officiating and most of all, nobody who cares about the dead man!" She exhaled, shaking her head. "No," she continued, "I would not call this a funeral or a memorial – it might be better called a celebration." She smiled slyly at both of them.

Andie felt a chill at her remarks and Max tried to laugh it off.

Morgana looked at Andie keenly to see what her response provoked. Andie was nonplussed and glad to hear the elevator bell ring at Morgana's floor.

Morgana looked disappointed but quickly recovered, "Well, here's the floor. Salut, mes chères," She gave them a little wave as she walked away down the corridor while the elevator doors closed.

"*Quelle femme ètrange, n'est-ce pas?*" Max said facetiously in French.

"A real wackadoodle, as we say in L. A., *ella es muy loco*!" Andie replied.

Morgana chuckled to herself as she walked to her room. Those two kids were cute, and the Pretymans were a distinguished family – how did they produce a musician? She shook her head; what has happened to the nobility? You just can't tell anymore who's who. It's one thing to compose classical pieces of music that may or may not be performed but working in a hotel … well. Nonetheless, they were smart, attractive and talented, and worth the price of admission.

She quickly focused on the other members of François's mourners and the responses to her suggestion that maybe someone didn't like François at all. That should put the cat among the pigeons, she chuckled grimly. She had no doubt the guilty party would crack, and the reveal would be wonderful. She loved drama and spectacular failure – as long as it wasn't her own.

Morgana shook her head as she took her clothes off. So many questions, so many curiosities. Suddenly she felt the familiar painful stab in her heart when the memory of her tragic loss throbbed like an old wound at the advent of a thunderstorm. I miss Charlie so much, she shook her head sadly. Oh, Charlie. Every once in a while, without warning, she would feel the same racking wrench, as if a giant was throwing her around like a rag doll. Morgana still reeled from the death of her husband.

The late Charles Malcolm Standish died seven years ago at the age of seventy-seven when he had a fatal heart attack. He had been a vigorous man in robust health; he still skied in the winter and sailed in the summer. It was unfathomable that he should suddenly be dead.

After his death, his family – Morgana's step-children - asked for an autopsy. They were told he had a previously undetected heart condition, which made the final diagnosis - a heart attack - plausible. The shocking death was so unexpected that the cause of death predictably resulted in speculation and rumor – some of it unkind and malicious.

Morgana never knew a greater loss than the loss of her Charlie. He was always her greatest supporter – he believed in her. She loved only Charlie in her life. She had never loved anyone before him, and she doubted she'd ever find that kind of love again, so why bother?

She only felt bitter at the injustice of the limited time she and Charlie had together. They each had more years behind than ahead of them when they met. After all, he was almost thirty years older than Morgana. He was old enough to be her father, but he was much kinder and more loving than the mean, brutal man who ran the miserable household she escaped at the first opportunity. Her mother was a lost cause, weak and willing to do anything to stop the yelling. Morgana was the oldest and bore the brunt of the physical violence.

She had a sharp tongue from birth, it seemed to her. She reflexively contradicted everything her father said from an early age. It made no sense – not to her, not to her mother and not at all to her father. He used a belt to spank her. It was endurable, and Morgana never cried. He was always too drunk to effectively hurt her, and she used that knowledge to scorn him and make fun of him. Her mother told her she was crazy and would suffer for it someday when she went too far.

"There's no telling what your dad might do – he's filled with hate - and you deliberately make him angry. You've got to stop provoking him, Morg, please!" She pleaded with Morgana over and over again, and finally that day came.

Morgana was dressed for a date and was at the top of the stairs. She had only been on two other dates, and they were nerve-racking and meaningless; she was nervous but defensive, with a chip on her shoulder. She had learned to wear armor over the years, to protect herself. She was tall, skinny and a ginger – the butt of jokes at school and abuse at home. She was sixteen – young and anxious.

Suddenly, her father burst through the front door with his arm around the uncomfortable shoulders of Morgana's date, David Hiller.

"Look who's here, Morg!" Her dad leered at her and started up the stairs, stumbling drunkenly. He was talking to Morgana and looking at her, but his eyes were focused over her shoulder – he was seeing double.

Morgana was furious, disgusted and deeply embarrassed. It was humiliating. She waited until her father was almost to the top of the stairs, and then she pushed him. She hated him with her entire being, and she wanted him to die. He crashed down the stairs and landed with his head smacking the newel post at the bottom.

He was unconscious for a few moments – the happiest moments of her life! - and then he groaned. David, the by now very reluctant date, stood frozen and mute, and Morgana couldn't find words to speak. Her thoughts were too complex to articulate, and her feelings bounced from emotion to emotion. She waved her hand down towards the landing - and her groaning father collapsed on the floor - in a dismissive gesture to David, a sort of a 'good-night and good bye' wave; then she turned into her bedroom to pack. She was leaving.

London was hard on her. She didn't have the looks to get breaks. She had to put in the hours and the hard work – whatever the job, she had to do it better than the cute little blonde just to stay employed. Oh, there were always cute little blondes – the bane of her existence. She began to stockpile resentments in small, imperceptible amounts that caused occasional flashes of bitterness in her demeanor. But she never lost her humor, and she was capable of laughing at herself which saved her and gave her a taste of humanity.

She was ambitious and not surprisingly not at all interested in men. Lacking a personal life, she stood out at her job and was promoted, solely on her merits. She started out as a teller at the Tottenham branch of McCallum Trust. She quickly learned the ropes and was promoted into administration, becoming Asset Manager at Tottenam MCT. Her sterling business acumen raised the profile of the Tottenham bank so much, it was brought to the attention of Sir Charles Standish, the owner and Chairman of the Board of McCallum Trust.

Morgana had reversed the downward slide of Tottenham MCT, and it became the most productive of all the neighborhood banks. Nobody seemed to know much about her; she was at work before anybody, and she left after everybody. She never spoke of her personal life; she was all about business. Sir Charles knew that whoever she was, this woman was someone Sir Charles wanted nearby, preferably just down the hall from his own office.

Sir Charles wanted her to come to London, and he went to Tottenham to ask her. He was delighted by her appearance. He loved her long, skinny body and angular face with its large hooked nose, all topped off with the reddest cloud of hair he'd ever seen. Morgana was very nervous but pleased with his interest, and she wanted to make the most of this opportunity. She kept her eyes down as she walked to her desk across the room. As she turned around the desk, she bumped into it and said, "Excuse me" without thinking. She stood still, and then, after a couple seconds, she laughed at herself. She bent over her waist in hilarity. Sir Charles joined in, and when they stopped laughing, and looked at each other - they fell in love. It was a true *coup de foudre*.

But how cruel to be married for such a short time! Oh, I miss you, Charlie.

She washed her face with cold water, examining her white, flawless skin. She looked tired and had purple shadows under her eyes. The only recourse was a nap – the answers to all her questions might well be in her dreams.

*****

In their room, Andie quickly retrieved her bag, Max put more cash in his wallet, and they went downstairs to leave the hotel to find a café. In Paris a café is always just down the street or around the corner, and in a matter of minutes, Andie and Max were seated outside at a small table waiting to order.

The café was not crowded; there were only a few tables and, judging by the cups of coffee on the tables, these customers would probably be there for hours while they talked, read the newspapers, and then talked about what they had read. Café owners in Paris expected some patrons to spend the entire day sitting at a table nursing a petit cafe or pastis and conversing quietly. It was one of the many charming features of their establishments. And there were customers like Andie who couldn't get enough of watching people walk by as she sat on the terrace.

They ordered omelets, coffee and tea, and Andie looked over her shoulder to see who was seated inside.

"Max!" she whispered urgently, "Look who's here – my mystery lady! And she's with the lawyer!" Then she added, "Don't look!"

Max, in the middle of turning around, stopped to look at her and answered, "You should have led with 'don't look'."

"What's going on?" she whispered loudly again.

"No idea. Especially if I can't look."

"She's leaving!"

Max suggested, "Maybe she's going to the bathroom."

Andie didn't appear to hear him and continued her close watch. Then she saw the lawyer get up and put some money on the table. He started to leave and noticed Andie watching him. He smiled and tipped his hat at Max and Andie as he passed them and then turned and walked up the sidewalk in the opposite direction of the hotel.

"I'm going to the ladies' room," Andie said as she got up quickly. As she expected, the room was empty. I knew it, she said to herself and then returned quickly to the table.

"I knew it, Max – she's gone!"

Max laughed, "Calm down. This doesn't mean anything. She must have gone out the back exit. So what?"

"I think she was avoiding us," Andie insisted.

"Why? Why would she care if we saw her?"

"I don't know but there's a mystery here and I want to find out what's going on."

******

CHAPTER TWO

That night, Andie wore her new-old vintage scarf she bought that day. It was navy blue chiffon with little embroidered silver stars on it, and she was wearing a navy silk trouser suit with a white camisole to show it off. Max called a medium up-tempo swing version of "*Beyond the Sea*" which Andie sang first in French, then with the English lyrics. The groove was bright and comfortable, and Andie felt as if she were bouncing gently on top of the rhythm provided by Benoit, Bernard and Adrien. The three sidemen were tops in their field in France, and Max and Andie were very grateful they had been able to hire them for the Orchidea Rose gig.

The set moved smoothly through jazz classics interspersed with Brazilian tunes which were Andie's specialties. She loved singing in Portuguese, especially to the sinuous and seductive Brazilian rhythms Benoit played on his bass.

Throughout the evening, Andie kept her eye on the group she had come to think of as Eddie's charges.

Her eye was immediately caught by the lovely Celeste. Her hair tonight was a mass of shiny red curls, and her dress was a classic vintage Courrèges 'Mondrian' shift. Instead of the iconic white boots, she wore black Tod's loafers. No wonder Eddie liked her so much – she was something beyond chic. She was sitting with the family, Marie-Claude and Hassim; and Bella and Fan, who wore their clothes as if they were uniforms.

Bella was fresh in her usual Liberty print full-skirted dress, and Fan wore grey pants and navy blazer to no effect at all. "Mother wrote of you in her diary often. You were sort of a heroine to her – someone who was independent and strong."

"That's sweet to hear, Bella. Your mother and I - we had fun! She wasn't afraid of anything, truly. She must have forgotten how strong she was. We went to so many exciting places with exciting people – oh, Bella," she said looking down, remembering and smiling, "We had fun!"

Bella and Fan nodded as Marie-Claude and Hassim huddled in a quiet conversation. They were, once again, wearing similar relaxed pants and tunics in a light knit. Andie realized they were always dressed for comfort and seconded the fashion immediately. Why not always be ready to lie down and take a nap?

At the next table, Morgana was regaling Danielle and Jean-Paul with a story while Chantal was sulking. Chantal wore an impossibly orange brocade dress with a black fascinator in her helmet of hair. Carter looked like an ad in *GQ*. Andie thought it was boring, but appropriate, and she always looked forward to seeing what Chantal would wear next – especially on her head.

Sitting between Chantal and Morgana, Carter attempted distractedly to soothe the former while keeping an eye on and trying to connect with the latter. He was frustrated by a feeling of distance he sensed from Morgana although she sat only inches away from him.

She was dressed all in white in a suit with an exaggerated collar, and her lips and fingertips were bright red. Andie enjoyed watching her, she was quite a creature. Danielle wore a ruby red dress and Jean-Paul was, as usual, sleek and handsome.

Andie was just finishing her fashion critique when Max called "Wave". She waved at him – her little joke - as the band played the intro to the Jobim tune.

The rest of the night went smoothly and at the end of the night, the band was spent but mellow. It was a good night for Eddie's group as well.

When Andie and Max went back to their room, Andie was restless and suggested they go to the spa for a soak. "I'm too wide awake to sleep. I think if I can soak in that warm, bubbly water I can relax – get the kinks out. Come with me,"

Max shook his head, "No, I'm beat. Why don't you go up and soak and I'll start a mystery on DVD."

"Well, I don't want to miss the beginning," Andie complained.

Max laughed, "Andie, it's going to be a movie we've seen countless times – don't worry, you'll be back in time for the ending."

"You're right. Go ahead and start it; I won't be long and we can watch the ending together." She gave him a kiss and changed into her swimsuit and the huge terry-cloth robe provided to all the guests in the Orchidea.

"Don't go to sleep without me," she warned him with a smile.

All the Orchidea Group hotels were equipped with very deluxe gyms and spas, complete with ambient lighting, soft contemplative music, a slight scent of incense, deep carpeting and up-to-date equipment. Andie thought it was ironic that she was in her best physical condition when she was working and living in a hotel. She found herself exhaling when she used her key card to enter the facility. Walking in was relaxation in itself because she knew how blissful the jacuzzi would make her feel.

The large physical fitness center was divided into a gym side and a spa side. As she walked over to the spa entrance, Andie heard a treadmill in use. Andie liked to walk at a little less than three miles an hour when she used the machine, and this loud sound indicated someone running at top speed. She peeked into the gym to see who was trying to outrun the devil.

She was shocked to see Morgana, her face twisted demonically as she pushed herself to her limit. Her entire body seemed clenched to Andie who marveled at the thin pale body with feet flying. She drove herself relentlessly, periodically checking herself in the floor-length mirror at her side and straightening her spine in response. The combination of extreme physical endurance and vanity impressed Andie. She backed away from the scene and walked quickly to the jacuzzi, not wanting to interrupt Morgana at her exercise.

She took off her robe, pressed the button to turn on the bubbling movement of the jacuzzi, and as she sank into the warm embrace of the sparkling water, she wondered if Morgana had any other secret occupations. She wasn't in any way what one would call 'still waters' but she certainly ran deep. Andie shook her head, laughing at her own nonsensical metaphor. Soon, she lowered her head to the cushioned coping and sank into a meditative mood. Wait 'til I tell Max, she smiled.

*****

Wednesday

The next day was sunny and warm, returning to the end of summer as opposed to the beginning of winter. A bright stream of sunlight appeared as a large halo over the group of catacomb visitors as they gathered in the hotel's lobby. All, save Bella, were still waking up, yawning discreetly, while they waited for Eddie. Bella was chattering like an amiable monkey to anyone who caught her eye. Andie was the only one who engaged with her, but she mostly nodded and smiled, no more alert than the rest.

Nonetheless, she was not too sleepy to notice what everyone was wearing. Bella wore a Liberty print shirtwaist again with good, worn walking shoes. Fan wore chinos, shirt and sweater, and he also had good, worn walking shoes. Carter Philip was dressed like Fan, conservative and basic, although he wore what looked like Bruno Magli loafers and his ubiquitous neck scarf, this one a pale yellow.

Danielle and Jean-Paul were predictably chic in almost matching grey trouser suits, and they also had well-worn walking shoes. Andie was surprised; she expected this from Bella and Fan, but Danielle and Jean-Paul hadn't seemed like ramblers to her.

Morgana wore black with big Doc Martins on her feet, which made her ultra-thin frame appear to be on a platform. The sartorially challenged Chantal once again put her own twist on the macabre occasion. She wore a bright, flowery mid-calf dress, and accessorized with a large straw gardening hat, white gloves, and a long, chiffon, white scarf which fluttered around her, responding to the slightest breeze. Her only concession to the visit was her fisherman sandals with socks. Well, those are going to be wet and muddy, Andie thought. She looked as if she were going to have high tea at Buckingham Palace, Andie observed. How silly she is.

Celeste rushed out to join them. "Oh good, I'm not late," she said brightly. She was wearing navy blue canvas overalls over a long-sleeved white tee shirt and had a dark green sweater tied around her waist. On her feet, she wore dark brown Adidas suede sneakers with white socks. Her hair today was a black pageboy bob. I want to dress like her when I grow up, Andie thought.

"Sorry I'm late," Eddie's booming voice interrupted her interior fashion commentary when he called to them as he approached. "I had some issues to resolve before I could leave the hotel. But I'm here now – is everyone else?"

Andie noticed he was followed at a distance by the mysterious woman in a hat. That's how Andie thought of her at this point. Once again garbed in a face-covering scarf and sun hat topping off a dark trouser suit, she was largely unnoticed by the sleepy company due to Eddie's hearty greeting. But Andie noticed her and decided to approach Eddie when they left the hotel.

He commandeered several taxis, giving each driver directions to take the passengers to the catacombs. He ended up in a cab with Andie, Max and the lady of mystery. Eddie had tried to put Madame in a cab by herself, but Andie quickly jumped in, followed by Max, and then Eddie, who felt obliged to join them.

As soon as she settled into her seat, Andie extended her hand to the mysterious Madame and introduced herself, "Hi, I'm Andie and this is my husband, Max."

The woman looked startled and then turned to Eddie who spoke before she could answer, "This is Madame Chausson."

Andie gave Eddie an impatient look and wondered why he was interfering. "She can speak for herself, Eddie."

"Her English is not very good," he retorted sharply, "and I was just getting to the point without translation."

"Oh, I see," Andie said, surprised by the rebuke. Nonetheless, she continued to pour on the charm for the rest of the trip. Her French was not as good as Max's, but she could usually be understood.

Fortunately for Mme. Chausson, Andie's answers were easily answered by nodding and shaking her head. Eddie continued to interrupt, and Andie realized she would have to speak to the woman alone. The catacombs themselves would be the perfect place for a one-on-one with her.

When they arrived at the entrance to the catacombs, they were faced with a spiral staircase descending 131 steps to the limestone quarry over sixty feet beneath the city. The staircase itself was narrow and daunting – almost claustrophobic. At the bottom was a large, cave-like room with an exhibition of the history of the quarry which was turned into an ossuary to re-inter the bones of six million Parisians at the end of the eighteenth century. The cemeteries were overcrowded, and the quarry was no longer used for digging limestone. The quarrymen left marks on the walls indicating directions so that none of them would be lost underground. One of them had created a facsimile of an Italian castle where he'd been imprisoned in the war – a limestone sculpture revealing the artistry of the miner.

After a very quick perusal of the historical background of the catacombs, the visitors saw an overhead notice, engraved in stone at the entrance of the ossuary, read: "*Arrete, c'est ici l'empire de la mort*" - Stop, here is the empire of the dead.

"Maybe we should stop, like the sign says." Andie teased Max.

"This is your expedition, I'm only coming along for the tea and cookies at the end," he joked.

Then they were silent as were the rest of their little band of explorers. The ground was dirt, like the floor of a cellar, and it was uneven with puddles here and there. The air was humid and dank, with moisture gleaming on the bones in the low light from the lightbulbs placed far enough apart to force the visitors to pay close attention to where they were walking. At first, the sight of the walls of bones shocked viewers into silence, but then it was the overwhelming presence of death that compelled quietude.

"This is the only tourist site I've ever visited where people are quiet," Andie whispered to Max.

"Except you, naturally," he riposted.

Eddie addressed the dozen of his charges, "At first, they just threw in all the bones – they made a pile of them. But perhaps to keep them in place, they created walls around the bone piles made up of tibias and skulls. And somebody decided to make these decorative and you can see the designs of stick men and hearts - whatever struck their fancy."

"How lovely!" C.C. exclaimed. "The artistic spirit is unquenchable."

Andie nodded vigorously. Max smiled at Andie, recognizing a new star in her firmament of iconic women. He tended to agree with her appreciation of unique and shining females who lived to their potential. He watched C.C. scamper ahead down the corridor, full of energy and delight in the morbid collection of old bones.

The low ceilings were made of carved stone, going back to when the quarrymen worked in the tunnels. And along the walls of bones were engravings of bits of poems, epigrams and the like, with observations on the meaning of death. Oddly enough, the writings had an uplifting effect on visitors. Typically philosophical, these made death seem both inevitable and inconsequential – nobody gets out alive.

"Oh, look, Max," Andie whispered, pointing to one of the engravings.

'Si vous avez vu quelque fois mourir un homme, Considérez toujours que le meme sort vous attend,' she read quietly.

"What does that say?" she asked him. "I think I know but I know you know."

"*If at times you've seen the death of a man, remember always that the same fate awaits you,*" he answered. "French fatalism."

They continued to slowly ramble down the tunnels. The others in their group were also walking and pausing to read the engravings.

Andie heard a muffled cry at one of the writings. She hurried over but saw no one, only the words "*Elle est horrible, la mort du pécheur.*"

She turned to Max who had joined her, "Why is the death of the fisherman horrible?"

He laughed out loud and then lowered his voice,"*Pécheur* means sinner, not fisherman. An easy mistake to make," he allowed, still chuckling.

And then they both heard a loud sob further down the corridor and quickened their pace to find Marie-Claude weeping quietly in Hassim's arms while Celeste read the words and wept also. Andie looked up at the engraving:

> "*Ainsi tout passe sur la terre,*
>
> *Esprit, beauté, grâces, talent*
>
> *Telle est une fleur éphémère*
>
> *Que renverse le moindre vent.*"

"Ah," Max sighed and translated,

> "*Thus passes everything on earth,*
>
> *Spirit, beauty, grace and talent,*
>
> *Such is an ephemeral flower*
>
> *That is blown away by the slightest breeze.*"

"Oh," said Andie, "how beautiful."

"That is François," Hassim murmured, and Celeste looked at them and repeated through her tears, "*Oui, c'est vrai* - that is François."

"Yes, of course," Andie agreed.

In front of them was an enormous barrel-shaped floor to ceiling column of bones and skulls. They stopped suddenly at the sight of it, and gasped.

"It's called the Crypt of Passions, and those are ankle bones among the skulls," Eddie told them. He had suddenly appeared beside them.

"Oh, Eddie, you gave me a start." Andie exclaimed.

Celeste chimed in, "Yes, I agree. I thought you were the Grim Reaper. You scared us!"

"Pretty easy to do down here," he answered her with a grin.

"Indeed," Max said to him.

"By the way," Andie said to Eddie. "Where is Mme. Chausson?"

"Oh, she's around here someplace," he said quietly.

"Why are you keeping her from me?" Andie was nothing if not direct.

"I'm not --"

"Yes, you are." She was insistent.

Eddie hesitated and then, realizing he wasn't going to be able to come up with a plausible explanation, said to her with a sigh, "I can't tell you here. I'll fill you in later, back at the hotel."

C.C. watched them both keenly throughout the exchange. Max tried to distract her attention, "I think you may have baby-sat me when I was a child. Do you remember the Pretymans in Sussex?"

C.C. turned away from Eddie and Andie and said "I don't think I ever babysat any child - ever. I did babysit Keith Richard once when he appeared to overdose, and I babysat many girlfriends who drank too much, but children? I should say not."

Max nodded.

Then Celeste turned to him and asked, "The Pretymans? In Sussex?" She gave a short laugh that sounded like little ringing bells, "I do know you! I remember a dance – a ball – at your home. It was lovely. I came with my parents who were friends of your grandparents. I met your father – he was very handsome but already moon-eyed over your mother. I don't think either of them ever considered anyone else romantically. It really was a heavenly night for me. I think it was the last time I went out with my parents to a party." She gave him a warm smile, "Why you're practically family!"

In the meantime, Andie wasn't happy being put off by Eddie's evasions about the veiled lady but knew there was nothing she could say to change his mind. She was happy to at least get an acknowledgement that he was trying to keep her away from the mystery lady and would explain later.

They continued down a long pathway which had the appearance of being literally endless: with no exit in sight, there was only darkness; the vanishing point was as frightening and unknowable as death. Out of the corner of her eye Andie saw what she believed to be white doves fluttering in the distance.

"Max, look!"

"What?"

"I thought I saw doves at the end of this tunnel, just before a curve."

"Andie, I doubt very much there are birds down here."

"Of course, there couldn't be, right?" she answered doubtfully. "But what did I see?"

"Very small ghosts."

"Oh, Max."

She noticed she and Max were alone again. Celeste and Eddie were either in front of them or behind them. It was hard to keep track of everyone in the dark tunnels. There were lightbulbs wherever there was an inscription, but they were strung far enough apart that they didn't light the corridors sufficiently. It always seemed as if one was walking into darkness.

Morgana had gone ahead of everyone. She was not as fond of the catacombs as the rest of the group and only wanted to get out. She found the inscriptions morbid, and she was especially unhappy with the one about the terrible death of a sinner. First of all, everybody is a sinner, she rationalized - it's only a matter of degree. Certainly, a murderer's death must be worse than a pickpocket's. It's probably a Catholic's argument for confession. Well, she was not a Catholic and had no need of confession. She could live with her little sins; she had no need for confession.

But there were others – at least one other that she knew of – who needed to get down on their knees and beg for forgiveness. Not only the ones who had hurt and damaged her, but the ones who committed mortal sins against innocent victims. Morgana wondered if she had ever been innocent, but she believed all babies are born without sin and at one time, she had been a baby, too. So long ago, she sighed, so long ago.

The group had been underground for almost an hour at this point, and they were scattered throughout the tunnels. Andie and Max seemed to have fallen behind the others due to their attention to the writings. Behind them, Eddie had paused for longer than usual in front of one of the engravings.

Andie saw his head haloed by the dim light behind them and walked back to him where she read:

"*Ou est elle la mort? Toujours future ou passée.*

À peine est-elle presente, que deja elle n'est plus."

Eddie looked at her and said: "'Where is Death? Eternal in future or past. As soon as she appears, she's already gone.'"

She sighed, "These are wonderful observations. The French seem to have a way with death. But I have to wonder why death is a woman. That doesn't seem fair."

"Hmmm," he answered.

"You know," he continued, "Robespierre and Danton are here, somewhere in the pile."

"It's so wet – and they're not turning to dust. Some of these are centuries old – do bones in the ground last as long as these?" Andie had a lot of questions. "I mean, don't we all go 'ashes to ashes, dust to dust'?"

Eddie and Max both smiled indulgently at her, and Eddie answered, "No, sweetheart, that's just a very poetic way of saying we go from nothing to nothing."

"Well, this is something," He gestured to the wall opposite them. "The leg bones and skulls had been arranged to form a heart."

"Yes, and Max and I saw some other figures and forms – it's so strange to see artistic expression down here."

"Well, look at all the poetry and epigrams written on stone down here," Max suggested. "It seems to have moved a lot of people to say something about death. Perhaps the workers were also moved, and they felt compelled to transform the hideous bones into something beautiful"

Eddie shuddered, "I could never have worked here. I cannot imagine how horrible it must have been to be digging up and carrying and tossing human skeletons – good God!" Then he laughed, unexpectedly. "I just thought of Peter O'Toole singing 'the hip bone's connected to the thighbone' - hilarious."

"Yes!" Andie cried and then, noticing how loud she was, she lowered her voice, "That was an excellent movie."

"Oh," Eddie perked up, "I just remembered something about the process of the bone re-internment. They moved the bones at night, and priests performed a ceremony which included their singing as they walked to the catacombs." He watched Andie as he said this.

Her eyes grew wide, as he'd expected, "What a scene – what a scary scene! The chanting and swinging those metal incense globes, with hooded cassocks!" As she spoke, Andie grew more excited, nonetheless keeping her voice quiet.

"You're going to have a nightmare tonight," Max admonished her, laughing.

She laughed in response. "I know," and turned to Eddie, "You are deliberately winding me up."

Eddie laughed "It's so easy, Andie. You know I love you. And I didn't make that up, it really happened. I mean, after all, the French were not animals – they were humanists, weren't they?"

"Philosophers, absolutely," Max said. "Some of the greatest minds of the time were dedicated to philosophy. That's why Paris is called the City of Light – it refers to the Enlightenment".

"And the French have a wonderful authority in their voices, don't they?" Eddie pointed out. "Is it the language? Or is it the people speaking the language? Which came first?"

"Oh, I don't know, maybe they just like to hear themselves talk," Andie smiled when she said it. She knew she was a Francophile and tried to temper her passion whenever possible.

"You are a funny girl, Andie," Eddie smiled as they kept walking down the ghost laden corridors of skulls and bones.

Bella and her brother were taking their time but only to closely regard the bones. They were not as interested in the French writings. Neither Bella nor Fan spoke much French, but they were both fascinated by the arrangements of bones.

"Do you suppose they were always aware they were stacking bones, or do you think they eventually regarded them as simply building blocks?" she asked Carter Philip who had been discreetly hovering in the background.

"I should think the latter," he suggested. "I suppose it was the only way to deal with what they were doing. After all, who could handle the remains of so many human beings without distancing themselves from the reality of what they were doing?"

"I suppose so. Fan, what do you think?" Bella turned to her brother who was closely examining the skulls and leg bones that made up a decorative section of squares and crosses.

"Oh, I think so, too. It's too ghastly, just too horrid otherwise. Unless, of course, the workers were all sociopaths."

Bella laughed quietly, "Well, we don't know how they got the job. Did they volunteer? Did they raise their hands and beg 'me, me, choose me – let me move the bones'?"

Carter gamely joined the siblings' amusement, but he felt intimidated by their easy familiarity with death. Although he was uneasy in the suffocating tunnels of bones, Bella and Fan seemed delighted by the macabre display. A little insensitive, he thought, but maybe it was the same enjoyment of morbid curiosities often found in children.

Behind them, Danielle and Jean-Paul were closely reading the engravings,

"Jean-Paul, you read Latin, don't you? What is this?"

"*Omne crede diem tibi diluxisse supremum; Croyez que chaque jour est pour vous le dernier.*" Jean-Paul read out loud.

He turned to Danielle, "Well, the translation is in French already - 'think that every day will be your last'."

Danielle nodded, "Ah, I see. Look - it's Horace. Did you study him?"

Jean-Paul laughed, "Dany, I studied many things, and most of them are lost somewhere in this old grey head."

"Cher," she cooed softly, "If you are old, then so am I, and I am not old yet."

"You will never be old," he assured her.

"Where is that woman with the hat? I want to see what she's wearing today," he asked Dany.

"Oh, she is the most loathsome creature – I avoid her when I can. I believe she left before we did, but I'm sure she's here somewhere. Just look for a big gardening hat – that's what she's got on today. You can depend on her to always be inappropriate. A gardening hat for the tombs!" She scoffed derisively. "She is an awful woman." She turned away from Jean-Paul in a huff and walked quickly away.

Jean-Paul caught up with her and asked, "Why are you so angry with this woman? It seems out of proportion to her bad taste, *n'est-ce pas?*"

Danielle stopped short and answered him, "She fell in love with her gigolo! Who does that? An American, maybe – but not a Frenchwoman. A gigolo is not *l'amour véritable*, is it?"

"*Non, mais nous avons l'amour véritable, oui?*" Jean-Paul smiled.

"Oh yes, Jean-Paul, we do have a true love. Once you are old – as we are now - then you discover what is real."

Soon, Bella, Fan and Carter caught up with them in the corridor. Everyone muttered greetings and mingled for a time, discussing what they'd seen and how they felt. Then the group split up again as they all disappeared in the dim light. Andie, Max and Eddie remained behind, examining the poetic sentiments inscribed on stone as well as the signs indicating from which cemetery each group of bones came from. There were also street signs, and Eddie told them he didn't know if they referred to a road above ground or were specifically for the tunnels.

"After all, it was very easy to get lost down here. We only see the small portion open to tourists –it's a labyrinth of two hundred miles of bones down here. And there are caves and rooms and pools: one wrong turn, and you could disappear forever." he shook his head, "As I said, for me this would be the worst job in the world."

"Amen," Max agreed.

In front of the group, walking quickly, was Morgana. She found the catacombs increasingly oppressive and the excursion heavy going. It was hard to breathe the thick, humid air, and she kept stumbling into puddles in the dark. She was slowly beginning to feel the stirrings of claustrophobia and tried to walk faster, still stumbling on the uneven floor in her giant shoes. She felt like she couldn't breathe and that she was going to hyperventilate if she didn't get back into the sun and air outside this mass grave of bones.

Worst of all, she was certain there was someone following her. It wasn't another tourist, she was sure. It was someone specifically trailing her, Morgana. Whenever she slowed down, the padding footsteps behind her stopped. She tried to pick up her pace, but it was impossible. The only way she could navigate the bumps and puddles in the floor was to go slowly, but it was maddening when someone was stalking her. Finally, she saw the stairs leading out of the ground up ahead and rushed forward to the very faint light.

She tried to run up them, but there were almost as many ascending stairs exiting the catacombs as those descending to enter it. Her legs were already tired when she'd started running up the steps, and now her feet felt as if they were encased in concrete. She wished she could run up the steps like a cat – basically flying, barely touching the ground. There was no doubt someone was not only following her, but chasing her, and now beginning to catch up with her.

When she slowed the pace for an instant to take a breath, she noticed the sound of footsteps was fainter, but it returned as soon as she started to run again. And this person was much closer. She looked around desperately, but below her it was too dark to see anyone. Still, she could hear the footsteps getting louder.

There were so many steps, she was gasping for air. She started to sob; she wasn't going to make it, oh, my God, please, please God ---

Suddenly she felt something on her ankle. Before she could turn around, she slowly but surely lost her balance, and flailing her arms in an attempt to regain her footing, she fell backwards and tumbled down the stairs. She let out a scream before she went silent.

*****

Andie, Max and Eddie caught up with Celeste who was ahead of them and had paused to wait for them after she heard a scream.

"For a moment I thought I'd taken a wrong turn and was lost, and then I heard a scream. It's silent now, but I know I heard a scream. I couldn't hear or see anyone until you showed up – I was so happy to hear your voices. It's not a place to be alone," she shuddered dramatically and linked her arm in Andie's who was thrilled by the familiarity.

When they arrived at the bottom of the stairs of the exit, they waited for the others, but after fifteen minutes they concluded the rest of the group must have exited already.

"I saw almost everyone pass us in the tunnels. Well, except for Mme Chausson," she looked at Eddie as she spoke.

"I think she may not have come down; I think she looked at the museum at the start and then decided to skip the ossuary."

"Really? How do you know that?"

Eddie turned and addressed her in a serious tone, "Andie, I try to look out for everyone. And I don't always feel I have to keep you up to date."

Andie blushed at his rebuke. "I didn't mean to offend you, Eddie."

"No, I'm sorry – I was thinking of something else. I didn't mean to offend you."

Max laughed, "Oh, come on. Is this one of those 'after you, no, after you, no, I insist, after you' routines?"

Eddie smiled at Andie, "I think it may be."

Andie smiled back, "I'm sorry to keep bothering you about Mme Chausson. Sometimes I cross the line from curiosity into rudeness."

"No," Max said with exaggerated wide eyes. "You don't say."

Andie mimed smacking his head and they all laughed.

At that point, Chantal joined them. "That was one long walk, n'est-ce pas?"

Andie immediately looked at her shoes – she couldn't help herself. "Wow," she said to Chantal, "your feet are completely covered with mud – what a mess."

Chantal agreed with her, "I knew when I got dressed this morning these would end up covered in dirt, but they're the only flat shoes I have."

"You'll have to throw those out, darling – don't you dare leave them outside your door. They don't even look like shoes anymore," C.C. added.

"Let's blow this joint, eh?" Eddie said.

They started to climb the long stairway and as they reached the top, they heard the noise of a large crowd. When they came outside into the light, it took a couple minutes for their eyes to adjust to the bright sun. They noticed Bella and Fan crowded with others in a small group. As they approached the knot of onlookers, they also saw policemen who were trying to make room around something on the ground.

"Oh my God! It's Morgana!" Andie cried.

Bella turned at the sound of her voice. "Oh, Eddie – something horrible has happened – Morgana is dead!"

"What happened?" Max asked.

"We think she fell down the stairs. Her body was halfway down when Fan found her, and the police carried her up here. She must have tripped and fallen." Bella informed them. Then she brightened as she repeated, "Fan found her! He's the one who first came across the body." She seemed quite proud of her brother.

Fan looked bashful, as if he'd been awarded a prize he didn't deserve but was very glad to get. "It was horrid, actually. She was spread out all over the stairs – you know how tall she is."

"Was," Bella corrected him.

"Yes, well, she was like a great big – enormous! - crow collapsed on the stairs. Really something, I say." Fan shook his head.

"What are the police saying?" Eddie asked them.

"They're not telling us much. They seem to think it was an accident, but we don't really understand them. Fan and I are horrible at languages." Bella laughed self-deprecatingly. "But they told us they will need to speak to all of us from the hotel because we know her. At least we know her more than anyone else around here."

"Do you know her family?" Andie asked her.

"No - not at all," Bella laughed again.

Andie wondered at her ability to enjoy herself in the worst circumstances. She was always cheerful, laughing at anything – what was initially charming was beginning to wear on Andie. Where was her sense of grief? Their friend – or at least traveling companion – was dead; without warning, she was gone forever.

Just like François, she suddenly thought. These people were either exceptionally accident prone, or something else was going on. She pulled at Max's sleeve, "Max," she whispered, "I think this is very peculiar. This is the second person in this group who has had a fatal accident. I think something is afoot!"

Max turned to look at her, "'Afoot'? Pray continue, Sherlock."

Andie looked at him quizzically and nodded emphatically, "I know - why did I say that? Where did that come from?"

"Elementary, my dear wife, Sir Arthur Conan Doyle."

Andie shook her head, chuckling. "I really do have a mystery addiction, don't I? Is there a rehab for that?"

"Not yet but give it time."

Eddie walked up to them and interrupted, "Well, she's not dead after all. Thank God. She is unconscious, however, and will be taken to the hospital."

Andie, Max and Celeste all said "That's a relief" or words to that effect.

Eddie continued, "Look, I've got to get back to the Rose. The police are going to want to know as much as possible about Morgana and I need to look over the paperwork for this group. I'll need to contact le Maître, Mark Redmond. I think that's his name. Oh joy", he continued sarcastically, "ever since they got here, this group of people have been nothing but death and misadventure. What's next?"

"Or who's next?" Andie replied eagerly.

Eddie stared at her, and then at Max, "Well, that's an odd way to look at it. And why do you look so gleeful at the possibility?"

"I'm not looking forward to it, but these people do seem to be in danger, don't they? This is no coincidence," Andie protested.

Max spoke up, 'You know, Eddie, she has a point. What are the odds?"

"Look, I've got to run, but I'd like to discuss this later - as in never," he said dryly. But he had enjoyed spending the day with the two musicians and was looking forward to seeing them later in Le Salon Jazz.

"I'll see you kids later," and he air kissed them both before walking ahead briskly to hail a taxi.

"Hang on, Eddie!" C.C. called to him, "I need a lift."

Nothing would please him more than to do a favor for the charming Celeste, and he gladly obliged.

"I'd like to go, too, Max," Andie said. "We've been on our feet all day and I'll be on my feet all night so …" she smiled with a little shrug. "I've often thought I would like to get a sort of invisible chair – maybe plexiglass! - to put on stage so I can rest when you take a solo."

"You're not moved? To dance? To sway to the music? Really?" He feigned shock and outrage.

"I can sway sitting down - it's a gift. Come on, my legs really are tired, and I'd love a long bath." She added, "You know, it's a big tub."

"I'm already there," Max said as he hailed a taxi.

*****

Bella and Fan spoke to the police at the greatest length because Fan had found Morgana. When they approached Danielle, she was immediately accorded great deference; she had been the face of

Marianne at one time; every Parisian – *tout le monde* - knew her face. The police were just as impressed by Jean-Paul who had famously starred in several movies as a police detective. He was a hero to them.

Danielle explained to the inspector that she and Jean-Paul had arrived after Morgana was discovered on the stairs and had seen nothing else – no one passed them going either way, as far as they could see in the dark corridors. They had nothing to offer the investigation, and they had only met Morgana at the banquet in India and saw her again the day before. The police were delighted to excuse the glamorous couple and send them on their way. Jean-Paul was particularly friendly and left the gendarmes positively glowing with satisfaction as they waved farewell, as if to an old friend.

Carter Philip left the scene as soon as Fan found the body of Morgana. His immediate thought was to avoid speaking to the authorities. He had never found any dealings with the police to be beneficial, and in fact they usually cost time and money. So, over the years, another ruling principle of his life was developed: never volunteer to speak with the police. As a professional social climber and would-be playboy, he had set for himself necessary rules of behavior. In order to project an image of wealth and family connections, he had learned names of aristocrats with a very large number of relations and schools in the U.S. known for educating rich ne'er do wells. He had made many visits to museums to learn who the donors were; he studied *Tattler, Town & Country* and *Country Life* for the names of debutantes. And widows.

He was not a fugitive from the law, but his constant travel and dependence on the wealthy friends and acquaintances he assiduously sought precluded a permanent address, and he had learned that this was a red flag all over the world to the authorities. He was not a con man, but he was not independent - a status which gave him no security or stability. He was beginning to get down to the serious business of courting a wealthy wife. He noticed the invitations for dinners and vacations to fulfill the role of the extra man were declining. He was no longer fresh and there were always other young men on the make right behind him. He needed to focus on one susceptible woman to secure his future.

He had had hopes of building a romance with Morgana who was definitely his type - a rich widow - but she seemed to be impervious to his charms, as the expression goes. She hardly glanced at him when he tried his best to attract his attention. Now that she was unconscious and perhaps out of action, he realized he was just wasting his time featuring her in his calculations. The best candidate at this point was Bella, although she seemed, if not sophisticated, nobody's fool. Still, he was running out of options. Best make a good impression tonight, he thought. Perhaps she would need comforting after the traumatic incident this afternoon – that would be a good way to insert himself into her life. He needed her to depend on him, not Fan.

*****

The police finally told Bella and Fan they could go home. Bella was enjoying the attention from both the police and the crowd of onlookers and was reluctant to return to the hotel, but Fan had had enough of the spotlight.

"Bella, please," he said to her quietly, "I want to leave. We don't need all this -" he gestured to the noisy crowd, "this is unseemly, vulgar – please, we need to go."

She reluctantly acquiesced and the two of them hailed a taxi. As they got into the cab, she said, "Fan, I'm sorry. I felt as if I weren't in control of myself. It was as if I were in a whirlwind – it was strange – and I was getting swept up spinning into the sky."

Fan looked alarmed, "Bella, I hardly recognized you. You didn't seem to be yourself."

"I know – that's what I'm saying. When I heard your voice, it was as if you were on the ground and I was at the end of a rope in the air – like a balloon - and you pulled me back down to earth. I don't know what would have happened if you hadn't been there."

Fan nodded, "You need to be careful. When you were talking to the police, I didn't know what you were going to say. You were going on and on … I was so afraid of what you would tell them."

"It's all right, Fan," she said quietly. "I know better than that. I'll be good." She patted his arm. "And isn't it nice that Mrs. Standish is still alive after all?" She shook her head, "She really looked dead, though," sounding a little disappointed.

"Yes, it's nice," Fan answered perfunctorily; his thoughts were elsewhere, lost in contemplation.

CHAPTER THREE

That evening, the mood in Le Salon Jazz seemed a little less energetic than usual. Max, Andie and the rest of the band recognized it as soon as they started to set up onstage.

"They need to wake up, non?" Benoit asked.

"*Mais oui*! And I'm too tired for heavy lifting," Andie replied.

"Maybe a big, loud drum solo?" Bernard asked with a grin.

"What was that surfing song with the drums? *Wipe Out?*" Andie asked.

None of them knew the tune, and they all looked at her blankly.

"Moving on ..." she said drily and laughed.

Max called out *"That Ol' Black Magic",* and the band hit it and hit it hard with Andie front and center singing against the swinging rhythm section. The musicians were tight and flying, and it seemed to them that the entire audience did sit up when they heard the tune. From then on, the set built a nice momentum song by song so that by the time they took their break, the band was feeling good.

"Wow," Benoit exclaimed, "Hot sauce," as he waggled his hand and blew out of his mouth.

They all laughed. It was going to be a good night after all.

The night proceeded in a similar fashion, and everyone's expectations were satisfied – those of the audience as well as the band's. By the third set, everyone who had been at the catacombs was in the Salon – except C.C. Andie couldn't help keeping track of them all. If nothing else, she thought, I'm making sure no one has suffered an 'accident' since we got back to the hotel – unless that's why Celeste wasn't there. She put the thought out of her mind, however, believing C.C. was invincible.

Chantal, looking worried and anxious, was sitting with Marie-Claude and Hassim who both appeared to be offering comfort to her.

She was wearing a surprisingly subdued caftan-styled dress in navy blue and was hatless. However, should anyone not recognize her, she wore sequined, four-inch tall platform shoes.

"Why hasn't he called me? Wherever he is, he can call me, don't you agree?" she asked Marie-Claude.

"We can't speculate, Chantal. There is no way to know what's going on, so you need to try to stop worrying ..." As soon as she said it, she knew it was pointless.

As if to prove the point, Chantal interrupted her, "Stop worrying? Just like that, I suppose. Sasha has disappeared off the face of the planet! All I *can* do is worry!"

Hassim tried to calm her and spoke in a quiet soothing voice, "Chantal, Chantal, we only want you to feel better. Perhaps we don't express it well ---" Marie-Claude made a small huffing noise and rolled her eyes ---" but we want to be helpful, we do, Chantal."

Hassim had taken her hand as he spoke, and it seemed to have a positive effect on her.

She gave him a little rueful smile and thanked him, "Merci, Hassim." Then she drank her brandy and caught the eye of the waiter. He quickly brought her another brandy.

Whatever works, Hassim thought.

Andie watched them and wished she could read lips – not for the first time. She turned her attention to the rest of the room. Danielle and Jean-Paul were sitting close together at a table in a dark corner of the room. They looked beautiful lit by candlelight. Andie couldn't help but hope she and Max would look as loving and comfortable with each other when they had been in love as long as Danielle and Jean-Paul.

"I hate to worry you, Jean-Paul," Danielle said. "Please trust me when I tell you I have considered all the possible outcomes, and I am not at all afraid. I don't want to add to your burdens."

He looked at her with an eyebrow raised, "You could never be a burden, Dany. You are a part of me. If you have a problem, I have a problem – that's all. It's not a burden. It's just something that has, oh how to put it? It's a new element in my mind – that's it. A new element."

"You love to talk, don't you?" she chuckled and kissed his cheek.

"You love to listen."

Jean-Paul beckoned to the waiter and asked him to invite Andie and Max to join them on the next break.

"What a lovely idea," Dany said approvingly.

"They are bright and lively – I think they bring a lot of joy with them," Jean-Paul mused. "And their music is sublime," he added.

Max and Andie were happy to join them, and Andie vowed to herself not to be starstruck in their presence, although she knew that would be difficult.

Danielle and Jean-Paul stood up when Andie and Max reached their table; Dany to kiss them both on their cheeks and Jean-Paul to shake their hands vigorously. Jean-Paul offered them wine which Max accepted - "Just a glass, merci" - and Andie declined graciously, "I still have one set to sing, and it takes a little concentration."

Danielle spoke to her, "You make it seem effortless, though. But I know how difficult it can be to make it look easy. Performance is about hiding the effort, n'est-ce pas?"

"Absolutely," Andie concurred. "You must always hide the strain and make it look as if you're not concerned but are somewhere in the clouds, floating with the music."

"It is the same with us," Jean-Paul allowed, "you must never appear to be trying to act, trying to pretend – it must always be as easy as breathing."

"And sometimes that is hard," Max agreed. "But if you practice, and the band supports you, then it becomes easy to perform."

"Oui, c'est vrai," Dany said emphatically. "The support of the rest of the ensemble is crucial. I need to have the director on my side. If I am unsure, it will be a disaster," she chuckled self-deprecatingly.

"What part of the states do you come from?" Jean-Paul asked Andie. He turned to Max and said, "I know you're English – it's all over your face."

Max grabbed his napkin and rubbed his face, "Is it gone?"

"It's a compliment!" Jean-Paul insisted. "The faces of the English are strong and constant – reliable."

"Such stirring words," Max said facetiously.

They all laughed, then Andie answered Dany, "I grew up in Los Angeles, but now we live wherever we go." She smiled, "I guess we live in hotels, and I must confess, I love it! The clean sheets every day, the amenities - it's very comfortable, and of course for us it's so convenient for our work."

Dany lit up, "I agree! I live here, in the hotel and I love it. I travel so much that it doesn't make sense to maintain a home when I can live so well in this hotel."

"Do you live here too, Jean-Paul?" Andie asked.

"Non - I have my own pied-à-terre in town. I don't travel as much as Dany does - I don't have the lipstick contracts you know."

They laughed and he added, "But Dany and I do share a house, just outside the town of Honfleur, on the coast in Normandie. It's very wild and refreshing, and we spend time there as often as we can."

"We will grow old there," Danielle said.

"We will grow old wherever we are," Jean-Paul said in a soothing tone.

Dany barked her odd laugh, and the rest of them joined her.

Just then, a woman's voice cut through the room, "How can I? How can I go on from day to day, never knowing where he is. Sasha! Oh my Sasha!"

It was Chantal. She stood up abruptly and was addressing Marie-Claude and Hassim, and she was sobbing and shouting in equal measure. She rushed away from the table while the rest of the guests in the Salon pretended not to notice although they hung on every word.

"Goodness, what was that?" Andie asked Danielle and Jean-Paul. "You know her, don't you?"

"Yes," Dany answered grimly, "we know her."

"And who is Sasha?" Andie continued.

"Ahhh, Sasha," Jean-Paul said. "He was a part of our group of travelers in Mumbai."

"He was a gigolo, Chantal's gigolo, and she was obsessed with him," Dany said sharply.

Jean-Paul said, "You mustn't mind Danielle – in many ways she is a Puritan. Yes, he was a prostitute, but I don't judge prostitutes – you never know what has brought them to this sordid life. It's not something you dream of as a young man, or young woman."

"I told you, it's not Sasha who angers me – it's Chantal. If he had not run away from her, she would have destroyed him. Obsession and possession are deadly."

"Did he run away from her?" Max asked.

Danielle and Jean-Paul looked at each other.

Jean-Paul answered, "Well, the last time we saw him – at the banquet as a matter of fact – he told everyone he was going to Bali and would be gone a few months or more. He was going as a guest of a minor royal, I believe."

"Sasha was always a guest. That was his life." Danielle turned to Jean-Paul, "I have sympathy for him, I do. But he is a silly boy, a very silly boy and he needs to be careful. He is playing with fire. Chantal is not a normal woman."

Jean-Paul said to Max, "In fact, I don't agree. I think she is *typique* – you know, like all women."

Both Andie and Danielle appeared ready to pop in anger, when Max quickly stood up. "We need to get back onstage, Andie."

They made their farewells. Jean-Paul said "*merci*" quietly to Max, and Andie and Dany promised each other they would go out somewhere in Paris very soon.

******

When Andie and Max were setting up for the final set, Andie said "Wow" to Max and he nodded, "Yeah - that was a lot."

"*You'd Be So Nice to Come Home To*", Max called to the band. It was an up-tempo but smooth groove to start the last set of the night.

Andie saw Carter accompany Bella and Fan into the room halfway through the last set. He had persuaded them to join him for a night cap. Although Bella had first demurred because she was tired – her earlier burst of energy having worn off – she finally gave way to his persistence only when he begrudgingly agreed Fan was welcome to come along.

Carter ordered champagne cocktails for the three of them. As he'd hoped, Bella showed the effect of alcohol quickly. She wasn't used to drinking and apparently had little or no tolerance.

"Let's not overdo it, Bella," Fan warned her.

"But it's been such a day," she exclaimed, "and I could use something to relax me."

"Of course, you could," Carter agreed. "And I'm surprised you haven't been traumatized, Fan. Literally stumbling across somebody you thought was dead – well! if that's not an unpleasant shock to the system. I can't imagine what is!"

"I didn't literally stumble on her," Fan corrected him, giving him a sharp gaze. "I saw her – I didn't step on her."

"Of course," Carter murmured, keeping his eye on an increasingly tipsy Bella.

Meanwhile, the band was bringing the evening to a close. Max called *"Corcovado"*, a Jobim tune, typically sensual and seductive, for the last song. Andie sang the lyrics in Portuguese, and when Max took a solo, she looked out at the audience and saw a happy audience – now that Chantal had taken her leave. It turned out to be a good night, including the exciting "Sasha Show".

*****

Thursday

Andie stood up and stretched her arms over her head and exclaimed, "I'm hungry."

"You look like a lion waking up and yawning and then roaring for food," Max laughed.

Andie laughed back, "I can't imagine a better compliment than comparing me to the king of beasts – and a cat at that!"

"Why don't we have omelets downstairs? It's a nice room and close by. I don't want you to have to wait to eat."

"Oh, great idea. You're right – it's a pretty room and very luxurious for breakfast."

"My wife likes her luxury," Max said as he got up out of bed.

"I'll shower when we get back – I feel faint," she laughed as she said it while getting dressed.

They took the elevator downstairs and walked through the lobby to the rear of the building where the restaurant, Le Jardin des Oiseaux, was located. It was a two-story extension of the building with a glass roof and walls. When the weather was warm, skylights on the roof and the glass doors were opened and birds occasionally flew into the room attracted by crumbs of food. Sitting in the restaurant was like sitting in an aviary.

The small garden behind the hotel building was heavily planted with aspen and birch trees so that the restaurant appeared to be in a clearing in the woods. There was a water fountain in the center of the room – fish spouting water on a cherub in the middle of a small pool - and trees in pots were also placed in and about the large space. Due to the presence of birds, Le Jardin had erected light linen tasseled umbrellas which only added to the charm of the romantic scene.

"This might be my favorite restaurant in Paris," Andie said as she ate a buttered roll.

"Do you realize you have said that about a dozen places at this point?"

"Now that you mention it, I do love a lot of restaurants in Paris."

"And patisseries – don't forget how many of those make the best pastries."

Andie chuckled, "Well, I guess my enthusiasm carries me to superlatives, it's true. But how lame would it be to say, 'this is one of favorites ...' or 'these are some of the best pastries ...'? No, I say go for the best, the most, *ichiban*, the maximum – *el supremo*."

The waiter brought them two fluffy omelets with pommes frites.

"Do you have ketchup, please?" Andie asked him.

"Of course, mademoiselle."

"You know," Max said, "I think your willingness to ask for ketchup for your omelet in a French restaurant is one of reasons I fell in love with you."

"And you've noticed, haven't you, that I am always served my ketchup with a smile."

"The French love brave women. Jeanne D'Arc, Eleanor of Aquitaine ..."

Andie glanced over Max's shoulder and saw C.C. and Bella enter the restaurant followed by Fan, Carter and Hassim. They found a large table and were soon joined by the rest of the group. She was surprised to see Dany and Jean-Paul with them. The entire cast had assembled.

"I'm sorry," she addressed Max, "I was distracted. All of my favorite characters just came in. Don't look!"

"Once again, I'm rendered sightless," he sighed.

"And isn't it surprising to see Danielle and Jean-Paul?"

"And again, I would be very surprised to find eyes in the back of my head – which is the only way I could see! This is ridiculous," he said turning completely around in his seat.

He quickly turned back. "And what about them?"

She laughed in response then sat up straight excitedly, "Look - it's Morgana. Oh, that's great. She seems to have recovered."

Everyone at the table rose from their seats to hug Morgana when she reached the table. The relief and affection were mingled with wariness. One by one, they embraced her. Andie realized the reason for the group event: they knew Morgana would be released from the hospital that morning. Maybe Eddie told them.

Morgana took a seat waiting for her and smiled her snarl at the group as she slapped a bug off her neck. "Damn thing bit me," she muttered. "So, did you miss me?" she asked brightly to the group, looking around at their faces. Like a herd of Holsteins, she thought dismissively. Except for one of them, she realized, remembering what she'd said the last time they all gathered around a table. She looked at them intently, wondering – who among you?

Andie was watching her as she suddenly jerked her head and said, "I feel a little dizzy. The doctors said it was a concussion and that I had to wait patiently – no drinking, naturally. But I think I need to lie down. Just a little dizzy ..." she smiled almost apologetically.

The others nodded – this time with genuine relief. Morgana made you concentrate on every word, Carter thought, she was too much work to make time with her enjoyable. The others at the table shared his feelings silently. Morgana could be frightening.

She stood up and seemed a little unsteady on her feet as she bade them farewell, but then she arched her back and held her head up and started to walk away. She seemed to have regained her strength. Her first step was fine, but then she lurched and struggled to stay on her feet. She was stumbling towards the fountain and pool in the middle of the room, and when she reached it with outstretched arms, she fell head-first into the water with a surprisingly big splash for such a slender body – it was dead weight.

After a beat, the entire Jardin des Oiseaux broke into shrieks, exclamations, cries of distress and calls for a doctor. Some, like Andie and Max, simply sat with their jaws dropped and mouths open.

"Good heavens," Max broke the silence first.

"Wow," Andie answered.

Across the room, Bella looked at Fan and nodded, "Well, she's dead again."

*****

Andie turned to Max, "I guess we should stay here and wait for the police, right?"

"I suppose it would be easier in the long run to give our statements now. But I doubt we'll have a choice."

"Good - we'll stay," Andie said. "I would really like to finish my breakfast."

"Naturally," he responded while he sipped his tea.

"You know," he continued, "this puts the 'accident' in a whole new light, wouldn't you say?"

Andie nodded as she took a bite of her toast.

"And it also reveals a very persistent killer," he added, savoring the moment he had the floor because Andie's mouth was full.

Not for long, she swallowed and replied, "Right. 'If at first you don't succeed …' " She took a sip of coffee, "And why her? What did she have to do with François?"

"I have no idea. When you think about it, we don't know much about anyone in this group. We've spent time with them, but I don't feel I know any of them."

"That's true. We think we know Danielle and Jean-Paul because we've seen them so many times on screen. But we know nothing of their personal lives except tabloid gossip that is probably not true. And the others? Chantal puts her life on display, so we think we know her. How can they maintain their, what can I call it? Their remoteness – that's it. They stay remote from us."

Max frowned, "I'm not sure ---"

She interrupted, "Maybe that's not the right word - they're not remote, they're all just well-masked. Yes. Not completely disguised, just the ---"

"It doesn't matter," Max stopped her. They both laughed.

"Are you done eating?" Max asked.

"Yes," she answered with a smile.

"Let's go then. They know where we are. I'd like to write a little."

"The breakfast made me sleepy, but I'm still trying to read that Dickens, and this might be a good time to tackle it again," Andie agreed.

"Well that guarantees a good nap."

"Ya think?"

They stood up and looked around the room. Most of the guests had left and the rest were milling around the exit. As Andie and Max neared the doors, they saw a uniformed policeman taking names from diners as they walked out. They waited their turn, gave their contact information and happily rode the elevator back upstairs to their home.

*****

The local Commissaire's right-hand man, Christophe Legrand, always arrived first at any crime scene. He found out the basics so Commissaire Montclair would not have to waste his time on preliminaries. Legrand was the *chef de groupe* from the OPJ - Officiers de la Police Judiciaire. Today he had five men under him who were making forensics recovery while he met with the hotel's executive staff. Eddie was included in briefings because he knew the woman who had died and the other people at the table.

"From what you tell me," Legrand said to the manager of Le Jardin, "it sounds like a heart attack, yes?"

"I don't know. I've never seen a heart attack before. My waiters told me it looked as if she were seized and struck down by something like a heart attack or a stroke. You need to talk to them; I was in my kitchen." Chef Grouillet was impatient to get back to his restaurant. "I know nothing about this woman – and I know nothing about her death. Please excuse me," he stood up and Legrand nodded his permission.

"Why don't we have the waiters here?" he asked the trio of managers, M. Gillet, the hotel's executive manager; Mme. Foucault, the food and beverage manager; and Silvain Amoux, the housekeeping manager.

"I believe they are waiting in the service room," Eddie offered. He was the fourth executive in this meeting with the OPJ. The service room was in the basement where the chambermaids, bellmen and facilities workers met for meetings with management.

"Merci, monsieur. We shall join them." He continued to address Eddie, "In the meantime, please advise the people who were traveling with Mme. Standish to be here at the hotel tomorrow. I will see them at that time. You may go ahead and schedule the interviews, about thirty minutes for each one. I want to get the results of the autopsy before I speak with them, and I am hopeful I will know the cause of death by the morning. But the waiters – I need to talk to them now while their memories are fresh."

The four men went downstairs to the service room to interrogate the hapless waiters, and Eddie went to M. Gillet's office to call his new-found, troublesome friends.

*****

Marie-Claude and Hassim decided to have coffee in the lounge off the lobby. They were still shocked by Morgana's violent death and were undecided about their next steps. Neither wanted to go back to their suite, but they were unusually nervous about leaving the hotel – their home ground. Due to Hassim's peripatetic occupation, filming documentaries all over the world, he and Marie-Claude, who often accompanied him, were used to a vagabond life. But literally watching Morgana die was traumatic, and they were still processing what had transpired.

Neither was hungry nor did they want to go shopping; they waited for inspiration and purpose.

The young woman pianist began to play quietly in the background, and Marie-Claude began to relax which in turn relaxed Hassim. Music had always had a beneficial effect on Marie-Claude. It worked the same way meditation and prayer worked – gently persuading the mind to focus so that it could be free to wander.

She started music lessons – piano – when she was eight years old. She asked for them; nobody had noticed her affinity for music. She was six years younger than the oldest, François, and by the time she was born, he was already the star of the family. He was precocious, he was charming, he was everything a parent wanted. Marie-Claude was a mistake, a surprise. She was born three months after the death of a sister, Diane, François's only sibling until Marie-Claude was born.

Although she never knew her, Marie-Claude heard about her so much that she felt she had. Diane was also a star. She was beautiful, smart and as charming as François. The death of Diane overshadowed Marie-Claude's birth just as François's life overshadowed her own. Her parents seemed resentful that this ugly little runt of a baby should live, but the glorious Diana should die. But this was what she thought, although not necessarily evidently true, and she was inclined to forgive them because she couldn't be sure they were neglectful; and she had no recourse if they were.

François was wonderful to be with, and she was as beguiled as everyone else was by him. He loved his little sister and was aware she needed more than he did from their parents. Nonetheless, he went away to school when she was a child, and she was alone with the Desenfants through her formative years. She suffered through an awkward adolescence but so did most of her friends – she was sensitive to a painful degree to the feelings of people around her – and she treated her own failings with a mature objectivity she had acquired living as an only child since François was no longer there.

Furthermore, she knew she would get out and away when she turned eighteen. She had no plans at all; she was ambivalent about more schooling – university didn't appeal to her because the idea of meeting new students and new teachers frightened her; and she was equally frightened of moving to her own apartment in Paris. Her parents' pied à terre was certainly large enough for her to pass days without seeing them – especially because they traveled and lived mostly in the Desenfants family estate in the Loire Valley - but she craved a home of her own.

She fantasized about what her little apartment would be like. She would have at least one cat, but probably two; she would have window boxes with flowers all year round, including holly in the winter; she would clean her home herself – no maids or housekeepers; she would play music on a record player all the time; and she would have a piano – a spinet – and play whenever she felt like it. She didn't cook, but she knew she could learn; furthermore, in a big city there were many places to get meals. She pictured herself eating a pastry with dark coffee in the morning on a little terrace off the living room.

She had no idea how to create her own home nor did she have any career plans. She wasn't raised to earn money – except through marriage. But not long before her eighteenth birthday, she overheard her parents, Clemence and Renny, discussing her future after her inheritance. Inheritance? She had paused on the stairs outside the library when she heard her name mentioned. Now, she very quietly crept down the stairs and stood next to the open door to listen.

Her mother's voice was raised, "What could she have been thinking of? Marie-Claude has no use for that kind of money – what will she do with it? Marthe must have done this just to annoy me!"

Marie-Claude couldn't make out her father's words, it was a low grumble. Her mother responded angrily, "That makes no sense at all. I don't think she even knows about this bequest. Why should she?"

Her father lost his temper, and his words were loud and clear, "This is her money. Marthe loved her and wanted her to have something of her own. We have a legal and moral responsibility here!"

Clemence interrupted with her typical fluttering words of comfort she used whenever he lost his temper, and she conceded the point. "Very well. We will present her with a big check on her birthday. I cannot imagine what it will mean to her, but we will give it to her at a dinner. We can call François! He will want to come for a birthday dinner – how lovely it will be to see him." Marie-Claude could feel her mother's happiness at the thought of seeing François through the wall that separated them.

"Still," she continued, "what will she do with twenty-five million francs?"

Marie-Claude had to put her hand over her mouth to quiet her gasp. Twenty-five million francs? She could go anywhere, do anything!

Now, in yet another hotel with Hassim, she remembered how giddy she'd been with joy. She shook her head as she remembered her certainty that twenty-five million francs would bring her happiness. How silly she had been as a teenager. Her parents had more money than anyone could possibly need, and their daughter had grown up lonely, feeling unloved. More than anyone, Marie-Claude should have known what an empty legacy that money was.

She called her aunt 'Marthe-Marthe'. No one knew why but Marthe thought it was clever and wonderful. She was Marie-Claude's biggest booster, her number one fan. Marie-Claude wished that Marthe-

Marthe was her mother and that she lived with her. Her own mother could tell, and it make her vindictive towards them both.

Clemence never missed a chance to humiliate Marthe at family gatherings, mocking her lack of fashion, her ignorance of social politics, her gaucheries and endless faux pas. Marthe was a widow and Clemence found a way to mock that too. Marie-Claude shook her head again. Sometimes the only feeling she had for her dead mother was hatred – pure hatred.

"What's the matter? Marie-Claude, you look frightening, like you could kill someone. What's the matter? What are you thinking about?" Hassim was disturbed by the look on her face. Marie-Claude's emotions could be volatile – like a roller-coaster. He never knew what would set her off. She was a sweet soul, but she was incapable of controlling her feelings. He was always a little afraid that she might go too far one day.

She looked startled by his question, "Oh, nothing. I was just thinking – it's nothing, Hassim." She reached for his hand across the table. "Let's go for a walk in the nearest park. I want to be surrounded by trees and grass and flowers … eh?" she gave him a bright smile. "Please?"

Hassim returned the smile and stood up. "Whatever makes you happy." He took her arm and pulled her into an embrace.

"Hassim - I would be lost without you," she murmured.

"That will never happen." He kissed her on the top of her head; and they left the lounge and the hotel.

*****

The rest of the breakfast diners shared the same unease as Hassim and Marie-Claude, and they also felt adrift, suddenly floating without a rudder, from whirlpool to whirlpool in a vast and mysterious river. Andie decided there was only one solution for her malaise, a good steam in the spa, followed by massage – serious relaxation. She had a lot to process.

Max said he wanted to read and maybe nap, "but have a good time. Try to get past what happened."

"Thank you for not saying 'try to forget it'."

She threw on the big, soft terry robe, grabbed her shampoo and left for the spa. What would a world be without spas? she wondered. Just as she was chastising herself for being so frivolous, she walked into the heavenly ambiance of the spa.

"Is that you?" a voice rang out from the massage room, just off the foyer.

"It's Andie," she called back walking towards the voice.

"Darling, come join me – what a horrid affair! I'm so glad you're joining us – we can give each other moral support."

"Who else is here?"

"Dany, Chantal and Bella. We're all just shocked to our bones! They're still soaking. Go join them and then come back for a good rub."

Andie's spirits lifted at the sight of C.C., and she found herself looking forward to seeing the other 'girls'. She walked into the jacuzzi room and both Dany and Bella called out 'hello's' to her. Chantal was looking off into space.

Bella spoke as Andie lowered herself into the warm bubbling water. "I guess we all had the same idea: horrible experience? Go to the spa." She giggled as she said it and the others joined her. Bella couldn't be offensive if she tried and it was funny that they all responded to Morgana's violent death the same way.

"Are we the most superficial, insensitive people in the world?" Andie asked with a laugh.

"I don't know any other kind," Dany quipped.

Andie sank deeper into the bubbles. This is heaven, she thought. She said, "I feel as if every single muscle is slowly un-tensing – is that a word?"

"If it isn't, it should be," Chantal agreed.

Bella rose up out of the water, "I'm moving on to my massage. I've been in the water so long, she's going to have to unwrinkle my skin."

"Perhaps as she untenses the muscles," Dany laughed.

One by one, the soakers went in to be massaged. When they were all lined up side by side on tables, C.C. said, "Well - wasn't that a ghastly scene this morning?! I have never seen anything like it!"

Dany turned her head towards her, "Well, I should hope not. I would have preferred to go to the end of my life without watching someone die."

"It was so exciting," Bella said.

"Bella - it was a tragedy," Andie argued gently.

"I know, but it was a matter of life and death and there's nothing more exciting than that." Bella explained.

"I guess. I think I understand," Andie said slowly, thinking, in truth, Bella was a very strange person and she would never understand her.

"Does anyone know what happened?" Chantal asked the group, turning her head right and left.

Bella raised her head to ask "Heart attack?"

"I thought it looked that way, but I've never seen anyone have a heart attack so …" C.C.'s voice trailed off.

"It seems awfully peculiar she died twice," Bella said.

"What do you mean?" Dany asked.

Andie knew what she meant and the inevitable conclusion: someone wanted Morgana dead.

"Well, she fell down the stairs at the catacombs and Fan and I thought she was dead, and now she had a heart attack and she really is dead. I would say she's a very unlucky woman who died twice."

Chantal made a noise like a grunt, and C.C. sounded exasperated when she spoke, "Bella, you have a very, uh, unique perspective on the world, dearest. But does anyone here actually know anything? Is there a murderer loose in the Hotel Rose?" She was slightly mocking but Andie wondered if she knew the truth: there was indeed a killer in the hotel.

"What makes you think it was deliberate?" she asked C.C.

"Deliberate?" asked Dany.

Andie explained, "If someone killed Morgana, then that person tried twice and that's pretty deliberate and cold-blooded. It's not a crime of passion in a hot moment."

Dany nodded, "I see." She shuddered slightly, "That's a frightening thought."

The unspoken conclusion was that the murderer was probably someone they all knew. Each woman processed this, and the conversation slowly died down as they fell silent.

Dany was the first to get up and bid the others *bonne nuit;* she was followed by C.C., then Chantal, leaving Andie and Bella bringing up the rear.

What had started as a giggling girls' night out turned into a solemn internal re-examination of every moment they'd spent together. Murder was not as titillating when the murderer might be one of your close friends. It was spooky, Andie thought as she walked down the hall to her rooms. She was grateful Max was on the other side of the door.

******

Thursday Night

Andie was distracted and Max was distracted when they entered Le Salon that night to find Eddie distracted as well. They exchanged limp greetings of commiseration.

"We need to buck up," Eddie said. "I'm counting on you and your music to lift spirits, especially mine.

"Well, that's fine for you, but who's going to lift ours?" Andie asked.

"Perhaps that enormous man with a guitar who's chatting up your band mates," he replied.

They turned and Max called out, "Balls!" and rushed to the stage.

Andie looked and called out "Ally Ocho!" and she too rushed to the stage.

Eddie stood and watched them happily run to the huge Latino. Alejandro "Eight Ball" Ocho stood six foot four inches tall with just under three hundred pounds on his frame. Eddie shuddered at the name 'Balls', fearing the worst. Aly was a very big man.

Aly was a genial giant and a brilliant guitarist. Nobody knew where he was from, but most assumed somewhere in South America. He spoke Spanish, Portuguese and English when he spoke - which he never did at length. He was a shy man but lovable and was becoming an international super star.

"Aly! What a nice surprise – what are you doing in Paris?" Andie said as they embraced.

"I have a gig at the Olympia – big room, but we're sold out. I heard you were here, and I couldn't miss the chance to see you."

Musicians who travel tend to make an effort to meet each other when they land in the same cities, and this was such an occasion.

"Do you think I might sit in?" Aly asked in his shy manner. As formidable as his talents were, he was nonetheless modest to a fault and generous in his appreciation of other musicians. He listened to everyone in the band and played complementary accompaniment which enhanced each musician's performance. In addition to his own heart-stopping solos, he made everyone sound good.

The band members eagerly assured him he was welcome.

Ally Ocho – also known as "Balls" – could play anything on his guitar, but his heart was in Latin jazz, especially Brasilian.

With that in mind, when the set began, Max called out *"Samba de Orfeu"* from Luiz Bonfá's score for the French film "Black Orpheus". The English name of the tune, *"A Sweet, Happy Life"*, and the upbeat feel made it one of Andie's favorites. They played a couple more songs from that soundtrack and then segued into a number of Jobim tunes. When the first set break came, the band settled into a large table to catch up with each other. Andie held back a little to ask Max why he called Aly "Balls".

Max laughed, "Well, his name is 'ocho' which means eight in Spanish, and you know how musicians are – at first, he was Aly Eight-ball which turned into Balls - which is also an apt name for some of his solos, now that I think of it."

"Naturally," Andie answered facetiously, "I mean, you can't really call him 'Ball'. Or 'Eight'. Certainly not Alejandro, his name." She shook her head, "Men."

Amidst laughter and beer, the musicians had a good break, dispelling the mood of distraction and anxiety in the face of the recent death.

Aly Ocho played the second set as well and when that ended, he invited the musicians to a special gig on a boat on the Seine.

"We're playing for an engagement party for some very rich people on Sunday and I would love to have you join us. It's a romantic boat ride on the Seine," he looked at Andie and Max and winked, "and I think you would all have a wonderful time."

"Sunday is our night off!" Adrien exclaimed. "I'm in."

"Me, too," the others chorused enthusiastically.

"Hasta la vista," Aly answered and with a big smile he moved like a mountain – if a mountain had legs - off the stage and out the room.

******

Before the final set, Dany and Jean-Paul came into Le Salon and took seats at the bar. As Andie and Max passed them on their way to the stage, the musicians gave them both a big smile and welcome.

"I was afraid you'd taken the night off," Andie joked to them.

"No, no – we wouldn't miss you. You're the night-cap for us now," Jean-Paul assured her.

"I guess that's a compliment, but I can't help but feel you're comparing us to a glass of warm milk," Andie joked.

Dany and Jean-Paul laughed and Dany responded, "Not at all, you're like a warm snifter of brandy sending us off to sweet dreams."

"Oh!" Dany exclaimed, "I almost forgot. I wanted to take you to one of my favorite places in Paris, le Musée d'Orsay. It's so exciting, especially if you like impressionist paintings."

Andie answered quickly, "Oh, I've heard so much about it, and I do like the Impressionists. I would love to go with you."

"Bien. I'll meet you in the lobby at one o'clock tomorrow. Is that good? I know you work late, and you must eat before we go."

Max laughed, "You never have to tell her to eat – she's always hungry."

"I don't believe it – you don't have any fat on you," Dany protested.

"That's because she's always moving," Ben commented.

"Like now," Andie laughed, "Max, our audience awaits."

Their spirits lifted considerably by Aly Ocho's visit, the band played a joyous, sparkling final set. As she listened to Max's solo on "*It Never Entered My Mind*", Andie saw a familiar figure in the back of the room talking to Eddie. She was both very surprised and happily validated by his presence. If he was here at the Orchidea Rose, there could only be one explanation – murder.

She managed to catch his eye and he mimed a shrug in response. Right, she thought. Don't even think you can fool me, Commander Ben.

When the song ended, she said excitedly to Max, "Look who's here! We knew that it wasn't a heart attack. He wouldn't be here if everything was kosher with these people. Here he comes."

Commander Ben Sinclair approached the bandstand with a smile, "And who else would be here but my favorite team of detectives: Andie and Max! I should have known – wherever you go, murder follows. Maybe I should be investigating you."

"It's murder, I knew it!" Andie said triumphantly.

"Good to see you again, Ben," Max had the presence of mind to welcome their friend.

Ben and Max shook hands, and Andie gave him an embrace.

"How did you get here so quickly?" Andie asked him.

"We weren't far away – in the Loire valley on vacation – when I got a call from the Orchidea Group chairman for a little help with a death on the premises."

"If it were simply a death from heart attack, you wouldn't have been called, Ben," Andie pointed out, "and what do you mean by 'we'?"

"Well, I think you'll be happy to hear that I'm here in France with Grace."

As expected, Andie was delighted, "Grace? Oh, that's wonderful Ben. Where is she? You didn't leave her there? Is she in a château waiting for you to return? Is she here?"

Ben laughed at Andie's rapid-fired questions, "You never change. I am sorry to tell you that she's on her way to London as we speak. That's her home base now. Our vacation was almost at an end, and she decided to go straight home. She is not as fascinated with murder as you are. She told me she had enough crime in London and didn't need to learn how the French solve a homicide. After all, she's with Scotland Yard now."

"Cool", Andie said, and Max nodded in agreement.

"Listen," Ben continued in a more serious tone, "I need to talk to you as soon as you pack up. I hate to say it, but you may be able to help me --- I know, I know," he laughed as Andie started to interrupt to remind him how much she and Max had helped him in the past, "but this is different. You two are actual witnesses. Come sit with me and Eddie, have a glass of wine, and try to remember what you saw in the restaurant."

"We'll be right there," Andie assured him as he walked away to join Eddie at a table in the back of the salon.

She turned to Max, "This is cool! We'll be in on it from the beginning."

He laughed in return, "Aren't we always?"

*****

Max and Andie joined Eddie and Ben at a large table on which Eddie had placed a bottle of very good Chateau Margaux and four glasses. He served them all and then Ben toasted the group.

"May we have success in this, our latest adventure."

They clinked glasses and Eddie said, "So you know each other, is that right?"

"Yes," Andie spoke first, "We worked on a couple cases in Hong Kong and Tokyo."

"I didn't know you were detectives."

"They're not – I was joking. They happen to run in murderous circles," Ben replied.

"To be fair, one could say the same for you," Max said in his usual measured tone.

"Could we please get to Morgana?" Andie interrupted.

Eddie said, "Yes, enough pleasantries, can we get to the matter at hand? Why are you here?"

Ben apologized, "I'm sorry, Eddie, I never did give you an explanation. As Andie and Max know, I have more or less retired from a law enforcement agency --"

"MI6," Andie stage whispered.

"An agency I'd rather not name," Ben continued with a sharp look at Andie who responded with a wide-eyed look of innocence. "And I now work for the Orchidea Group as a consultant in matters that may cause local police to pay unwanted attention to the hotel's guests."

"You're a liaison for the Rose with the local cops, is that it?" Eddie asked.

"Yes, in so many words."

Eddie continued, "And if it was a heart attack that killed Morgana, then why do you have to deal with the police at all? These things happen."

"Well, as it turns out, once the body went to the coroner, he was able to very quickly determine that the woman's death was not due to a heart attack. She was poisoned." Ben stopped speaking as the others responded.

Andie responded with a gasp, Max gave a whistle of surprise and Eddie blanched.

"Are they sure?" he asked with a note of desperation.

"There is no doubt. She was murdered."

"I knew it," Andie whispered loudly and dramatically.

Then he assumed a serious tone, "I need you to tell me everything you know – about the victim, how she is related to the other people she was with --- everything you know about the victim and her friends."

Eddie, Andie and Max looked at each other.

"You go first, Eddie. You met them first, and a lot of what we know is what you told us."

Eddie sighed, "I suppose that's true. Yes, Andie's right, I do know some things about them."

He turned to Ben, "Do you know about François Desenfants? His death in Mumbai?"

Ben nodded, "Yes, but you can take it from here, when you first met them. And how did they all get here? I mean, why are they here?"

Max answered, "His lawyer - François's - notified them and told them to attend the memorial because that was a requirement for any bequests – that they all gather at the Rose. Apparently, François made the arrangements and reservations in his will. Mark Redmond is the lawyer."

Ben nodded, "I see. Eddie, would you continue?"

Eddie nodded, "As I recall now, the first one I met was the sister of the late François. She approached me in the Salon Jazz at the end of the night. She was concerned because the group was going to view François's grave – well, not exactly a grave, a marker – in Père Lachaise. She needed my help in making the arrangements to get the group to the cemetery and then to a small reception in the hotel lounge when they returned."

"Isn't that usually the responsibility of the concierge?" Ben asked.

"Yes, but she felt more comfortable asking me." Eddie explained, "When I greet guests in La Salon Jazz, I meet them, and more often than not we become friends."

Andie interrupted, "Eddie is famous for that. He's attentive, sensitive and funny. People respond to that, Ben. You might learn something from him."

Ben looked at her, "Always so quick on the trigger, Annie Oakley. Please go on, Eddie," he nodded at him.

"Well, the trip to Père Lachaise went well, apparently, and then the deceased's cousin, Bella Jardine, asked me about a trip to the catacombs, and of course, I helped set that up, which is where Morgana fell."

"Fell? She must have been pushed or tripped," Andie blurted.

"How did little Miss Marple end up on this jaunt?"

Andie guffawed, and Max smiled.

"I know Andie and I knew she'd want to go – and she did. Her keeper, Max, came along per usual, perhaps to make sure she didn't wander off and get lost."

"My keeper?" Andie exclaimed.

"Still, someone died." Ben offered.

"Yes - and I know something none of you knows about her," Andie boasted.

"You do?" Max asked her. "Why didn't you tell me?"

She looked at him, "I haven't had time, and honestly, it hasn't come up."

All three men looked at her and chorused, "She's dead!"

"Yes, well, they said it was an accident and then a heart attack; and what I know only seems relevant now," she responded defensively.

They looked at her expectantly.

"Yes, uh, well, I was walking to the ladies' room in the lounge, when they were all sharing memories about François, and Morgana disagreed with them that François was well-loved. She said that it didn't seem plausible that his car would break down and roll over the cliff in flames. She made a good point, actually, that he would never let his car fall into such disrepair, and that he had driven in much more difficult terrain than a well-traveled city road in Mumbai. She had me convinced there was something shady about the accident."

"You're not exactly an impartial observer, though. You are willing to believe any death is a homicide," Ben pointed out.

"I don't think Morgana was wrong, Ben. What she said made sense. And, as you all just said – now she's dead. I think whoever caused the car accident in Mumbai killed her because she knew something."

"Did she say anything else about the car accident? What could she know about it?" Max asked her.

"Well, no. But she saw me and lowered her voice so I wouldn't hear her," she answered. "What other reason do you have for her murder?" she asked Ben. He gave a small wave of his hand in dismissal of her question and asked, "What can you tell me about the others? I need to know the connections they have to each other and to Morgana."

"Andie and I only know what Eddie told us about them, which wasn't much." Max said.

"Exactly - I know his sister seems quite distraught, and she is married to the cinematographer on François' films. I told you about Bella Jardine – oh, and she has a brother whose name is Wei Fan – don't ask. They are here as representatives of the family as far as I can see. There were two more people at the cemetery – two elderly Desenfants – but they left and didn't return to the lounge. Who else, Max?"

"Well, the very famous Danielle Dufault and Jean-Paul Toussaint, and no, I don't know how they connect to François. Andie?"

"Right. Morgana, of course, who was English. A playboy type named Carter, but I don't remember his last name. He told me, but I don't recall it now. He was quite pleasant. American, I'm pretty sure, but he was kind of putting on a little English accent off and on. Oh, and Chantal! Now there's a tale."

She paused to take a sip of wine. "Yes, Chantal. Well, she is very upset that her gigolo isn't here." She looked around to see their reactions, but there were none. "Apparently, according to Danielle Dufault, Chantal is obsessed with Sasha. That's his name, and he was also at the banquet in Mumbai. She is in love with him and is desperate because he hasn't arrived yet. He told her he was going to Bali the last time she saw him which was in Mumbai. She assumed he would be here for the funeral because he was quite fond of Francois, but he's not here. She's practically hysterical wondering where he could be."

She looked at them and shrugged her shoulders as if to say, that's it.

Suddenly she looked at Eddie and exclaimed, "And you! You have been hiding that lady from me – Ben, he knows some woman who also attends these group affairs, and she's always hiding her face – Sasha! It's Sasha!" she said triumphantly to Eddie.

He stood up and said loudly, "No! It is not Sasha. I don't know whom you're talking about, but I have to finish up in my office. It's been a long night and it's going to be an early morning call for me, isn't it?" he asked Ben.

"Actually, the police are going to want to question all of you, and yes, it will be fairly early in the morning for someone who works at night. Andie, Max," he stood up and extended his arms, "You know I am glad to see you. And Grace will be very sorry to know she missed seeing you." He became serious again, "And please – do not tell anyone about me." He turned to Eddie, "Your executive manager called me, but nobody else here knows who I am. I am something of a secret agent."

Andie rolled her eyes, "Oh, please."

"Good night, Andie," Ben said firmly.

Both Max and Andie saw that they were dismissed and stood up to go. They wanted to get back to their room and compare notes, in any case.

Everyone kissed and hugged and said good night.

Andie and Max took a waiting elevator, and Eddie and Ben walked slowly to catch another one. They entered where the doors opened, and Ben said to Eddie, "So, what is it that you need to tell me, Eddie?"

Eddie started to answer, "It's rather complicated ... you see ---" and the elevator doors shut.

Andie and Max took off their performing clothes and changed into sweatpants for Max and yoga pants for Andie and breathed big sighs of relief to be alone and free to talk about the latest news.

Max opened the bottle of wine they kept in the room and gestured to Andie asking if she wanted a glass too.

"No, the sugar will keep me up. I've already got too many thoughts in my head to sleep. Hand me a bottle of Evian, please."

They settled into the soft couch and easy chair, and once comfortably ensconced, Max initiated the conversation.

"I have to tell you, Andie, you need to stop haranguing Eddie about your mysterious veiled lady." He raised his hand to quiet her protest, "Clearly, this person does not want to be recognized. I agree it's maddening, but I think your approach is getting you nowhere. I think you might want to try the opposite – befriend this woman. Get her to open up naturally. Demanding answers from Eddie is obviously not going to work."

"All right, you have a point. But how can I get close to her? At this point, she'll avoid me as soon as she sees me."

"I don't know, Andie. But I know this isn't working."

Andie sighed, "You're right. I blew it. Now Eddie is going to avoid me, too."

"Not necessarily. After all, he's now working with Ben, and you always manage to get Ben to tell you things he's trying to hide. See if you can do the same thing to Eddie. To tell the truth," he laughed, "I don't know how you do it, so I can't be more specific than that. It surprises me as much as it surprises him."

"Usually, an opportunity presents itself and I don't have to do much more than zero in."

"You know, Danielle seems to have taken a shine to you. Maybe she can give you more info to go on. Maybe she knows more than she knows ---"

Andie interrupted him, "You're beginning to sound like me!"

"No kidding," he answered ruefully. "When are you going to start sounding like me?"

86

"Not gonna happen - that ship sailed in 1776," she laughed in response.

"Another thing – it occurs to me that the mysterious lady may be in danger from the murderer. Maybe that's why Eddie is trying to keep you away from her. Two people have died suspiciously ---"

"Been murdered," Andie interjected.

"Perhaps," Max continued, "and it's possible that the veiled lady is the target now."

"Hmmm, that's a thought. Let's call her VL for short."

"VL?"

"Yes, Max. Veiled lady, VL. Then you and I can talk about her in front of other people if we need to without tipping our hand."

"VL. Andie, for some reason I find that hilarious," and he laughed.

"Nonetheless," she replied.

"VL it is."

He added, "Let's go to bed. I have a surprise for you. I got a DVD from the concierge."

"Goody! What is it?"

"If I told you, there's be no surprise. Wait for the opening credits."

There was a television in all the rooms with a DVD player. Max and Andie would lie in the king size bed and frequently watched movie mysteries while they fell asleep. This was one of those nights. When they were settled, Max hit the play button on the remote, and as it started, Andie exclaimed "Maigret! Oh Max, you are a darling," and kissed him on the forehead.

"I try."

******

CHAPTER FOUR

Friday morning

As the train pulled into the station, Samia took a deep breath and forced herself to relax as she exhaled. She was excited and anxious in equal measure. She was fifteen and this was her first trip to Paris. It was also her first trip anywhere alone. She had gone to London with two classmates at the end of term, and because the trip went smoothly and the girls' mothers spoke to them by phone frequently, Samia's mother reluctantly allowed her to go to Paris on her own. Someone would be meeting her and she had her phone. The train slowly came to a noisy stop.

Samia stepped off the train and moved away from the passengers behind her. The station was huge. Daisy, her roommate and closest friend, had been to Paris and told her the Gare du Nord station was the biggest in Europe, but Samia was unprepared for the size - and sound - of the crowd. It's just one big roaring and rushing mass, she thought. They all seemed to know what they were doing and where they were going. The steady barrage of sound made by the noisy crowd of travelers - apparently all speaking at the same time - was due to the high, glass ceilings that seemed to bounce the noise back and forth like an enclosed echo, never fading away. Samia remembered an old song about feeling lonely in a crowd of people; she felt invisible and very much a foreigner.

She joined the group of passengers departing her train as they moved ahead, presumably towards an exit. Samia didn't really know where she was going, but believed since everyone else was headed in the same direction, it would be best to follow them. Soon, however, the group of passengers dispersed in different directions. Samia stood still. What to do? She decided to go outside and try to get a taxi. Perhaps that's where he was – he was going to meet her outside. Of course.

It took a surprisingly long time to get to the street outside the station, and the suitcase was heavy. She came to a stop not far from the curb, but saw no taxi.

Just then a man who looked African came to her,"Pardonez-moi, mademoiselle. Ça va?"

He looked at her and thought she was a prize. She was petite, slender and very pretty: light mocha skin and shiny black hair in a short bob that framed her fine-boned face and set off her deep black eyes. And, best of all, she was young, too young to be on her own in the Gare Du Nord.

Samia didn't know how to answer the stranger. He looked Moroccan, familiar, like someone from home. Maybe she could trust him. He was friendly and had warm eyes.

"I'm supposed to meet someone; he should be here."

"Ah," the stranger replied. He stood with her and looked around with her, but nobody was looking for Samia. "Perhaps I can help you get to your destination. Do you have an address? A phone number?"

Samia searched her bag for the address. It was in her wallet on a small card. As she looked for it, the friendly man looked over her head to signal a driver.

"I have a friend with a car. We were just dropping off my auntie and I took her to her train. She's old and I wanted to make sure she would get on the right train. I saw you and thought you looked lost. My friend will be happy to take you to your destination."

Samia responded with assurance, "I wouldn't want to take advantage." She felt if a grown man used the term 'auntie' and took care of the elderly woman, he must be a good man; she was confident he was trustworthy. And he appeared to be West African, someone her family might know.

"Oh, it's no trouble at all. You have to be careful in a big city like Paris. It's easy to make the wrong turn and get lost."

Samia handed him the card.

"This is where you want to go?" he asked her, and she nodded. He continued, "I know where it is. It's just a short distance."

"Really?" Samia asked. "Are you sure you don't mind?"

"Not at all," he replied. "Ah, here he is now. Let me take your bag for you."

"How kind you are," Samia told him as she handed him her suitcase.

The two of them walked to the white van at the curb. When the man slid open the side door, he put her suitcase inside and then turned to her and very quickly grabbed her and threw her inside, immediately putting his hand over her mouth and yelling at the driver to go.

Before she had a chance to realize what was happening, he tied a dirty handkerchief around her mouth and tied a rope around her hands that he had forced behind her back. Finally, he put a hood over her head. She was completely helpless and immobile. Paralyzed, blind and silenced, all she knew was terror.

*****

The next morning was hectic for everyone who'd been in Le Jardin for breakfast the previous day. Messages had been left on their phones to please come down to the front desk and ask for Eddie Bancroft who was acting as a liaison for the police. Since everyone knew and liked Eddie, Dashiell Montclair, the Commissaire, reasoned the guests would be more likely to respond to him than an unknown police detective.

Dashiell Montclair stood no more than five foot eight inches tall, but his penetrating eyes intimidated most people when he questioned them. He had thick, dark hair and bushy eyebrows that framed his almost black eyes.

Commissaire Montclair, Eddie and Ben had a brief conference before the interviews took place. They ran over the questions that needed answers, and Commissaire Montclair proposed an easy way to take everyone's fingerprints.

"When they come in, you, Eddie, will offer them a drink of water or juice – something in a glass. After they leave, we'll label each glass and put it away for fingerprinting back at my station."

"Excellent thinking. Dash." Ben said.

"Merci, Ben."

Eddie asked, 'But what if they don't want a drink?"

Both Ben and Montclair laughed. Ben answered, "Everybody is nervous with a dry mouth when questioned by police. Whether they are innocent or guilty, they always want to wet their mouths."

Eddie smiled and answered, "Of course, that makes sense."

Ben and Montclair agreed that Ben should not attend the interviews - the guests didn't know him and at this point, his presence might not be helpful. He retired to his room to wait for the results from the Commissaire.

The remaining two inquisitors sat in the office of the concierge, behind the front desk. Eddie sat at the desk and Montclair took a seat against the wall of the room in order to appear less imposing.

Bella and Fan were, not surprisingly, the first to arrive for an interview.

Eddie asked them if they would like something cool to drink – juice or water – and they both requested orange juice. As he handed them their glasses, Eddie asked them if they had anything more to contribute since the previous day.

"You seemed to have been interviewed at some length when Mme. Standish had her accident; what can you tell me about her death yesterday?"

Bella answered, "We're just responding to the message on our phone. We were there at breakfast, of course, but we have no particular knowledge of her heart attack."

"I see. Well, I thought Commissaire Montclair would like to meet you, you know, put a face to the name. He's interviewing everyone who was at Le Jardin when she died."

Montclair nodded, drawing the Jardines' attention to himself. "Yes, I have read the transcripts of your interview, but I thought I would take this time to introduce myself in case you have additional thoughts on the, uh, accident in the catacombs or her death in the restaurant yesterday." He turned to Fan, "You found her when she fell at the catacombs, yes?"

"Yes, I did. I was climbing the stairs to the exit, and I saw her body."

"Did you try to help her? Or did you think she was dead?"

Fan cleared his throat, "It seemed quite clear to me that she was dead. I turned around to tell Bella and keep her from the awful sight. Then we exited and used the first phone box we found to call the authorities. Of course, she was only unconscious."

"And did you see her body on the stairs, Miss Jardine?"

"Yes, I did. It was horrible," Bella answered with relish. "Fan tried to shield the body, but Morgana was a tall woman, and she took up a lot of space. I also thought she was dead. She was so still," Bella shook her head at the memory, "and that's why I thought she was dead. Not even a slight tremble – she was as still as stone." Then she brightened, "And then yesterday, she really was dead! It was out of the blue – she was sitting there and then she got up and died. At first, I thought she had another spell, but she died, ker-plop into the water!"

"I see," Montclair said. "Do you know what kind of 'spells' she had?"

"No, I just assumed she fell both times because she had spells of some kind. But I don't know what they were. Maybe she had a weak heart?"

"Hmmm," Montclair murmured.

He continued, "Did she have any enemies that you know about?"

Bella thought for a moment. "Well, she was somewhat abrasive, but if that's what triggered it, then everyone would be a suspect – she annoyed everyone. Not me, of course, or Fan. We don't take offense. Irritating people are just a fact of life, no?"

Montclair nodded, "And you?" he asked Fan.

"I never take offense – it's useless. Some people are just annoying – as my sister said, it's a fact of life."

"Non, I meant do you have anything to add?"

Fan replied quickly, "I know nothing. I thought the way my sister thought – that the woman had spells that caused her to collapse and appear to be dead. We really don't know anything more about her," he spoke with finality.

Montclair thanked them for their help, such as it was, and told them to please stay in Paris until his investigation was completed. Then Eddie gave them a big smile and escorted them from the room.

"What do you think?" he asked Montclair after they left the interview room and Montclair collected and labeled their used glasses.

"Ah, they are a little, how can I say? Disturbed. It is hard to find the truth with people like that. Perhaps they know more than they say – or perhaps they want to be important, who knows? I need to find more answers before I can evaluate this Bella and her protective brother."

They spoke as they labeled and put the glasses in plastic bags.

Eddie nodded, "Bella is one of a kind, and her brother obscures anything she says so that you end up with nothing – he's good at protecting her."

"That is an excellent observation, Eddie, and just what I was thinking. Now, who is next on our list?"

"I think you will enjoy these two: Danielle Dufault and Jean-Paul Toussaint."

Montclair loved the cinema, but not celebrity. He looked forward to meeting the two film stars, but he had no illusions. It was one characteristic that all homicide detectives shared; the overwhelming desire for truth gave no one a pass, not for beauty, fame or charm – everyone and anyone was capable of murder.

Danielle and Jean-Paul came in and sat down, and Eddie asked them if they would like a drink of juice or water. Dany requested sparkling Evian and Jean-Paul had juice.

"Mme Toussaint," Montclair began, but Danielle stopped him by holding up her hand and shaking her finger,

"Non. 'Dufault'," she corrected him.

"Ah, of course," he said. "Forgive me, I haven't kept up with the times, I am afraid."

"It's been a long time since I was his wife."

"I am sorry, but you are here together, non?"

"We are friends, very old friends."

"Oh, not so old," Montclair said diplomatically. "How do you happen to be here, a part of this group? Do you know these people?"

Danielle sighed, "I am sorry to say we do. I have known the family of the young man who died in India for many years. When François was a young man, he spoke to me often about his desire to use film to tell true stories – documentaries – and when he began his last project, he was looking for financial investment and approached me. Jean-Paul and I decided to back him because we agreed with him that film was powerful and could be used to enlighten and inform an audience instead of just telling fairytales which we have been a part of, and we felt that helping François was a chance to show another side of cinema."

Montclair nodded.

"Perhaps," she continued, "it is because we have both seen how easily people can be fooled, and this was a way to *équilibrer la balance* - balance the scale, so to speak."

Jean-Paul nodded as she spoke and added, "You have seen how successful I am as a detective in movies, and you - most of all – know that that is a lie. My movies are great adventure stories that please people who want to believe justice is always triumphant, but that is not true, not true at all."

Montclair spoke evenly, "Yes, you are correct. Many murderers are never caught. Justice is often elusive, *n'est-ce pas?*"

He turned back to Danielle, "But I must always endeavor to find the truth. Who do you think wanted Morgana Standish dead?"

The directness of the question disconcerted her for a moment. "I don't know. I hardly knew her. She was very vulgar, but that is not usually a fatal flaw."

"What did she have to do with François? Was she also an investor?"

"I suppose so. She was at the dinner in Mumbai and most of us there were investors, so I suppose we can assume she had put money into his project."

Jean-Paul spoke up, "It's not safe to assume, Dany."

Dashiell Montclair was amused by this movie detective's attempt to live out the role in real life.

"No," he answered, "it is not, but since everyone makes these guesses every day, it is worth hearing them."

Both Jean-Paul and Danielle looked chastened, surprisingly, in Montclair's view. Were they trying to impress him with their attempt at being transparent and well-intentioned? Were they covering up something or did they take him for a fool? He had seen both so often it was a cliché in his business.

"Do you know her occupation?" he continued.

Danielle and Jean-Paul again looked at each other, and Jean-Paul took the lead. "I'm not sure. She seemed to have no money worries, but I don't know where the money came from. Dany?"

She smiled and said, "Nor do I. As I said, we hardly knew her at all."

Montclair realized the two of them were such well-practiced a pair that he would not be able to find anything of value from a conversation with the two of them. He would need to separate them in the future if he wanted to find helpful information from either of them.

"That is all I need for now," he said to Jean-Paul, "but I may need to trouble you again, so I must ask you to stay nearby if at all possible. I know you have obligations, of course, but I hope you will leave your contact information for my office if you leave Paris."

"Bien sur," Danielle answered while Jean-Paul nodded in assent as they left the interview.

What a pair, Montclair thought as he collected their glasses.

Eddie said the same thing, "They seem to be as strange a pair as Bella and Fan, don't they?"

"Absolumente, Eddie," Montclair replied. "Do we have any solo acts this morning?"

"Yes, first we have Carter Beauregard Philip."

Montclair gave a little smile, "How important he sounds, yes?"

Eddie smiled back, "Indeed." He walked to the door and opened it for Carter Philip.

Hardly disguising his displeasure, Carter entered the small room and sat down. He refused anything to drink.

"I can't imagine how, but I would like to help," he said to the commissaire, trying but failing to hide his annoyance.

Montclair nodded.

"Do you know how Morgana Standish made a living? Her occupation?" He came straight to the point.

Carter looked a bit taken aback by Montclair's directness.

"Well, no, not really. She appeared well-off ---"

"'well off?" Montclair interrupted.

"She seemed to have money – a lot of money," Carter explained. "But I don't know where it came from. I hardly knew her."

Montclair was beginning to get impatient, "It is surprising to me that everyone tells me they hardly knew her – but she was a part of your traveling circus, wasn't she?"

"Well, that hardly seems fair. I wouldn't characterize us as a circus."

"How would you characterize this group?"

"We seem to be traveling companions, that's all, based on our friendship with François. Nothing more than that."

"*Eh bien*," Montclair waved his hand dismissively, regretting his loss of temper. "So, what was your relationship with François?"

"Like most of the people at the banquet, I was an investor in his recent film."

"I see. And if you don't mind my asking, where does your money come from?"

Carter puffed out his chest, "I mind very much. How do my finances figure in this woman's death? I fail to see any connection."

"It is not important what you do or do not see. It is only important to me. Now, please, would you answer my question?"

Carter was at a loss and decided to tell the commissaire the same thing he told new acquaintances, "I used to be in the financial sector and with the advice of some close friends, I made some wise investments so that I am able to live on my dividends."

"How fortunate for you. Where did you meet François? I am under the impression he is not what is called a jet-setter – is that true, would you say?"

"Well," Carter began, "that is true, but his family is large and some of the Desenfants do travel in the same circles I do. I met his sister, Marie-Claude, when I was seeing a friend of hers. It was at her wedding to Hassim Barkat where I met François. My friend and I were no longer together but I went to the wedding at Marie-Claude's invitation. And, well, you know the rest."

"Mais non – no, I do not know any of the rest. Please go on. How did you come to be here?" Montclair said sharply. This man was the most foolish of the people he had spoken to today, but he was also the weakest, the easiest to break. Montclair had met many hustlers, and Monsieur Beauregard was just another hustler – better dressed, but a hustler - *vraiment*.

Carter turned to Eddie and asked him for a glass of sparkling water before he answered Montclair's question.

"How did I come here? Everybody at the banquet came here," he said, nonplussed.

"I apologize – my English is not very good. I meant to ask how did you come to invest your money in his film project?" Montclair was very polite. There was no point in attacking him now; he could inadvertently tell Montclair something of use if he were comfortable.

"Ah, I see, yes, of course. Well, Marie-Claude told me about the documentary and that François was looking for investors. Naturally I was interested, and I approached him and that was that – I became an investor."

Montclair was tired of talking to this man. Nothing he said was believable. Hustlers don't invest their own money – ever. *Jamais*.

"M. Philip," Montclair pronounced it in French, "I think I have all I need today. But please don't leave Paris until this investigation is over."

Carter looked up sharply, then relaxed and asked, "I suppose that goes for all of the group?"

"Yes. All of you must remain."

Marie-Claude and Hassim came in for their interview next, and Hassim spoke to Eddie and Montclair before they had a chance to speak to tell them he hoped they could get through this procedure quickly.

"My wife just lost her brother to a terrible accident and another sudden death is too much – she's fragile," he said as he sat down.

Without a word, Eddie put the water carafe and two glasses on the table. He then poured each glass and handed them to the couple. Marie-Claude picked hers up and took a sip.

Montclair raised his eyebrows and answered, "I will try not to keep you. Perhaps you would like to leave and come back after your errand?"

Hassim shook his head, "No, let's just get it over with now."

"*Eh bien*," Montclair nodded. "I need to know where you were when Mme Standish died. Also, do you have any thoughts about any enemies she may have had?"

Marie-Claude cleared her throat and answered first, "We were at the table with everyone else. It was a sort of celebration because Morgana had returned from the hospital, and we all wanted to show our support for her."

"And our happiness that she was not badly hurt," Hassim interjected and drank some of his water.

"Or dead, yes?" Montclair suggested.

"Well, that goes without saying," Marie-Claude objected to his tone. "I know we were all relieved, but only Fan and Bella thought she died at the catacombs. The rest of us thought she had had a mild heart attack."

"And isn't that how she died?" Hassim argued.

"Perhaps," Montclair answered.

Marie-Claude started to speak, and Montclair noticed Hassim checked his watch.

"I don't know anyone who would wish her dead. No one, surely, would want her to die just because she was annoying."

Montclair noticed the sweat breaking out on Hassim's forehead and lips. He was nervous. Why?

He answered Marie-Claude, "Yes, Mme Desenfants, usually annoying people are not killed for that alone."

"Killed?" Hassim asked. "Was she killed?"

Both Hassim and Marie-Claude were clearly worried about this turn of events.

"You are telling us now that she was killed?" Marie-Claude seemed about to break into tears. "That's not possible. We were all there at the table and none of us could have killed her – we would have seen it."

"Yes, we would have," Hassim was emphatic. "How can you make such an outrageous claim?"

"I am sorry if you are offended, but we have proof that not only did she not have a heart attack, but she was poisoned. Anyone at that table could have poisoned her without being noticed," Montclair retorted.

Montclair was a little offended by Hassim's tone, but he was used to angry witnesses. People always made the mistake of thinking the best defense was a strong offense when in fact that approach only insulted the interviewer, and an insulted policeman was then likely to view the witness as a suspect. Montclair was philosophical, you can't overcome your nature.

Hassim checked his watch again, and his voice quavered a little when he assured Montclair he knew of no enemies Morgana may have had.

"We hardly knew the woman, and certainly we had no reason to kill her." Hassim couldn't believe he was talking about murder.

"Not at all," Marie-Claude shared the sense that the scene was surreal and senseless. How did they come to be speaking of murder? She shuddered.

"Are you cold, Madame?" Montclair asked solicitously.

"No. I'm just appalled that we are involved in a homicide! I still cannot believe ---"

"Are we done here?" Hassim interrupted. "My wife is upset, and we have nothing to do with this matter." He was agitated, begging for release.

Montclair regarded him for a moment then said, "You may go." He waved his hand, "I will probably need to speak to you later as the case develops, but since you are providing me with absolutely nothing," he paused, "you may leave now."

After Commissaire Montclair interviewed the Desenfants, he told Eddie he needed to take a break. Eddie left the room, and Ben came in.

"Dash, ça va?"

"Oh, mon ami, tous sont fous! And they are all liars."

Ben laughed, "Isn't that true of all suspects?"

Montclair smiled in assent. "This will not be easy, I fear. Unless they all were involved – which I doubt – why must they all lie?"

Ben nodded sagely, "I don't know, but everyone is afraid of the police. I suppose everyone has a secret."

The two detectives compared notes and then Ben thought it would be better if he gave his friend advance notice before Andie and Max came in for their interview.

"Before you meet them, I want to explain a little about Andie and Max, the musicians, who were at the catacombs and the restaurant. They are not part of the group, but Eddie wanted to bring them along on the trip because he knew Andie would enjoy it. And because they are the musicians at the hotel, they live here and often have breakfast in Le Jardin. She is a funny young woman who thinks she is a detective; her husband is quite charming, as well."

"Oh, that's all I need – an amateur detective!" He shook his head.

"In truth, they are very smart, and they can be helpful in an investigation." Ben assured him. "And you know, I was thinking, if these people are lying to you, then perhaps I can step in as a threat or friend? What do you think? And which would make them tell the truth?"

Montclair snorted, "I have no idea if they even know the truth anymore. Perhaps you could befriend them, as a guest in the hotel? They don't seem to respond to authority at all."

"That's a good idea. You're right – if they are able to stonewall you ---" he paused when Montclair looked confused, "If they refuse to answer you, then there is no reason to believe they would be any different with me. All right, I'll be a fellow guest. Brilliant."

"I still have to interview -" he looked down at his notes, "- a Celeste Colewood and Chantal de Caqueray. Do you know them?"

"I know of a woman named Colewood – she was a famous friend of musicians and artists in the 1960s. She's English. I have no idea what she is doing now, but she is probably a friend of François's. And I know nothing about Chantal de Caqueray. I'm afraid it's up to you to find out who she is and what she's doing here."

"I am afraid, too, that I will learn nothing more from these two women than I learned from the others. I think it will be you, Ben, posing as a hotel guest who will find answers."

Ben smiled, "One hopes."

*****

By the time Chantal came for her interview, Dash Montclair had come to expect verbal fencing from her and the next woman he would see. Eddie offered Chantal a drink, and she chose orange juice with effusive expressions of gratitude.

"I fear I am losing my mind, Commissaire," she had turned abruptly to Montclair. "I have lost a dear, dear friend, you see, and it's driving me mad."

"Are you referring to Mme Standish? I didn't know you were close to her," Montclair responded.

Chantal looked at him blankly. "What -- no, no – we were not friends." She scoffed at the idea. "I am talking about someone who should be here but is not – he is missing!"

Montclair looked at Eddie who very slightly shook his head.

"Mademoiselle de Caqueray, I will ask one of my men to get the particulars from you after you have answered a few questions for me. Then we will look into this missing friend of yours."

"Merci," she said dramatically in a loud whisper.

"Now, you said you were not friends, but you knew Mme Standish, yes?"

"Well yes, I knew her but we were not friends – she didn't like me, and I am not friendly with people who don't like me. She was like a mosquito in your ear, you wanted to swat her away. And nobody seemed to like her. She was loud, vulgar – and she liked to stir up trouble. I do not think she was friendly with anyone."

"I see," he answered. "Do you have any idea what she did for a living? How she made her income?"

"I haven't the slightest idea. As I said, we were not friends – just acquaintances. If that is all, I would like to leave." She stood up as she spoke. "To whom must I speak to raise an alarm for my missing friend?"

Montclair was dumbfounded but saw no reason to make her stay. None of these people seemed to realize a woman was dead, and they were all suspects in the homicide.

"Eh bien," he waved his hand dismissively at her. "Speak to my *chef groupe,* M. Legrand outside this office. He will arrange the alarm," his mustache twitched at that idea. "And don't go away from Paris. There will be more questions as we proceed to discover the murderer." He thought if he referred to the crime as murder, perhaps he would shake her façade a little. But she acted as if she hadn't heard him and departed the room.

As he and Eddie packed up her glass with the others, Montclair exclaimed, "Mon dieu – these people! They could not be less helpful," he declared with exasperation.

Eddie laughed and then apologized for it, "I'm sorry but you're correct – they are only wasting your time, Commissaire, I am afraid."

Montclair sighed, "Well, we must be getting to the end of the list, non? Who is next?"

Eddie smiled as he told the Commissaire, "Celeste Colewood, an Englishwoman whom you will be happy to meet, I am certain."

Montclair was taken aback, "Really? Well, that would be wonderful. After meeting all the creatures in this zoo today, I would be very glad indeed to meet a different animal altogether. Please, bring her in."

Eddie escorted C.C. into the room and asked her if she would like something to drink - water, juice?

"I know just the thing – a mimosa!" She clapped her hands, "I would love a mimosa, darling," she beamed at him.

Eddie melted, looked at Montclair and told him, "It will only take a minute, sir. I'll be right back." He rushed out of the room too quickly to be stopped and made his way across the lobby to the bar in Le Jardin Oiseaux.

Montclair cleared his throat, "May I introduce myself? I am Commissaire Dashiell Montclair, and I am investigating the death of Morgana Standish."

C.C. nodded. She was wearing black hair today, a longer cut that swung around her shoulders when she spoke. She looked almost demure in a bat-wing linen shift in pale pink. She had well-worn Olvera Street huaraches on her feet and her toenails were also pale pink.

"And I am Celeste Montgomery Colewood," she extended her hand and gave Montclair a smile and small nod.

Just as Eddie had predicted, Montclair was already happier.

*****

It didn't take Eddie long to deliver the mimosa to a delighted C.C., but by then the Commissaire seemed to have come back to life with a renewed vigor for his job.

"Eddie," he said to him, "I am happy to tell you I have learned something from Mlle Colewood – forgive me, Baroness Colewood – that will actually help me with my case."

Eddie gave her a questioning look.

"It is entirely my pleasure," Celeste said to both of them. "And, if I may call you Dash, please call me C.C. All my friends do. And I only have friends – I have no enemies." She laughed, sounding like the ringing of little silver bells.

While C.C. sipped her mimosa, she, Eddie and Montclair spoke about Paris and England; what was good about one? What was bad? Where did the best detectives live?

"Even *Poirot* lives in London!" C.C. insisted.

"Well, he's not French, as he will tell you. We have *Monsieur Lecoq* – and *Maigret*!"

C.C. said excitedly, "Written by a Belgian!"

The three of them laughed, and C.C. stood up, "If that's all, Dash, Eddie, perhaps I may go? I've enjoyed this immensely, and I hate to cut it short ---"

"Bien sur, Mademoiselle." If he'd been wearing a hat, Montclair would have tipped it.

"I'll see you tonight, Eddie," she kissed him on both cheeks, then turned around and left.

"Quelle femme," Montclair murmured.

*****

Andie and Max were next. They had a leisurely coffee and pastry breakfast in their suite and then left for their interview with the Commissaire. When they exited the elevator, they found Ben at the front desk waiting for them.

"Are you hiding from me? I thought you two would be eager to tell the police your ideas."

"We have no ideas, Ben," Andie said.

Ben made a face, "You can't expect me to believe that, Andie. You see homicidal intentions when someone stubs a toe."

"Good one," Max agreed.

"You're no better, Max. You just have a better poker face."

"Ben, we're here now," Andie interrupted his train of thought, "So, where is the Commissaire?"

"Come with me."

He took them to the concierge's office behind the front desk and opened the door. Eddie was no longer in the room since Ben had vouched for Andie and Max and no fingerprints were necessary.

"Commissaire, allow me to present Andie Kirkness and Max Pretyman," Ben said with a flourish. He then left, closing the door behind him.

Montclair stood up and said, "I am Commissaire Dashiell Montclair. Please sit down."

"Dashiell?! Your name is Dashiell?" Andie asked gleefully. "Wonderful!"

Montclair was a little taken aback, "'Wonderful'? I don't know about that, but I'll tell my mother how pleased you are with the name."

"Now," he continued. "I understand you were at the catacombs when Mme Standish had her accident."

"When she was first attacked, you mean," Andie felt compelled to correct him.

"When she fell. We don't know any more than that, and I would appreciate it if you would not repeat this. We don't want to frighten people. Do you understand?"

Chastened, Andie nodded affirmatively, "Of course. Sorry."

Montclair nodded. "So, what do you know about Mme Standish? Or perhaps I should ask, do you know anything about her? Anything at all?"

"We just met her the day before the catacombs trip," Max broke in. "So we don't really know anything about her."

"That's right – we just met her," Andie concurred quickly. "We were having breakfast in Le Jardin when she came in, met her friends and died."

"*Naturellement*. Nobody knows this woman. *Eh bien*, you may go, *allez, allez*." he said in disgust and waved his arm towards the door.

"That's it?" Andie asked as she and Max stood up.

"*Oui* - go away, please," Montclair waved his hand at them. "I'm getting a headache."

"Nothing serious, I hope," Max offered, standing by the door and holding it open for Andie.

"I think it will go away once you do."

Andie couldn't help but laugh, "If you think it will help, au revoir, Monsieur le Commissaire."

She and Max gave a little wave and left the room. Montclair put his head in his hands and growled.

*****

When Max and Andie left the Commissaire, they went to the front desk where Andie would meet Dany for the museum trip. The day was grey with enormous thunderhead clouds that threatened but never delivered rain.

"As long as it stays dry, it's a really stunning day – those clouds, so many shades of gray." Max said. "Maybe I'll go for a walk in the park while you're painting-gazing with your movie star friend."

"Oooohhh, how jealous you are," Andie teased him.

"I prefer to fly under the radar, and I'm very comfortable with the little people."

Andie looked at him, "What kind of mixed metaphor is that? You sound like a bat."

"Good one. Well, I'll be leaving you now; don't get into any trouble until I get back," Max said to her.

"How much trouble could there be in a museum? Don't be silly." She gave him a kiss before he turned to leave the hotel.

He started out on his way to the Parc Monceau, arguably the most elegant of Paris' parks. He had researched it and knew it was created by the Duke of Chartres in 1778, perhaps not the most fortuitous time for an aristocrat to make a public display of his wealth or his fondness for English gardens.

The man who designed the garden, Carmontelle, said of his aims when he planned the garden while, perhaps unwittingly, exposing the contemporary zeitgeist: "The true art is to know how to keep the visitors there, through a variety of objects, otherwise, they will go to the real countryside to find what should be found in this garden: the image of liberty."

The image of liberty he sought to display failed to protect the Duke who lost his life in the Revolution. It was a bittersweet history of the park, and Max realized Andie would love it, and with that in mind, he was already planning to revisit the park with her before he arrived there himself.

When he arrived at one of the four iron gates, he was immediately swept into a world of beauty. It was a lush landscape. Here and there among the dark green foliage were shots of bright yellow, orange and red as autumn entered the park. He saw big, thick clumps of lupin, chrysanthemums and roses, lots of roses. He smiled and nodded as he marveled at this English garden in Paris - the Duke had succeeded brilliantly.

Throughout the park there were green iron benches. Max found one in a pool of sun and sat down to read the Parc Monceau pamphlet he found in the Rose lobby. There were people in the park, but he had accidentally found himself in a very quiet, unpopulated clearing. The stillness was seductive especially combined with the warmth of the sun on his back. He listened to the occasional bird call, the hum of bees and the wonderful absence of human speech. He was beginning to enter a pleasant meditative state of mind.

The silence was soon shattered, however, by the sound of an argument. Ah, he sighed. It would have been easier to accept the interruption had it been the billing and cooing of a couple in love. But no – two cranky people unable to appreciate their surroundings were destroying the ambiance. The voices grew louder, and he realized they were coming his way. The only word he recognized was 'François' which was said several times before the argument stopped abruptly followed by the sounds of a scuffle at the entrance of the clearing.

Then the two figures entered the space and saw Max. To his surprise, it was Carter and Fan. When they saw him, Carter immediately turned on his heel and left quickly. Fan brightened and visibly composed himself by pulling his shirt and jacket into place and walked over to sit down beside Max.

"Sorry you had to see that, but he is an awful cad, and somebody had to put him in his place."

Max nodded and murmured Andie's stock phrase, "I understand."

Fan cleared his throat, "I'm only protecting my sister. Before he died, François told me about Carter Beauregard Philip and warned me about him." He paused to gauge Max's interest. Max was a handsome man with a great talent, and Fan was not unaware of the appeal. He believed he could draw closer to the good-looking musician if he fed him gossip. After all, everybody was curious about the death of Morgana, and Max was no exception.

"How so?" he responded to Fan's remark about François.

"Well! I don't know how, but François had found out something about Carter's past, and he told me he was going to warn Morgana since it was clear to everyone that he was going after her."

"Just a moment," Max interrupted. "I'm a little confused. Who was 'going after' Morgana?"

"Carter Philip! And François found out something damaging about him, and he was going to warn Morgana to stay away from him – he was a gold-digger! He told me because he knew Bella was naïve and easily seduced." Fan looked uncomfortable for a minute and quickly turned away from the thought of his sister and back to Morgana. "You know that Morgana was a very wealthy widow, and that's the prize Carter is looking for – a rich widow. François told me that's what happened in New York: Carter was found out by the children of another wealthy widow, and they made a lot of noise about her untimely death."

"Really?" Max drew the word out with his eyebrows raised high.

"Yes," Fan was enjoying himself now that Max had taken the bait. "The children even called in private detectives and were going to contact the police when Carter left the country."

"Goodness," Max said, keeping the shocked look on his face. He, too, was enjoying this unexpected conversation with an unusually verbose Fan.

"I suppose you could say he was one step ahead of the authorities when he came to Mumbai."

"How did François know about it?"

"I have no idea. But François was not the benevolent circus master everyone says he was. Ask Danielle Dufault and Jean-Paul Toussaint how they really feel about him."

Max couldn't believe what a mine of information Fan was turning out to be. Naturally it couldn't be taken at face value, but still. "What happened to them?" he asked Fan.

"They sent their ten-year-old son to François's home on Lake Como and he was killed in a boating accident -- François ran over him!"

"No! Really?" Max was incredulous. He couldn't believe Dany and Jean-Paul would come to a memorial for the man who killed their child.

"I don't understand," he said to Fan. "Why would they have anything to do with him after that? Why are they here?"

"Le Maître contacted them just like he contacted us, and I guess they couldn't turn down a bequest."

Max shook his head. He needed to hear it from Dany herself before he accepted it as truth.

Fan continued, "And speaking of le Maître - Mark Redmond – I believe he and François were very, very close."

"Yes," Max answered. "I think they attended Le Rosey together and were good friends ever since."

"No," Fan said, leaning closer to Max, "I mean very close – as in lovers." He sat back with a nasty smirk on his face.

Max didn't know how much longer he could tolerate Fan's gossip. Granted, it was information he could share with Andie and Ben about the suspects, but Fan's delight in these sordid rumors was repellent. Max had to swallow his angry revulsion and play along with the man.

"Well, that's hardly a crime."

"But it used to be. It hasn't been that long, you know."

Max was ashamed that England persecuted homosexuals for as long as it did and answered, "No, it hasn't, and it is a stain on any democracy to strip the civil liberties from a group of people simply because of their sexual preference when nobody is being hurt. It's horrid what was done to people, horrid." He shuddered.

Fan suddenly looked warmly at Max, "I had no idea you felt that way."

"Any civilized person feels that way."

Fan felt his hopes rise. Was it possible that Max had shared a physical relationship when he was at boarding school? As a Pretyman, he must have gone away to school. Fan fervently believed bisexuality was common in the upper classes in England. He found great consolation in this. Fan was raised with tutors and never attended boarding school himself, so it was entirely speculation.

"What about his sister and her husband?" Max decided to steer the conversation away from this subject so he could find out as much as possible about the Mumbai group and then make a precipitous exit from this mudhole.

"What do you mean?" Fan was mildly annoyed that Max had changed the topic.

"Well, they must have loved François - didn't they?"

Fan snorted, "Hah! Hassim must have hated him. François was going to fire him. He had already hired another cinematographer for the next project."

"Are you sure? I thought Hassim was upset because he didn't know how the new film could get made without François."

"No - I happen to know Hassim was absolutely not going to be on the new film." Fan was smirking again.

Max couldn't believe the change in Fan. The previously staid, decorous, conservative and dull beyond belief Fan Wei flipped a switch and turned into a nasty, salacious, rumormongering and quite vicious gossip. His head was spinning, and he stood up to make some kind of excuse to get away from Fan.

"You know, I was supposed to arrange a passage in a song today, and the band is counting on it for tonight. I hate to leave, but I must go," he said, extending his hand.

Fan looked content as he shook Max's hand. "It has been lovely. So glad I ran into you. I suppose I'll see you again tonight."

Max almost blanched at the prospect, but recovered and said, "Oh, absolutely." He turned and forced himself to stroll out of the clearing.

As he headed back to the Hotel Rose, Max smiled to himself as he pictured Andie's face when he brought her to Parc Monceau. It would be exponentially better to visit the park with Andie instead of Fan.

*****

Andie didn't wait long for Dany. She watched Max leave the hotel and then turned to see C.C. and Marie-Claude with Danielle as they turned into the lobby, coming back from Le Jardin. They were chatting and as they approached, Dany said to Andie, "I ran into these ladies, and they are going to come with us to the musée."

C.C. added, "We had no plans; we just wanted to go out somewhere, and Dany appeared out of nowhere to give us a destination. How lovely!"

Andie was charmed, as usual, by C.C.'s enthusiasm, and even Marie-Claude seemed less morose than usual. The four women left the hotel in high spirits.

Andie was having a lovely time with Dany, C.C. and Marie-Claude, and when they came to the entrance of the museum, she exclaimed with delight, "It's a railroad station! A very old, very big railroad station. I forgot – the Gare D'Orsay, of course."

Dany smiled, "Yes, and wait until you see the inside."

Andie gasped when they entered, "It's huge; it's magnificent. How old is it?"

Dany answered, "Well, it was actually built at the end of the nineteenth century so it's not that old, but the designers wanted it to look old. Eventually, though, it wasn't big enough for long trains, and was going to be torn down in 1970. The government – the minister of culture - stopped the demolition and put it on the list of historic buildings. Eventually it was turned into a museum – in the eighties, I believe – and now it has the biggest collection of impressionists anywhere in the world."

Andie, C.C. and Marie-Claude stood still, transfixed by the sight of the enormous train station dedicated to the Belle Epoque aesthetic. It was beautiful and Andie thought how French it was that there was an office in government to protect the culture of France. She grew up in California where the public couldn't wait to tear down the old and then build their own new monuments. Nobody wanted history in California. Most of the people there came from another place with another history they were happy to forget. It's the 'Now' state, she thought. Andie knew and loved the parts that had escaped the bulldozers and the magnificent countryside - 'from the mountains to the sea', as an old newscaster used to say when he signed off.

Dany smiled at their reaction, which is what she had hoped to provoke with her invitation to visit the museum. "Come, come," she said to them. "I have something even more amazing to show you."

She led them to a large room with a glass floor. Underneath the floor was a true to scale model of Paris.

"Exquisite, non?" C.C. said to Dany who smiled in return.

"I love this," Andie said as she walked slowly looking down at the city beneath her feet.

"Look," C.C. said to Andie and Marie-Claude, "there's the Opera Garnier, in the middle."

"*Incroyable*," Andie used her favorite French word with dramatic exaggeration.

"Yes," Dany answered with a smile, "unbelievable."

They heard a gasp and turned to see Marie-Claude bent over with her hand on her forehead. C.C. also turned to see her and asked her, "Are you alright?"

"I'm just a little dizzy. It makes me dizzy to see this under my feet," she looked down at the city under glass and swayed a little.

"Of course, you can get vertigo from such a sight," C.C. said as she put her arm around Marie-Claude's shoulder.

"Maybe you're pregnant!" Andie suggested brightly.

The three women turned to Andie with frozen, white and shocked faces.

Marie-Claude burst into tears and walked quickly away from them towards the other hall. C.C. rolled her eyes and said softly, "Oh, Andie" then turned to her with compassion.

"What? Please tell me, what have I done?"

C.C. reached out to her with open arms, "You couldn't have known."

"No, cherie, you didn't know. It's all right," Dany said to Andie. "She lost a baby, not that long ago. She was pregnant for the first time, and it was a difficult pregnancy. She was frightened and wanted Hassim to stay with her. They live in the south of France out in the countryside. It's lovely, but isolated and far from a hospital. Hassim couldn't stay with her because François needed him on set and couldn't find another cameraman. So Hassim left her alone, and she had a miscarriage. It was very traumatic because she almost died, and the doctors told her she will never be able to get pregnant again."

"Oh my God. I am so sorry I said that. What should I do? What can I say?" she asked the older woman.

"It will be fine, Andie," Dany reached out and put her hand on Andie's shoulder. "Follow her cue. Whatever she talks about, talk about it with her. She will be fine."

C.C. said, "Yes, it will be fine. Marie-Claude knows you meant nothing by it. She knows it was an innocent mistake. Just don't bring it up – don't apologize because that just brings it up all over again. She knows you're sorry."

Dany stood up straight and clapped her hands, "*Eh bien*, let's go find her and we'll go see the Impressionists. It's the greatest collection in the world."

They found Marie-Claude in the gallery room off the central hall. C.C. hailed her and she turned with a smile to the women. She walked up to Andie and hugged her, "It's all right. Let's have fun, eh?"

Andie felt a blush of warmth and was grateful for the company of these women. Even at her young age – not quite thirty – she realized that much of whatever life wisdom she had received had come from other women – from lessons in love and loss to the most mundane household tips. An elderly Irish-born woman whom Andie had never seen before had spoken to her in a market in New York once, and in her lovely brogue had advised her, "If you turn the carton upside down, the cottage cheese will last longer." Andie smiled at the memory.

Women seemed to have an urge to share what they had learned with other women. This was one of those moments, and Andie was glad to have C.C. and Dany as her teachers. Marie-Claude had also taught her something: how to move past an inconsolable loss and remain sensitive to the feelings of a gauche but well-intentioned girl.

Dany led them expertly through the Impressionists. Andie's jaw dropped at the bounty in front of her – incredible works by all the major Impressionists including Berthe Morisot, Claude Monet, Édouard Manet, Degas, Renoir, Cézanne, Seurat, Sisle, Gauguin and Van Gogh. It was almost over the top – how could this treasure trove exist in one museum?

The ladies wandered happily, murmuring to each other with delighted recognition of one classic painting and then another, then another, another, and so on. As expected in a museum, the group split apart as each woman paused at a different painting. Andie turned a corner and saw C.C. in front of a painting wiping tears off her face. Andie ducked back into the corridor she'd come from and then turned and walked away in the opposite direction. As soon as she felt enough time had passed, she walked carefully into the gallery where she'd seen C.C. weep.

She examined all the paintings closely and then came to one with a little brass plate saying that the Renoir had been donated anonymously to the museum in honor of Baroness Celeste Edwina Colewood. Good Heavens, she thought. She knew C.C. traveled in illustrious circles, but this was beyond beyond.

"Wow," she said softly.

"Yes," Dany was suddenly at her side. "That's a lovely way to express love, non? It will last forever."

"Who gave it to the museum?" Andie asked her.

Dany was amused, "It says so here - anonymous."

Andie gave her a sharp, intense look. "Are you teasing me? Do you know?"

Dany put her arm around Andie's waist and answered, "You are a clever girl, I can see. You watch people, and you know what's going on. But truly, I cannot tell you who 'anonymous' is. I think you should just enjoy the gesture. Whoever it is wanted to make the world see C.C. the way he did."

This Renoir was a bright and sunny painting of a woman, very feminine and light but with a slightly melancholic cast. Her head was tilted, and the eyes looked past the viewer with resignation juxtaposed with affection. Her mouth was smiling slightly, almost heart shaped in peony pink. The entire scene was filled with sunshine shaded by yellow-green trees. It was masterful, and, as Dany said, it was an accurate impression of C.C.

Because she had blurted out the wrong thing to say to Marie-Claude, Andie left Dany's cryptic comments about C.C. and the Renoir alone. She wasn't sure Dany knew who donated the painting anyway, and she accepted it may remain a mystery. Besides, Andie doubted it had anything to do with Morgana's death.

The ladies decided to go out for a late lunch/early cocktail, but Andie wanted to go back to the hotel. When Andie entered the lobby, Chantal was at the front desk, asking loudly if Sasha had arrived yet. When the concierge told her there was no record of Sasha Ivanov, Chantal appeared distraught to the point of hysteria, but merely walked away from the desk toward the elevator, mumbling to herself.

Still fretting, Chantal walked towards Andie on her way to the elevators when the elevator doors opened to reveal Mme Chausson. Chantal gasped at the sight of her and asked, "Sasha? Is it you? Sasha?"

The woman flinched and shook her head no, but Chantal would not be put off. She reached aggressively for Mme, Chausson, but Andie immediately stepped between the women and addressed the VL, "There you are. I was waiting by the front desk. Let's go, I've got a taxi waiting."

Chantal looked at Andie and asked her. "Why are you --- what are you doing?" Then she turned to Mme Chausson, "Sasha? Please, Sasha ---"

Andie interrupted her, "Don't be ridiculous. This is François's cousin from Montreal," as she whisked Mme Chausson away.

When they went outside, Mme Chausson looked at Andie gratefully with tears in her eyes. "*Merci*," she whispered.

Andie was surprised the VL was weeping but thought it must be nerves. "*Pas de quoi*," she answered, then continued in English, "There's no taxi waiting, but here you are," she said, feeling foolish for pointing out the obvious.

VL waved her hand dismissively, and then she took both Andie's hands in hers and clasped them firmly. "*Merci, merci*," she whispered

118

hoarsely and then walked away down the street. Andie watched her for a moment and then re-entered the hotel. She took the elevator back upstairs and let herself into the room.

"Max! Are you here?"

"In here," Max called from the living room. "Wait until I tell you what I've learned today."

"You're not going to believe what I'm going to tell you!" she exclaimed to Max, "I just had a very illuminating encounter with the VL."

"The who?"

"Max! We just decided on a code name for her – the veiled lady. Wait until you hear this!"

"Max," Andie paused for dramatic effect, "the veiled lady is a veiled man."

"What? Why do you say that? What are you talking about?"

"The hands!" she announced, ignoring the second question. "I noticed it the other day but didn't make much of it. Then today – oh, I'll have to tell you how I rescued her, remind me – anyway, she thanked me by taking both my hands in hers and I knew they were man hands. But she clinched it when she walked away. She did not have a female's behind."

"What?"

"Her bum, her behind, her caboose, her ass Max! She is a he."

"Wow," he was impressed with Andie's findings. "I guess it makes sense, though, doesn't it? That's why Eddie wouldn't let you talk to her, uh him. So he knows and is keeping it a secret. Why?"

"I can't imagine," Andie shook her head.

"Oh, come on, your imagination has never failed you before."

Andie laughed, "I know, but the problem is I can't figure out why anyone would cross dress to attend this memorial whatever-it-is. Could Chantal be right? Could it be Sasha?"

"I'm glad you didn't tell anyone else. Remember, the veiled man could still be in danger, and maybe that's why he's disguised as a woman."

"Exactly! We can't tell Ben; if we tell Ben, then the secret is no longer a secret. He'll want to interview and investigate, and the veiled man will be a target."

"But why not tell Eddie we know? Surely he's in on the secret and won't tell," Max suggested.

"Just because we assume so doesn't make it so. Maybe Eddie is still fooled and is only helping a woman in distress – and that's why he discourages me. I mean, we can't be sure he knows, and we'll give it away if we tell him we know."

"I agree. Wow." Max shook his head again, "It explains a lot about the veiled lady, but only makes the whole think more confusing."

"That's why I need your advice. She, or, he, trusts me now. Chantal was going to harass her in the lobby, and I interrupted and rescued her and took her outside – it's a long story, and all it means is that she considers me a friend now. Maybe I should initiate a conversation and tell him I know it's a disguise. How does that sound?"

"I don't know, Andie. I mean, what if that puts you in danger? It's possible this mysterious man is a killer."

Andie scoffed, "Nonsense. That's ridiculous."

"You don't know that." Max insisted, "We don't know why he's hiding. He's disguised – that's suspicious activity in a murder inquiry, don't you think?"

"I know what you're saying, but it's a long stretch from a possible victim to a killer."

"Yes, Andie, and that's my point – until we know which one he is, I don't want you to be alone with him. Promise me, please?"

"All right, Max. You'll just have to go with us."

"Where are you going?"

"When I know, I'll tell you."

Then she added, "And don't let me forget to tell you about Marie-Claude's motive."

"You look very pleased with yourself. But I have a lot of news – I bumped into the odious Fan and he spilled a lot of beans."

"Why do you call him 'odious'?" Andie asked.

"Turns out he's a very nasty gossip!"

"Fan? Meek, reticent, sobersided Fan?"

Max shook his head, "Well, it turns out he's got an entirely different and infinitely more obnoxious personality.

She told him about Marie-Claude's miscarriage and subsequent inability to have a child, and that it was believed to be caused by Hassim's leaving her to work for François who wouldn't give him the time off to be with his wife.

"Did she tell you this?"

"Oh, no," Andie answered, "Dany told me after I put my foot in my mouth and teased Marie-Claude that she might be pregnant."

Max grimaced, "Nice one. You must have felt terrible."

"Yes, once I took my foot out of my mouth, I kicked myself for saying it. But Dany and C.C. were very sweet and Marie-Claude showed me she wasn't angry with me. It was actually kind of a nice object lesson for me. I have to think before I speak."

"Really?" Max deadpanned.

She laughed, "But I just don't see her committing murder over it. She seems sad but not bitter or vengeful."

"Maybe she feels vindicated now that François is gone."

"Max, you don't believe that, do you?"

Max shook his head, "Not really. I never heard of a murderer finding peace after killing someone, but you never know."

"Maybe Hassim wasn't so forgiving," Andie suggested.

"Well, Fan said Hassim was going to be fired by François, and maybe the miscarriage and losing his job put him over the edge."

"Maybe."

Max said facetiously, "Anything's possible."

"Don't start!" Andie threatened. "I've got to get ready. You can tell me the rest of the tabloid news while I paint my face after my shower."

"Oh, I will. But I'm not sure you'll be able to keep your hand straight when you're drawing your eye-liner."

"That bad?"

Max nodded, "That bad."

*****

Andie noticed the message light on the phone was blinking. Max picked up the phone, and Andie watched his face as he listened to the voice mail.

"The skullduggery begins," he told Andie.

"Yes?"

"That was Ben. He's going to pretend to be a guest here to investigate Morgana's death. He's going to be my uncle, and you and I will introduce him as such to the suspects."

"You're kidding, right? Uncle Ben?" she laughed.

Max was nonplussed, "What's so funny about that?"

"I forgot again – you're English. Uncle Ben is the advertising logo of a very well-known rice company. He's portrayed as a black man for some reason. I would have thought a Chinese man would be more appropriate."

"I know why – he's supposed to be the good old servant in the kitchen, taking care of the family."

"Well, that's kind of awful then, isn't it?"

"Look at Aunt Jemima – you Americans have a funny way of dealing with the history of slavery in your country."

"It's pretty bad when you look at it like that." Andie shuddered. "Happy slaves gladly making rice for their master's family."

"Anyway," she continued, "Uncle Ben is a silly name, but he actually looks enough like you to be a plausible relative.

"Because we're both English? Don't tell me we all look alike."

"Well, I don't know, you're an island people – maybe certain characteristics get passed on, you know, in an insular population. Weak chins come to mind …" Andie laughed.

"Is that why all Americans are rude?"

Andie threw a pillow at him. "No, only the really smart ones."

He threw the pillow back at her, "I'd like to meet one of those."

"Allow me to introduce myself," she said laughing, then pushed him onto the bed and jumped on top of him.

*****

CHAPTER FIVE

When they finished their interview with Montclair, Hassim gave Marie-Claude a kiss and hugged her tightly.

"I won't be long," he promised.

She scoffed, "You don't know when you'll return."

"I don't want you to worry. Do you want me to call?"

She shook her head, "That would make it even worse – waiting for a phone call. No, no – just go and do your best." She felt ridiculous, as if she were sending her child off to school, 'do your best' - it was absurd.

Hassim smiled as if in response to her thoughts. "I will keep you in the front of my heart and return to you as soon as I can."

Marie-Claude crossed herself and whispered, "*Bonne chance.*"

Hassim kissed her again and left the hotel while Marie-Claude went down to Le Jardin for her brunch date with C.C.

*****

Hassim had debated taking a taxi to Rue Myrrha for the sake of saving time, but he knew he would stand out and be noticed in the neighborhood if he arrived in a taxi – and he did not want to attract attention. Besides, the number 4 line was only a few blocks away and it went to the Chateau Rouge metro station. He was going to the lower end of Rue Myrrha – the dangerous part – not far from the station.

Hassim had lived in the neighborhood around the Chateau Rouge metro station when he first immigrated to Paris as a young teenager. The neighborhood was sometimes called Little Africa because it was where newcomers from Algeria, Morocco, Egypt and West Africa first landed when they came to Paris. For an immigrant, it was wonderful and frightening at the same time. It was good to see familiar faces and hear familiar languages, but there were also hoodlums and hooligans who preyed on the newcomers or dealt drugs, just as in the old country. The criminals had also immigrated. For those who left Algeria to escape crime, the discovery that the same malefactors had immigrated too was devastating.

But Hassim had thrived in an environment similar to Algiers – a cosmopolitan city built by and for trade since ancient times. Africans, Moors, Arabs, Berbers, Egyptians – these were his people in a way Europeans would never be. He learned to avoid bad parts of town and was thankful his Algerian face could blend in and hide his upper-middle class status.

Hassim was not surprised he had been told to meet here. It was lawless; the police came in frequently with their big wagons and filled them up with suspicious people, but it changed nothing. The immigrants were expendable, interchangeable and relentless. They had nothing more to lose – they had already lost everything, and it made them invincible. It also made some of them reckless, larcenous and even murderous.

*****

Ben had become very curious when Montclair told him about Hassim's nervousness and anxiety, and he decided to keep an eye on him. He followed Hassim and was grateful for the crowds in the metro which allowed him to keep out of sight while shadowing Hassim closely. He was puzzled by Hassim's choice of metro train and couldn't shake the feeling that they were headed to the Chateau Rouge station. What could Hassim, an esteemed cinematographer married to a very wealthy member of a well-known aristocratic family, be doing in the dark street of Rue Myrrha? And what – if anything - did this trip have to do with Morgana? Or François? He and Montclair were predicating their investigation on a link between Morgana and François that resulted in both their deaths, and now a nervous Hassim is headed to Rue Myrrha – how could Ben connect the dots? He was certain Hassim was hiding something, and it was beginning to appear that it was something sinister. It was clear to Ben that Hassim knew where he was going and how to get there. It wasn't his first time in this neighborhood, and it suggested to Ben that Hassim might have a criminal past.

Ben was finding it difficult to keep up with Hassim because he blended in with the crowd so easily – he was *mahgrebian,* North African. He was also concerned because he knew unlike Hassim, Ben would stand out with his pink skin and blue eyes; he hoped he would appear to be a tourist slightly off the beaten path

*****

When Hassim exited the train at the Chateau Rouge Station, he stepped outside into the sunshine and was overcome with nostalgia. As he started walking to Rue Myrrha, memories flooded in of sights and sounds of another time, in another place. His earliest memories were the best ones, and he relished the reverie of a childhood filled with wonderment and magic, of the security that can only be felt in the arms of one's loving parents, a sense of peace that comes from the protection they provide. His thoughts returned to the time he spent alone on the beach when he was a little boy.

Born in Algiers on the African shore of the Mediterranean, he loved living by the sea in Boumerdès, the seaside neighborhood where the family had a waterfront villa. He recalled playing on the warm sand and pretending he was a pirate from Barbarossa's fleet who was stranded on an island, waiting for rescue. He watched the ships and used his father's binoculars to see their flags of origin; there were ships from all over the world, as in centuries past. Hassim's mother had told him the history of Algiers, the Barbary Coast, the invasions from foreign countries, and the centuries of pirates – especially Barbarossa. He loved looking out at the blue-green sea, calling up the ghosts of the brave pirates who fascinated him. Those sun-drenched days would shine in his memories all his life.

He reminded himself those days were long gone, however, and he needed to focus on today's mission – and how he was going to succeed at such a daunting prospect. Once again, he felt in need of rescue – where was Barbarossa?

*****

Ben followed Hassim into the crowded streets heading towards Rue Myrrha. He was struck immediately by the similarity to North Africa, where he had spent considerable time when he was with MI6. He felt as if he went underground in Paris and came up in Morocco. The sight of Little Africa was startling and yet familiar. He had always loved the bazaars not only in North Africa, but all over the faded trails and *caravanserai* of the Silk Roads. The colors and the smells were what he loved the most, and they were displayed abundantly here.

The women wore their indigenous colorful clothing and he felt he was walking among flocks of tropical birds. And the scents! The aroma of spices from faraway lands he vaguely remembered from his days in the Middle East and Central Asia made his mouth water, and he found he was craving coffee. He wished he could linger and explore this neighborhood that reminded him so much of North Africa. Then he remembered he was also under the gun, so to speak, on those occasions as well as now, here in Paris, and he wondered if he would ever have the time to leisurely enjoy a Moroccan dinner without having to cut it short to run after a malefactor.

*****

Hassim walked down Rue Myrrha and, as instructed, he turned and took one block to the left and then one block down to the right and found himself on a street with garages and small shops where the owners lived upstairs. The first rule of his life in Paris was to never turn left on Rue Myrrha. His uncle and cousin warned him repeatedly, and this was the first time he had ever turned left. He had to laugh – a short, bitter burst of sound. The streets were relatively empty of crowds with only the occasional local resident buying groceries and then scurrying back home. As usual in any city, there were a few men on street corners passing time. In spite of these pedestrian transactions, the area seemed dark and menacing. Hassim knew this part of town was ruled by lawless criminals, who respected no one and especially not each other. In every family down here on the left end of Rue Myrrha, there would be at least one child who saw the cash and the flash of the swaggering tough guys, and who then made the easy decision to follow that money. Every city had neighborhoods like this – from Moscow to Honolulu. Hassim knew this and had seen more than his share, but turning left on Rue Myrrha was the most frightening prospect he had ever faced.

He looked into faces as he walked, and it seemed to him that everyone knew he was in the wrong place. His brown skin garnered him nothing – neither acceptance nor acknowledgment that he was one of them. They gave him what seemed to be disapproving glances – what was he doing here? He felt oddly insulted; he had a right to be here - he belonged to the *mahgreb*, but he knew he had never been on these streets before - it was the dark side of Little Africa.

He made the right turn where he'd been instructed and, looking to the right and left for possible henchmen, he found the garage where he'd been told to bring the money. It was situated at the end of the block, in an alleyway. He tried to calm his nerves so he wouldn't make a mistake and do something stupid that could blow up the whole deal. He had to be calm and collected to pull this off. He wished he had a gun. He had never had a gun but thought this was the one time he needed one. The alley was dark and it seemed as if every window looking down to the street had someone watching him in it. He looked up but saw no one. Still, he knew they were there.

The shop had a roll-down door like a garage that closed the entire shop, with a smaller, regular sized doorway on the left cut into the metal. He slowly walked over to the small door, looking again to the right and the left for any potential threats. He saw no one and advanced to the little door and knocked. Nothing happened for a moment so he knocked again, louder.

Shadowing him was Ben, who was hiding behind a recessed doorway just across the alley and around a corner. He saw the door open and watched Hassim enter the dark interior. Before the door closed completely, Ben was able to cross the road and put his foot in the doorway, keeping the door open slightly. He waited a moment and then quietly and slowly opened the door wide enough to let himself in.

He closed the door silently and stood in the darkness just inside to get his bearings. He saw a white van immediately in front of him and to his right. It gave him cover, and he could see the only source of light was in the far-right corner in the back of the garage. He slowly crept alongside the van towards the back of the room.

Hassim had been led to the back corner of the garage where, under a dim hanging light bulb, there was a card table and two metal folding chairs. There were two men there, one of them pointing a gun at Hassim. Hassim had seen that the man who met him at the door had a gun in the front of his pants.

Ben couldn't hear all the words they were saying, but from what he saw, he realized Hassim was there to pay them off for something. Could it be the murder of Morgana? The man who seemed to be the leader of the group took an envelope from Hassim, opened it, pulled out the money in it and laughed. He shook his head and frowned, and Hassim raised his voice and gesticulated. The three men looked amused but the leader suddenly snarled at Hassim and told him to leave. "Allez-y!"

Hassim yelled back, "Not without the girl!"

As if on cue, Ben took a step forward in front of the van and saw a young girl gagged and bound to a chair behind the table. With his gun ready, he shot the man who was holding the gun dead center in his hand. The man cried out and fell to his knees clasping his bloody hand. Ben quickly turned his gun arm slightly and shot the man pulling his gun from his waist in his knee. He too cried out in pain and collapsed onto the floor, both hands grasping his bloody knee.

Ben advanced rapidly and spoke loudly to the leader, "Give me your weapon – or get a third eye. Hassim," he turned to him, "get his gun and the others'."

Hassim hastened to get the guns and handed them to Ben who told him to keep one for himself. Hassim hesitated, but Ben said, "Don't be a fool – take it! Get the girl and hurry - we have to leave."

Hassim untied the girl, and they ran towards Ben who said to him, "You need to use that gun to guard her – go to the door and wait for me, but for god's sake, be ready to shoot anyone who tries to stop us. Go on," he waved his arm at them, "get going."

He turned to the three men, two in pain and one ready to burst from anger.

"You're on the wrong side, gentlemen," he approached the leader, stepping over the one who was still writhing in pain, clutching his knee with both hands. Ben took the envelope of money out of his jacket pocket with ease – the man was not about to put up a fight.

"I'm on the right side," he continued as he backed away from them. He looked hard at the leader – the only man who was uninjured, "You don't have a weapon; you don't have any help; and I'm the wrong target – I have weapons, I have my friend with a gun, and I have Interpol to help me." He thought he'd throw in the last bit just for effect – and it worked. Ben saw the startled response in his eyes. But he knew there were others outside the garage that would do the leader's bidding - he wasn't entirely without help.

He backed out of the garage quickly and joined Hassim, who introduced the young woman who was named Samia – Hassim's sister. Ben was suitably impressed with this information, and he shook Samia's hand firmly and gave Hassim his warmest smile along with a gesture to hurry along.

The three of them turned down the alleyway towards the right side of Rue Myrrha. Ben walked backwards with his gun at the ready, and he insisted Hassim carry his gun so that it could be seen as he led the way. They walked silently as quickly as they could without attracting attention.

"We can talk when we get out of here", Ben had cautioned them. When they reached Rue Myrrha, they were relieved to find a big crowd of happy, noisy shoppers filling the street. They exhaled and joined the boisterous crowd.

They were immediately enveloped into the scene - the colors, the smells and the faces from all over the *Maghreb*. Some women were busy buying food, some buying fabric, some buying jewelry - all the shoppers bargaining loudly with the vendors; street musicians played drums in native styles that were inadvertently in counterpoint to each other; and on top of the cacophony was the sound of laughter – from belly laughs to dry cackling to the lilting sound of a merry aria of delight; these were the sounds most comforting to Hassim. He knew these people. Suddenly, he and Samia heard a familiar melody that cut through the crowd like a strike of lightning. They followed the tune into a small shop as if hypnotized.

Ben had been separated from them by the twists and turns of the unpredictable crowd. He knew Hassim and Samia still needed protection until they were safely back in the hotel and hurried to catch up. He frantically looked all around as much as he could in the packed street. Then, out of the corner of his eye he saw them duck into a small shop. There were lanterns of all shapes and sizes – some enameled with color, some plain tin with cut-outs – hanging above the entrance with brightly colored caftans and *djellabas* that looked like flags blowing in the breeze under the lanterns.

He followed Hassim and Samia into the small, dark shop and walked into a wonderful cloud of incense and African coffee beans. There were hundreds of items, from tape cassettes and CDs to Moroccan leather wallets, bags and belts; *balghas* - embroidered Tunisian slippers like Aladdin wore - side by side with Algerian *babouches* in turquoise and scarlet; silver picture frames glinted next to jewel-toned tea glasses on bright copper platters; honey-dripping pastries and glowing bottles of argan oil next to Moroccan blue tiles and *Tajine* pottery. Ben was overwhelmed by the enticing scents of leather and wood – cedar chests and puzzle boxes - in addition to the incense and perfume oils and all the legendary spices that spawned and spurred global trade for centuries.

Perhaps Ben would finally get his cafè Arabe. When he joined Hassim and Samia, the owner came over to them and asked if they would like a café. When he returned, he handed Ben a cup with a smile. Almost as if he knew, Ben thought. He brought the cup to his lips and smelled the aroma of cardamon before he took a sip. The coffee beans were full-bodied and the cardamon scent was like icing on a cake. Ben made a short moaning sound – it was more delicious than he'd remembered.

And all the while, Hassim and Samia listened to the recording of the singer transfixed, with tears in their eyes.

"It's Umm Kulthum," Hassim told him. "She is singing *Inta Umri*, one of her songs that everyone knows and loves. She is no longer alive, but she is still the most popular – the entire Arab world holds her in reverent esteem."

Ben had never heard Hassim wax eloquent about anything and was impressed by his passion.

"I would like Andie to hear this – she is such an inventive singer herself; I think she would enjoy this."

Hassim asked the owner if they had a cd for sale. "Bien sur", he replied and Ben made the purchase.

Then, hastily, Ben hailed a cab for the trip back to the hotel. As enjoyable as these last few minutes had been, they had to get out of this neighborhood. Each of them fell into a satisfied silence as they settled into the taxi bound for the Hotel Rose. Ben kept a keen eye out to make sure they weren't being followed, but Samia fell asleep on Hassim's shoulder and Hassim closed his eyes as well. "Just for a moment," he assured Ben. They were safe.

Hassim slept for a few moments, and when he woke up, Ben was able to fill in the blanks as to what had just happened. It was a short - and familiar to Ben – story of his sister falling prey to sex traffickers at the train station.

"Why didn't you call the police?" Ben asked him.

Hassim shook his head, "Maybe I should have, but I believed the kidnappers would kill her before I could get the money to them. They would have seen police cars and taken her away to get rid of her. That's what I believed, and so I paid the money."

"How did you get the million francs?"

"Marie-Claude is very wealthy although we never touch that money – until today. Her family left her a healthy trust fund – at François' insistence. He told his family if he couldn't share the estate with her, he didn't want it. It took courage, but François was close to his sister and wanted her to share everything he had."

Ben nodded, and he realized he could check him off the list of suspects in François's murder. Furthermore, he had no reason to kill Morgana.

"I still don't know what you were doing there – you saved my life, but I don't know how or why you were there."

Ben smiled, "I was following you; Commissaire Montclair thought you were acting strangely when he was interviewing you; he asked me to follow you." Then he laughed and continued, "It was lucky for you that you don't have a poker face."

Hassim smiled broadly and nodded in agreement, "Sometimes it seems God is watching out for me. I have been blessed more than once in my life, and I feel like a cat who is on his ninth life."

"Then you must be very careful for the rest of it."

"I will be. I haven't even given you thanks yet!"

"Well, we've been busy." They both laughed.

The taxi pulled up to the Rose, and they woke Samia up. As soon as she opened her eyes and sat up, she looked at Ben with such admiration that both men noticed.

"Uh oh," Hassim chuckled, "I think you have a real fan here."

Ben looked at Samia and smiled, "Your brother is the hero, Samia; I'm just along for the ride."

Sami cast her eyes down in shyness, but she knew who the hero was. "Thank you," she whispered to Ben.

*****

Hassim put Samia in the extra bedroom in the suite where she fell asleep immediately. Marie-Claude hadn't returned from the museum trip yet, and he lay down on their bed to rest. He was exhausted and in shock. How could he have ever thought he could rescue Samia? Thanks to Allah, Ben was there. Never in his own life had Hassim experienced such danger – not personally. Naturally he had seen violence all around him when he was young. He thought about his special childhood when he lived in a paradise and was loved and protected by his parents. He closed his eyes and let his mind wander to that time.

As usual, he was at the beach, his feet in the water as he gazed at the blue-on-blue horizon, deep in thought; he was on the lookout for a ship, any ship. He heard his mother's voice.

"Hassim! Hassim, come here now," Fatima called to him.

"Mama?" he turned to her.

"Hassim," she was a little breathless when she reached him, "we must go now. Papa and I have packed your things, and it's time to go."

"Go?" Hassim couldn't imagine what she was talking about.

"Yes, hurry now." She put her arm out and took his hand in hers. She pulled him gently towards her, but she could feel his resistance now that he was no longer a small child. He reluctantly allowed her to hold his hand.

"Where are we going?"

Fatima had an inspired answer, "We are going to the other side of the sea." She pointed to the Mediterranean.

"The other side?" Hassim looked up at her as they walked towards the villa. How could they know he wanted to go there? And now? Right now?

"Yes, the other side of the sea." Fatima congratulated herself on her quick thinking of the perfect destination for her son. He was now ten years old but his devotion to the sea was just as great as when he was a child.

Hassim picked up his step, excited now for the opportunity to see the other side. He was amazed they could read his mind - it was just what he wanted!

Hassim always looked at his life in two parts: before and after June 22, 1966 when his world changed forever. Earlier that day, Fatima had answered a knock on the door to find her close friend Dhiaka in tears. She rushed into Fatima's foyer, quickly closing the door behind her, and took Fatima's arms in her hands. She had come to warn her that a rogue group of ex-FLN soldiers were coming to arrest the Barkats and seize their belongings. Apparently, their material success during the French occupation provoked suspicions that the Professor was in the pocket of the French – a collaborator. It had taken four years for the powers that be to get around to them, but they had determined the Barkats' political status was deeply suspicious. Dhiaka believed the Barkats would be arrested and interrogated.

"That's absurd," Fatima protested. Yanis entered the room and when he heard the warning, he nodded.

Hassim's father, Yanis Barkat, taught at University of **M'hamed Bouguerra.** He was a chemical engineer highly valued by the French who invaded Algeria for her oil. Yanis Barat was rewarded well for his knowledge of not only how to extract oil, but where it was. The professor helped the French because he knew it was useless to resist, and he believed his family would benefit from the material rewards he earned with his knowledge. Nonetheless, he was an Algerian and celebrated when the French left in 1962.

However, as usually happens after revolutions, then all hell broke loose. Algeria was thrown into sometimes violent civil unrest as competing parties vied for power in the new state. Yanis was still in a protected profession due to the enduring value of Algeria's greatest natural resource – oil. But chaos reigned in post-revolutionary Algiers, and Yanis began to worry for his family.

He didn't care who ruled his country; he was happy Algeria was no longer a colony belonging to one of the imperialist European states. It was enough for him to be free of the French; but those who had fought against the French wanted representation – and authority – in the new power structure. And Yanis came to believe over the years his personal isolationist policy was failing him; with no political identity, he had no protection. He had to flee; his beautiful, ivory tower life had become collateral damage.

"I've been expecting this," he told his tearful friend and his frightened wife. "This country has been destroyed by the war, and now people look at us and how nicely we live, and they believe we are guilty of something. Why haven't we suffered?" He sighed, "I understand. When the French were here, everyone was united in rebellion. Now that they are gone, it's been four years of complete chaos while we determine how we will govern our country. Everybody has an opinion, and no one will compromise. They compromised too long under the French. Nobody can agree how to do it so they fight for position; they need new enemies to legitimize seizures of authority – and we are easy targets." He turned to Fatima. "Pack, now. We will leave tonight for Marseille."

Fatima gasped, "Tonight?"

Yanis nodded. Then he shrugged, "We could be arrested tomorrow morning, couldn't we? We could even be arrested ---"

"Don't say it – I will pack quickly."

When Hassim entered the house, Yanis wanted to pick him up, but although he was thin and unformed, like a colt, Hassim was already ten years old, and Yanis recognized the young man in him. Nonetheless, he opened his arms wide and then embraced him tightly. "My little pirate," he laughed.

"Papa, are we going over the sea? To the other side?" Hassim asked eagerly.

"Yes, little pirate – we are taking to the sea!" Yanis laughed.

That night they took a night-traveling fishing boat crammed with other immigrants to Marseille, the other side of the Mediterranean. Yanis was well aware of the irony in his taking refuge in France. He hated the French, but knew that once again he had to rely on them to provide for his family.

Hassim couldn't sleep. He was too excited and watched the moon glinting on the waves until the sunrise. His first view of Marseille was breathtaking. So many boats in the harbor! All the pale plastered buildings shone in the morning sun and Hassim delighted in the different facades – Italian, French, and Moroccan, he noted with pleasure. The port resembled Algiers so much that Hassim felt welcomed and not threatened.

His father Yanis, however, felt humiliation with every stranger's glance. He was an immigrant; he was not the intellectual academic lauded by his peers and rewarded by governments. He was a *Maghrebian* – an immigrant from North Africa; he was no different than anyone else on the fishing boat. Yanis was a proud man, but he had compromised his principles and suppressed his emotions for decades, and he was reaching his breaking point.

Fatima's brother, Said, lived in Paris, but he came to meet them in Marseille and took them to the neighborhood where other North Africans came when they landed – Noailles. As the family followed Said down the streets looking for a hotel, the scents in the warm air enveloped the Barkats like an old blanket and they smiled, Fatima and Yanis for the first time since they boarded the fishing trawl. Hassim hadn't stopped smiling; he was living in a dream, hardly touching the ground, with every new discovery sending him higher into the clouds. What a wonderful place, he thought.

Suddenly a cool wind blew over them. "The mistral," Said said. "It comes from the north."

Hassim spoke up, "It's the opposite of the sirocco, isn't it? That's the hot wind from the south. How funny."

Said smiled, "It's the same, but it's different, no?"

Hassim nodded and smiled in answer.

When he was going to sleep that night in a bed with a bumpy mattress and old linens in a dank room in a small, crowded two-bedroom suite, he wondered when they would go to the beach. He was certain his parents wouldn't leave the beachside villa in Boumerdès unless they were going to live in something just as good, or better, in France. This smelly, old but undistinguished hotel couldn't be the final destination. Maybe tomorrow they would go to the beach.

They did not go to the beach the next day, nor the next. Hassim asked, but his parents shushed him and consulted with Said and then with each other after he returned to his own family in Paris. Eventually, Yanis was able to get a part-time tutoring job to live on while he waited for openings and official clearances in the academic world. But his expectations of a quick and easy entry into a French university were not met, and over the ensuing months and years, he began to feel frustrated.

Professor Barkat was loath to react without great thought. He had always relied on his intellect and was naturally resistant to a knee-jerk emotional response in any situation. His words were measured and considerate. But he could never forgive the enslavement of his country by the callous brutality of the pompous and insensitive Europeans. And now he had his hand out in the very country who had enslaved him. His impotence and humiliation were brutal.

Over time, his resentment turned to anger, and then the anger turned inward; he became clinically depressed. He continued to tutor, but he did so emotionlessly, and he was boring. Students began to drift away. He spoke very little to Fatima and Hassim and was unable to communicate as a parent or husband. His presence was that of a boarder in a rooming house. It seemed to Fatima that he was locked behind an invisible screen. He would smile and nod at her, but never engaged in conversation. He seemed devoid of ideas.

The responsibility of taking care of the newly-arrived family fell more and more to Hassim. He didn't mind helping his mother since errands enabled him to get outside and explore. But when Hassim was twelve, his mother fell ill. She was overwhelmed with pain and by the time she went to a doctor, the cancer was fatal; it was only a matter of months before she would die. Yanis broke down completely in despair. He sat all day at the window, looking out at nothing, and appearing to be waiting for death, his own as well as Fatima's.

Hassim wanted to shake his father to make him respond to this emergency. He didn't know where to turn until Fatima told him to go to the apartment next door and ask for Laila. She was a recently arrived *maghrebian* who had been studying nursing when she left Algiers. Fatima told Hassim she would help them.

Laila was only nineteen and Hassim felt very shy with her. He had no idea how to speak to a pretty girl, but fortunately for him, Laila was kind and grateful to his parents; she never teased him. She came and lived with the Barkats for the few months Fatima had left. Yanis had managed to bring enough money with them so that they were able to pay Laila and keep Fatima in some comfort.

But Fatima was handling all the management of the house, and she grew weaker every day. She taught Laila everything she would need to know to run the house when she was gone. Laila had agreed to be a housekeeper and nurse for Yanis. And Fatima had planned for Hassim as well.

Laila brought him to her one day.

"Hassim, you know I am dying."

Hassim started to cry.

"We don't have time for tears, my little pirate," she shook her finger in his face with a smile. "You must listen carefully to me now. I have decided that you will go to Paris and live with Said and his family."

Hassim started to speak, with more tears, "But ---"

"No!" Fatima spoke harshly for a minute. Then she softened, "This is what I want you to do. Do you understand? I am your mother who is dying and I am telling you what I want. Do you understand?"

Hassim lowered his head, "Of course, Mama. But what about Papa? Is he coming too?"

Fatima smiled lovingly at her good son, "No. He will stay here, and Laila will take care of him. All right?"

Hassim was ashamed that he felt relief. He was happy for his father as well, but primarily he didn't want the responsibility for his father anymore. He wanted to be free.

Shortly after she made Hassim promise to do what she asked, Fatima died. Yanis was unable to do anything but weep quietly. Laila helped Hassim pack his few things and she accompanied him to the train station. She assured him Papa would be all right, and she would write him every month to tell him so. Hassim boarded the train after daring to kiss Laila good-bye, and then he turned to find his seat. He didn't look back and his spirits lifted as he realized he was already becoming free.

Within four hours, Hassim's train was pulling into the Gare de Lyon station. His uncle Said had told him to go to the Lost & Found in the station and he would meet him there. Hassim thought that was funny but practical. He asked a porter where it was, and when he found it, there was Said with a big smile on his face. "That was easy, no?" Said asked him.

Hassim laughed, "Yes, it was a good idea, Uncle."

They took a metro train to the Les Halles station and transferred there to another train to get to Chateau Rouge station. Hassim was beginning to feel oddly claustrophobic from the crowds of people in the stations and on the trains. Marseille was a big city, but Paris seemed so much bigger, it was frightening to Hassim.

Said noticed his anxiety and assured him, "Once you have been here a while, all this," he gestured to the crowded metro, "will be normal for you. It doesn't take long to get used to the crowds."

Hassim nodded and tried to assume a confident face. He was a skinny fourteen-year-old from Algiers without his parents in a new city in a new country. How confident could he be?

When they exited at Chateau Rouge and climbed the stairs, they emerged in a neighborhood that looked and smelled very familiar to Hassim. His face lit up, and Said noticed. "You see? It's not so strange after all, is it?"

Hassim laughed, "No, it looks like Algiers and Noaille – how funny. But where is the sea?"

A frown crossed Said's face very briefly, "There is no sea, Hassim. Not for now, but someday …" his voice trailed off in view of Hassim's disappointment.

"But you will enjoy Paris. My son, Dadi, is a student at the Sorbonne, and he will teach you what you need to know to go to school here; he will also tutor you so that you can go to the Sorbonne as well."

Hassim did go to the local school and Dadi became like an older brother to him. Hassim was very grateful to Said's family in part because they encouraged him to go outside on his own – to learn Paris.

He found he could go anywhere he wanted whenever he wanted in his new neighborhood, but he discovered there were invisible borderlines, criminals and ruffians - he had to be careful not to cross either. The gangsters were more deadly than the French authorities in Algiers – rather than imprisoning rebellious young men, they killed them. Nonetheless, he had more personal freedom in his new home, and with Dadi's help and his father's academic connections, he was able to go to the Sorbonne where he indulged his imagination with film studies.

He had always loved the cinema, and he discovered at school all the ways his flights of fancy could be realized. Ironically, he was drawn to documentary films when he saw "The Battle of Algiers", the masterpiece about the Algerian revolt against the French occupation. He burned with passionate fervor for the truth as opposed to fantasy fiction, and it was only a matter of time before his dedication and filmmaking prowess were discovered by a rising star in the world of reality cinema - François Desenfants.

François had come to Hassim's school to give a lecture and after he spoke, Hassim came up to him to ask how he could pursue documentary filmmaking. On the spur of the moment, François invited Hassim out for a beer, and they talked until midnight. François recognized a kindred spirit and offered him a job. Hassim learned how to film on the fly when he was given the job of the film's official cinematographer. François was amused and helpful whenever Hassim mis-stepped; he respected his diligence and ability to learn quickly. They found they shared a dedication to integrity and a passionate sense of morality; they had been a team ever since.

Hassim's little sister was born in Noailles. Leila had kept her promise to Hassim and wrote to him every month. Each letter was an update on Papa's condition after his mental collapse. With Leila's care, he began to heal from the daily trauma his life had become, starting long ago in Algeria. Leila drew him out and when he voiced his worst nightmares, long buried in his psyche, they dissipated in the light of day. One by one, the hideous memories faded, and one day he didn't think of Fatima at all. He realized it when he went to bed that night, and the next morning he asked Leila to marry him.

Leila had come to love the sad man closer to her father's age than her own. His instincts were good; and she eventually wore down the bitter resentments by exposing them for what they were – failed dreams anchored in place by Papa's living entirely in the past. Leila tricked him into the present by feeding him *maghreb* desserts and making strong Arab coffee for him every morning. He began to look forward instead of backward.

Two years after Hassim had arrived in Paris, he received the first letter written to him from Yanis. It began "My dearest son" and included an apology for neglecting him when they were in Noailles and ended with the triumphant news that he and Leila had married and were now expecting a child. Yanis was exultant, and Hassim felt a warm love for his father. He was grateful to Leila and wrote to tell her so. He knew his father belonged to the other part of his life – the better part, perhaps – and he was without regret that Yanis had created his own second life, just like Hassim.

When the little girl was ten years old, and decisions about her schooling needed to be made, Yanis started to contact every Englishman he had met in his career as a respected and highly valued chemical engineer who knew where the oil was in Algeria. It wasn't only the French who craved the liquid gold under the sands of Africa. Finally, it was the wife of a fellow chemical engineer based in London who helped Yanis place Samia in one of the best girls' boarding schools in England.

Samia shared her brother's wanderlust and went to England with an excited anticipation that was well-rewarded; she thrived at the school and made a group of friends that she trusted. Samia had always been a bright little bird, chirping sweetly and hovering over her family. When Sami left for school in England, Papa's tears of sorrow mixed with her tears of joy for her bright future, far away from tumultuous Noailles. Leila and Yanis believed Samia was safe.

Hassim knew that Sami was safe now, with him. Whatever the future held, he vowed he would never let her get that close to danger again. His mind went back to the beach and he drifted off to sleep to dream about the salt air, the turquoise waves that turned into foam around his feet and the warm sand he loved to sink his feet into when he walked.

*****

When they entered Le Salon Jazz that night, Andie and Max found Ben at the bar, waiting for them.

"Did you get my message?" he asked them as he accompanied them to the stage.

"Uncle Ben! So good to see you. How long has it been?" Max asked.

"Not long enough," he answered with a grin.

As Andie adjusted her mic stand, she told Ben, "If we're helping you, I expect you to tell us what you find out."

"Why?" He responded.

"Curiosity?" she suggested.

"Let's just take one step at a time," Ben told them both.

"Let's make some kind of plan," Max said. "Should we introduce you to everyone? Doesn't that seem obvious?"

"Right. Well, we'll have to play it by ear – something you might be good at."

Andie rolled her eyes, and Max groaned, "I forgot how much you like puns. Try and control yourself – these people are sophisticated."

"I think I can pull this off if you two don't get silly," Ben warned them.

Just then, Eddie approached the three of them and said to Andie and Max, "Danielle and Jean-Paul asked me to ask you to join them on your break. I'll seat Ben at a nearby table and then you can introduce him to them, and, ideally, they'll invite him to sit with them. O.k.?"

"I love this cloak and dagger action," Andie told him excitedly. "I didn't know you were in on it too."

"Well, yes, I had to be. After all, I know who Ben really is," he reminded her.

"This is going to be fun," she said.

"I don't know about that," Eddie said a little grimly. "It is a case of murder, remember."

"We have experience," she retorted. "Don't worry about a thing. We know what we're doing."

It was Ben's turn to roll his eyes. "I don't know why I decided to involve you in this. And as always, I must say, your enthusiasm is a little troubling."

Eddie joined in, "And I don't want a shoot-out in Le Salon."

"A shoot-out?" Max laughed. "I hardly think so."

"She's an American," Ben pointed to Andie. "They all have guns, and it seems to be the way they solve problems."

"For Heaven's sake, Ben. I've never had a gun in my life. Neither has Max."

Eddie spoke up, "Of course not. He's English. They're just the opposite – which is no comfort either. I have never understood how an English policeman persuades a criminal to just give up and surrender without using a gun. Why doesn't the criminal fight the arrest? Why put out your hands for cuffs if there's no gun on you? There's no threat - makes no sense at all. English villains seem awfully well-behaved." He shook his head and continued, "In any case, I've got to get back to my guests. Now be good," he shook his finger at them and turned away with Ben joining him.

Ben stopped when he remembered his gift for Andie "Oh, I bought you something today I think you will enjoy." He pulled out the CD and handed it to her.

Max laughed, "Nice try, Uncle Ben, but Andie is very familiar with her. When she was at university, she studied her."

"Well, no, not exactly. I was studying independently with an oud player and he introduced me to her music. She's phenomenal."

"Where was this?" Ben asked.

"I was at Columbia College in New York participating in a joint program with Juilliard – studying music. And through Juilliard I met the oud player and studied Eastern music with him. Umm Kulthum is Egyptian and she may be the most popular singer in the Muslim world. She died in the 1970s, but she's still everyone's favorite. Her voice is very powerful but also haunting – nobody sings like Umm. And "Inta Umri" is one of her most famous songs."

"Do you perform any of her songs?"

"Oh no, Ben. You need to be fluent in Arabic to sing them. There are melismas --"

"What?" Ben asked her, "What's a miasma in music? Something foul?"

Andie and Max laughed, "No, melisma, not miasma. Although there are miasmas in music too, I suppose." Max responded.

"We have to get to work now," he continued. "Andie can tell you all about it when we take a break."

Ben walked away and Max called out the first tune which Andie started singing to Ben as he walked towards the bar, "*Pack up all my cares and woes, here I go, singing low, bye, bye blackbird ...*" Ben turned around and waved at her.

The first set was upbeat and bright; all the musicians were having a good time and it showed. Whenever Max took a solo and the spotlight left her, Andie scanned the room. When the first break came, Andie and Max left the stage and went straight to Dany's and

Jean-Paul's table. As he'd promised, Eddie had seated Ben at the adjacent table for two where he looked suitably forlorn.

Andie and Max made a show of greeting Uncle Ben affectionately, and when they reached Dany's side, she asked them about it.

"It's my uncle Ben," Max offered. "He's always traveling so we rarely get to see each other. He called yesterday to say he'd be in Paris a few days, and I jumped at the chance to see him."

"Oh, please invite him to our table. It seems rude to talk with you while he sits alone. Please," Jean-Paul urged Max.

"If you insist," Max assented and got up to bring Ben to the table. Andie made introductions all around.

Jean-Paul hailed a waiter and ordered champagne. "This is a celebration – *une réunion de famille*! And this time, Andie, you must join us in a toast."

"I'll join one toast – just one. I need to stand up straight for the rest of the night," she laughed.

"*À la famille!*" Dany exclaimed, raising her glass. The others chorused the same, and all took a sip.

"So, you are also a Pretyman?" she asked Ben.

"My mother was. She married a Scot – my father, Fitzhugh Sinclair. The Pretymans were dismayed and threw her out of the family."

"No!" Andie, Max, Dany and Jean-Paul chorused.

Ben just laughed and shook his head. "I'm joking. They welcomed him with open arms and urged him to make his home in Edinburgh."

Max laughed, and Andie punched him playfully on his arm.

"What is the joke?" Jean-Paul asked.

"The English love to insult the Scots. I think it's because they are jealous," Andie told him.

"She's right. She's also Scottish." Max pointed out.

The table laughed.

"Max, I need to go over the arrangement of "My Favorite Things" with you. Would you excuse us?" Andie asked Danielle.

They returned to the stage. As she perused her music charts, Andie said to Max, "I can hardly wait to hear what Ben finds out."

"He never wants to share with us, remember."

"Yes, but he always does – remember?"

*****

"I am surprised to see you here, in a hotel. I would have thought you had a home in Paris," Ben said to Danielle and Jean-Paul

"This is my home. Jean-Paul has a pied à terre a few streets from here," Dany replied. "I love to live in a hotel – it's so easy, and I travel a lot."

"I live in hotels too most of the time," Ben said.

"Does your work keep you traveling?" Jean-Paul asked him.

"Yes, I have to oversee a global business. There are always communication problems when you do the same business in different countries; not only are the languages different, but the cultural customs must be addressed from place to place. Everyone wants the same end result, but the approaches vary from state to state. Unfortunately, I have become something of a problem-solver for the business, so I go from crisis to crisis."

Jean-Paul nodded. "I have found that to be true in film making also. The differences in the crew members' daily routines are tricky, not to mention the union rules in each country are so different," he said, shaking his head. "It's a wonder sometimes that we ever get a movie finished."

"I have heard that *Apocalypse Now* and *Fitzcarraldo* were uniquely difficult for the directors and actors because of the locations," Ben said.

Danielle scoffed, "Well, I know if you work with Klaus Kinski in the jungle, you may well go mad. And *Apocalypse Now* was also in the jungle. Maybe it's the jungle that drives some people mad."

Jean-Paul nodded vigorously, "Oh Kinski was a volcano; he was a *psychopathe*. I knew him, and I learned to avoid him always."

Dany disagreed, "I think *psychopathe* is perhaps too harsh."

She turned to Ben, "He's calling him a psychopath – but I don't agree. Klaus was made of anger – he had nothing else inside him. In his lifetime, there are maybe a few small moments of calm, little islands in the stormy sea - do you know what I mean?"

"I do, and I agree completely. I have met tortured men – and women - like this."

Then he looked up and said, "We were celebrating – let's continue celebrating. There will always be unhappy people in the world, but we don't have to join them."

"Of course not," Jean-Paul, ever the cheerful diplomat, agreed. "It has been difficult these past few days – because of the death of our friend – and some people don't seem to be able to move forward. They need to know It's all right to laugh. To drinking champagne and laughing," He raised his glass.

Danielle and Ben met the toast just as Andie and Max started the evocative, mesmerizing Jobim rhythms of "Corcovado" and Danielle exclaimed, "Oh! I love this song," and she swayed in her seat to the bossa beat.

"*Quiet nights and quiet stars ...*" Andie decided to start the song in English. She would switch to Portuguese after Max's solo. To her delight, C.C. and Carter walked onto the tiny dance floor and began to dance beautifully to the song. Andie expected nothing less from Celeste, but Carter's expertise was a surprise – a pleasant surprise.

Bella watched him from her table with a rapt expression. She, too, was pleasantly surprised. Fan was typically expressionless. Chantal sat at their table watching everything through a boozy haze.

She seemed to have finally accepted the reality that Sasha had left her, and she was going through a time-tested ritual familiar to every woman and man who has ever been dumped: she was getting plastered. On Grand Marnier. Andie saw her, and she recognized the sticky-sweet liqueur when the waiter refilled her glass. Andie enjoyed one glass spread over an entire night – little sips over time, the only way to drink Grand Marnier. But to each her own, she supposed.

Chantal was wearing a heavy black satin wrap-around dress with a bright diamond and silver brooch pinning the front together. Tacky and gorgeous at the same time, Andie thought. She couldn't see the shoes under the table but was sure they'd be dazzlers. If she didn't know better, she would think Chantal was enjoying her unhappiness – her gestures were so over the top; her beautiful hands were flying around. So dramatic. Still, everyone's different. As her dad always said "That's what makes a horse race."

Andie almost missed her cue while she was philosophizing, but she managed to come in fashionably late, not unlike Billie Holiday. As she came to the end of the song, she repeated the last line while the band played slowly and stopped for the last word – "*O, que é felicidade, meu ... amor*" - which she held for a few beats; then the band kicked back into the bossa groove. The audience loved the drama and applauded warmly.

C.C. and Carter clapped from the floor in front of the stage and C.C. reached up to clasp Andie's hand, "Lovely, darling – just lovely." Andie nodded her appreciation, and Max called out a classic, "The Lady is a Tramp". Bernard kicked out a hard and fast rhythm with his brushes, and the bank took off.

After the set, Andie and Max split up: Andie went to sit at Bella's table with Celeste, Fan, Carter and the morose Chantal. Max rejoined Ben and Danielle and Jean-Paul's table. The only ones missing were Marie-Claude and Hassim.

"You were terrific – just terrific!" C.C. said ecstatically. Andie glowed, and she realized C.C.'s enthusiasm for music was what endeared her to musicians long ago – she took great pleasure in a well–played tune.

"That Latin one, that was very romantic," Chantal managed to say through her tears, which she turned off and on periodically, depending on her audience. A drama queen, Andie thought as she turned to her with a smile.

Normally she avoided drunk customers when she performed, but Chantal seemed so bereft - genuinely or not - that compassion seemed more appropriate than a quick getaway. "Thank you, Chantal," she managed.

Then she turned to Carter and said brightly, "And you were quite the Fred Astaire, Carter – very good on your feet."

The others around the table agreed, and Carter blushed a little and said, "Blame my mother. She had me in cotillion ever since she found out an extra boy was always in demand."

He didn't add that she believed if he danced with girls from the upper classes, he might move up in society. And because he grew tall before other boys his age, was handsome and turned out to be a great natural dancer, he was invited to all the cotillions during his four years of Catholic high school. His mother worked with him every night - cajoling and threatening - to get his grades good enough to gain a scholarship to St. Peter's, and he succeeded. His school was not as fancy as the other boys' secular prep schools, but some of his classmates were sons of wealthy - but devout – Catholics, and Carter wooed them to make sure he was invited to all the parties. Carter parlayed his good looks into romances with what his mother would call "the best girls", and his occupation in life was set firmly and irrevocably: he would marry wealth.

He was surprised how long he would have to search for the right rich girl. Most of them had protective parents who did not see a son-in-law when they looked at Carter. Turns out, rich girls marry rich boys. But Carter never gave up hope. He believed there were bound to be rich spinsters whose parents would be happy to marry them off. Spinsters and widows. Widows very often had children, however, who were suspicious of their mothers' suitors. It could result in a very sticky situation – and it had. Spinsters were a much better bet.

"Well, I think your mother was onto something – you're a marvelous dancer. It's heaven dancing with you." C.C. said. "Bella, you should take a whirl."

"Oh, no, I couldn't. I'm not a good dancer – truth be told, I'm a terrible dancer. My mother thought I was so awful that she discouraged me from cotillions!" she said with a hoot of laughter that echoed around the table.

"Nonsense," Carter said firmly, "I can make anyone a dancer. I'll show you tonight or tomorrow night. One way or another, you're going to dance beautifully in Paris, I promise."

Bella's cheeks bloomed as he spoke. He painted such a pretty picture, and Bella wanted to believe. Andie looked at them and saw the dynamic. Cynicism aside, she thought they were perfectly matched in an odd way. This could work.

Andie saw Marie-Claude and Hassim walk into the room and pause to look around. They saw Bella's table, and as they made their way towards her, she realized she was taking one of their seats. She stood up and waved the newcomers over.

"I'm afraid I've taken your seat here," she apologized.

Max had just arrived at the table. Hassim smiled and put out his hand, "Hassim Barkat."

"Max Pretyman," he smiled and shook Hassim's hand. "And my wife, the lovely Andie Kirkness."

"Pleased to meet you," she said and shook his hand.

Hassim said to them, "And my wife, Marie-Claude Desenfants."

She smiled and reached out to embrace Andie, "Oh, I know Andie. We've spent some wonderful time together. But it's lovely to meet you, Max," she said as she shook his hand.

Andie and Max made their excuses and walked over to the bar. Max ordered a Guinness; Andie asked for a glass of room temperature water. Max drank the beer quickly and Andie took the glass onstage.

"You know, you drank that beer so fast, I think it may impede your performance." She started to laugh. "What happens when you're holding a note and you burp? I never thought about that before."

"Neither had I. Thanks for putting the idea in my head."

This made Andie laugh again, and Max couldn't help but join her.

"What's so funny?" Bernard asked.

"Life, Bernard. Life is funny," she smiled at him.

*****

CHAPTER SIX

Saturday

Too early the next morning, Carter woke up to the sound of the phone ringing.

"Hello?" he mumbled, trying to shake the sleep out of his head.

"Carter? It's Chantal."

He waited a moment.

"Carter? Are you there? It's Chantal," she repeated.

"Yes, yes, of course." He was awake now.

"I want to go to breakfast and I don't want to go unescorted. I don't feel like being alone. I will meet you at the entrance in half an hour. Don't be late."

"Chantal, I just woke up, I ---"

She hung up before he could register an objection. But he had none. He was awake now and had nothing else to do, and he knew how to clean up and get dressed in a hurry. He could write a book about the lessons he'd learned from illicit love. The final exam was making a public confirmation of the affair. He had a few passing scores, but he still hadn't made the big match that would allow him to relax, to finally let go of the endless stress – being a gold-digger was a lot harder than most people realized, he thought with his usual irony. For one thing, you had to learn how to reject the ones looking for a gigolo.

Carter was willing to do a lot for a rich woman, but never would he take money for sex – well, not for sex only. As long as he could remember, Carter had followed that rule, easily. The women he pursued were usually not so inclined – they weren't looking for sex without strings - and he kept his eye on the goal at the end of the long run. Sex might facilitate commitment, but that was the prize – commitment.

He never wanted to appear needy: he needed to be able to invite a woman for dinner and pay the bill; he needed to be able to buy little trinkets and flowers for her. With this in mind, he had squirreled away just enough savings to be able to approach his 'intendeds' as an equal. The inheritance he had just received was a gift from the gods. He had spent all his savings wooing the ambivalent Mrs. Woodruff, and his proposal was still hanging in the air when she died.

At first, her family found him devastated by her death. He greeted them when they arrived at her apartment with red eyes and a tear-stained haggard face. They were unmoved. They had never welcomed him into their mother's life and now that she was dead, they were ready to show him the door – preferably empty-handed. They actually accused him of causing her death. It was absurd, he said.

He did go to the safe, as alleged, and he did retrieve the will and found out he was rich due to her death, also as alleged, but *not* before she died. The vindictive children – who were all in their forties! - could not prove when he saw the will. He admitted he profited from her death, but he denied vehemently he had caused it. He smiled at the memory of their faces when the District Attorney – naturally an old family friend – told them in Carter's presence there was no evidence to pursue a wrongful death lawsuit, much less criminal charges. He cautioned them against continuing a public campaign against Carter because he could then sue them for defamation. Oh, how he loved that!

They all acquiesced; they received substantial bequests even after Carter took his share; the publicity was abhorrent to them; and they wanted him gone. For his part, Carter was happy to go. Anywhere in the old country would be fine. Europe, the British Isles, maybe India! He needed another identity, and now he had ample funds to establish Carter Beauregarde Philip in the jet set.

Since then, he had kept his head down until the storm passed, and then contacted this friend in London and that one in Rome until he met François Desenfants at a wedding and decided to become an investor in his next film. Carter realized this would put him in a perfect position for meeting the right people – the ones with money and an appreciation of artistic endeavor. Wealthy art enthusiasts formed a fluid, porous strata in high society, and Carter knew he had a better chance of joining them without the scrutiny more strait-laced members of that class would direct at him and his background. Soon, he was dining with widows and spinsters with money to spare and no one to share it with.

He had already moved on from Chantal but perhaps she had changed her mind when Sasha failed to appear in Paris. Frankly, he thought, he preferred Bella at this point. She was so much easier to read than Chantal who was complicated and unpredictable. He always felt off balance around her. He sighed as he put on his cream-colored linen jacket and tied a Liberty print scarf around his neck. Steel yourself, he thought, you're embarking on a bumpy road – be careful, curves ahead.

*****

Danielle and Jean-Paul had invited C.C. to breakfast with them, and she was hurrying to get ready. She had overslept due to a bad dream, not a nightmare, just one of those dreams from which you wake up exhausted as if you've been working all night. It was the usual scenario: C.C. was trying to leave a very surreal version of London and a man who could have been any prominent male figure in her life. He kept talking while she was moving from room to room in a strange, large house trying to find her clothes to pack. She couldn't find them and was in a hurry to catch a flight or a train – it was confusing and chaotic and she felt trapped by her own ineptitude. She was trying to leave but couldn't. She had had this dream, with slight variations, for many years. She was not interested in analyzing it; she just wanted it to stop. It was tiring, meaningless and robbed her of a good night's sleep.

She threw on a sheer red duster-style coat over a light green jumpsuit – no, she thought, I look like a Christmas tree! She tossed the duster and grabbed a pale yellow sweater. My hair! She grabbed the white bob from the wig stand, adjusted it, made a face at herself in the mirror and left her suite. As she rushed down the hall to the elevator, she shook her head at her unusually disheveled state. Maybe she should go to bed earlier. Or, better yet, don't make dates for breakfast. Thank God the restaurant was downstairs and she didn't have to catch a cab.

*****

"What do you say to breakfast? Le Jardin sound good?" Max asked.

"Sounds perfect! I'm starving, too. But be warned, this is going to cost you."

"I wouldn't mind so much if I could actually see the food show up on your body. Then I'd get my money's worth."

Andie gasped, "You don't like my body?"

"I love your body; I just don't understand where the food goes. It's a phenomenon."

She laughed, "I don't know how it works, but I'm happy it does, because as you know, I do love to eat. Are you ready? Let's go."

They were among the early diners for breakfast, but others wandered in as they ate. Max noticed the sporadic arrivals and said to Andie, "The usual suspects," as he gestured around the room.

They were scattered at separate tables: C.C. with Dany and Jean-Paul; Chantal, with Carter; Bella and Fan; and Marie-Claude and Hassim. A few of them nodded and smiled when they caught Andie's eye.

"Well, they're all alive at least," she said wryly.

"Maybe they're all innocent," Max retorted.

"Sure - anything's possible. But I tend to think the dead ones are innocent and one of these people is the killer."

"Hmmm," Max was chewing and made an ambivalent sound.

"For one thing, we still know nothing about VM," Andie took a sip of juice.

"VM?"

"Max, if it's not a lady, it's a man. Why do you have such a hard time with my pseudonyms? How can we talk in code if you don't learn the names?"

He laughed, looking around theatrically, "Nobody's here! You can't think we're bugged, do you?"

"You never know. But, and please pay attention, I'm changing the code name to VP – for veiled person – o.k.? That should be easy to remember. And I am going to pursue his identity. I can't help but think it's a clue that could give us all the answers."

"That's absurd, Andie. Eddie knows who he is, and we've met with Eddie and Ben, and if Eddie knew something that could help, he'd tell us. Surely you don't think Eddie is in on this? "

"No, of course not. And don't call me Shirley."

"But," she continued, "I think you and I are in a good position to find out more about our suspects. You know how strangers open up to entertainers – they think they know us. I think we can exploit that."

Max countered, "Normally I'm all in when you find a mystery. But there's something evil here – I can feel it. I don't know which one is the killer, but I have the strongest feeling they are all capable of it. And please, don't bug Eddie. He's not going to tell you anything and you're just going to annoy him. Can't you just put it out of your mind?"

Andie sat up straight in her chair, put a prissy look on her face and spoke loudly in a thick French accent, "My leetle grey cells are burning up! Zey work overtime! I will not let this go!" Her voice rose as she burlesqued her favorite character, Poirot. "I will not rest until I find out who committed this atrocious murder!"

Max applauded her performance – literally – while he laughed. "All you need is the little mustache. Otherwise – a dead ringer. Truly."

Max had noticed the room's attention shift to their direction when Andie was taking center stage performing her Poirot, and wondered if anyone in particular found it provocative – and if that was going to be a problem.

*****

While she and Max stood at the elevator bank waiting to go back to their rooms, Andie felt an electric shock go up her spine when they were joined by Mme or, more accurately, M. Chausson. This was her chance to solve the VP mystery.

When the doors opened, Max took a step back and indicated he/she should go first. He knew she was a he, but he looked like a woman and Max was a gentleman.

"Merci," the VP said and walked into the elevator.

Andie joined the VP, and Max joined them, and they started to ascend.

They reached the VP's floor and he/she nodded and smiled as he exited the elevator. Andie immediately put her foot between the doors to keep it open, and after a moment and without a word, she left Max – looking shocked but immobile - in the elevator and crept down the hall trailing the VP.

Andie saw her prey turn right around the corner into the next corridor and she scooted up to peek around the corner. Great luck! The VP entered his suite without a card key because the door was open with a chambermaid's cart in front of it. Andie raced quietly down the hall, and as she passed the room, she saw the hat and veil come off a male head. And the bare-headed man in woman's attire was facing Mark Redmond! She had to scurry past the door before Redmond saw her. She stood on the far side of the open door straining to listen. She was rewarded by the sound of the two male voices. They were arguing and speaking French very rapidly. Their voices were only slightly raised, however, and it seemed more of a heated discussion than an argument.

Andie's French comprehension was hopelessly behind the pace of the men's voices. The only thing she could hear – because it was said repeatedly – was "Sasha". She thought she heard "Souviens-toi, Sasha". Then she heard a man's voice say it again, and now she was certain: the mysterious veiled lady was Sasha. I knew it, she thought triumphantly.

The chambermaid came out the door to her cart and saw Andie. She started to say something but Andie gave her a big smile and asked for soap, "Savon? Por favor?" Oh my Lord, she thought. Now my bad French is mixing in with my bad Spanish.

But the maid understood her and handed her a pack of Hotel Rose soaps, which happened to be from Hermès. Naturally, Andie thought.

"Merci, merci," she said to the maid while bowing. What is the matter with you? she asked herself. We are not in Japan and we are not in Mexico. She turned and fled down the hall to the elevator and home.

"Max!" Andie called out when she breathlessly entered their suite. "Max!"

"Calm down," he called from the living room.

"I know it's Sasha! I have proof!" she said excitedly as she entered the living room.

"Really? Did he introduce himself?"

"No. He didn't see me, but he was talking to Mark Redmond and I could hear him saying 'Remember, Sasha'."

"What else did he say? What were they talking about?"

"Well," Andie was a little deflated by his questions, "I couldn't understand them. They were speaking so quickly – but I did hear that one thing. One of them told the other, "Remember, Sasha." And that had to be Redmond speaking to the previously veiled lady, man and person."

"Why do you say that?"

"Because he didn't say 'Remember, Mark'. He said ---"

"I know, 'Remember, Sasha'. So, what do we think now? What does this mean?"

Andie made a face, "That's what I thought you would tell me. I have no idea. I thought it was Sasha before this and that didn't tell me anything, but I thought if I were right, you might have an idea."

Max mused out loud, "Not a one. You know, I hate to say this, but I think we're going to have to ask Ben what it means."

"Maybe by the next time we see him, we'll have a plan and we can keep it to ourselves."

*****

Saturday night was the last night of the work week for the band. Musicians were the same as everyone else when it came to the day before a day off: full of happy anticipation that made the work fly by. In addition, Saturday night brought other Parisians into Le Salon Jazz for a date night, and the crowd was a festive one.

Bernard and Benoit told Andie and Max when they came onstage that a friend of theirs was there, and he played flute. Would it be all right if he sat in? When Max heard the name, he said "I would love to play with Marcel Blanc!"

He shook hands with Marcel when he came onstage and then called out "Afro Blue", one of Andie's favorite tunes. There was an ethereal quality to the song, perhaps because the African 6/8 rhythm had the mesmerizing quality usually found in a waltz. The audience responded warmly when they finished, and Max asked Marcel to sit in for one more tune.

Marcel asked "Caravan?"

"Absolutely!" Adrien said from his piano, and the others laughed.

Jean-Paul was in the audience with Danielle. He leaned over to Dany and said, "I love Marcel Blanc's playing. This is quite a treat for us. I have always wanted to see him play live."

Dany smiled and nodded in response.

When Andie looked out over the room, she was delighted because there were brightly colored fashionistas in the room. No doubt in Paris for the big engagement party on the boat Sunday, they were all in a celebratory mood and their excited, happy voices ebbed and flowed whenever the music stopped.

Andie recognized two of the top models of the day who were wearing the very trendy hot-off-the-runway looks from Gucci, accessorized with heavy yellow Timberland boots, the footwear worn by the most popular rappers. They were at a table with two older women who were dressed to the peak of chic. Must be editors, she thought. Also at the table was a long-haired man wearing earrings with necklaces on his bare chest. He wore blue jeans with his open cowboy shirt. Too old for the look, he had to be a photographer, Andie was certain. She loved these people – so entertaining and colorful to look at.

She was not too surprised when C.C. rushed over to the table to greet them all effusively. She was matched in enthusiasm by the older women and the photographer. Andie couldn't imagine what would elicit a response from the stone-faced mannequins. She found out quickly when Dany and Jean-Paul entered the room. Both models took notice, and they waved with big smiles. Everyone loves a movie star.

Bella, Fan, Carter and Chantal took their usual places at their usual table near the stage. Chantal was no longer drinking and weeping. She had made a conscious effort to shake off her disappointment, and it seemed to be working. After all, she was mourning a *gigolo*! How could she have ended up such a mess from a broken romance with a *gigolo*? On the surface, she knew who Sasha was and what that made Chantal. But she also had feelings – deep, obsessive feelings of possession, ownership.

When she was rejected, she was angry – not sad. And she was a firm believer in revenge served cold. She could wait, but she would make Sasha pay for this insult. In the meantime, she was on the lookout for a new boy – a fresh diversion. Someone young, innocent, full of dreams and plans and energy. Someone new. She glanced at Carter; maybe new was sufficient - he didn't have to be young. Or innocent.

Carter couldn't help but feel Chantal's sudden interest. He knew she was looking at him, assessing him. It was a little distressing; Chantal had a very strong personality and will, and now that he had decided to pursue Bella, he was anxious to avoid a scene with Chantal. He found himself genuinely fond of Bella to his surprise. He had never truly cared about anybody but himself and now he was worrying on her behalf, looking out for her. Could he be – in his own limited way – falling for the girl? She needed someone, someone besides Fan. Could he take on the responsibility of keeping her safe from herself? It was clear to him that she had mental issues – challenges, he corrected himself - and if he married her, he would have to watch over her. Could he do this?

Bella had no such doubts about Carter. When she saw him dance with C.C., she knew she had found her Prince Charming. He was so dashing! She recognized the feelings she had for Carter because once before, she had fallen in love. But this time she knew what to do. More importantly, she knew what not to do. Carter was the opposite of the other boy – Carter was a man and a gentleman. She had found her feet. She was certain she knew what she was doing, and she didn't need Fan's approval. Fan could go back home as far as she was concerned. She was grown up, and she was fine. She didn't want to hear Fan's opinion. He was of no concern. Fan should just leave.

Fan was just as certain Bella needed to be stopped. He had taken care of her and protected her since her last entanglement had landed her in a hospital, and he would be damned if he was going down that road again. She had no idea the trouble she had brought onto the family nor the extent of the damage control they had had to provide. No matter what it took, Fan was not going to let her current crush put them through that again. He was just breathing a sigh of relief due to François's death when she was off again on another fantasy romance. Over my dead body, he swore to himself.

They kicked off the set with a swinging "My Favorite Things", and when Max took his solo, Andie watched an extraordinary scene.

Chantal was standing at Dany's table, presumably saying hello, when an elderly, very well-dressed man approached her. Andie recognized him. He was a well-known fashion designer, who was already an eminence grise in his heyday in the 1960s and '70s, famous for being the exclusive designer for a beloved actress and for being the first couturier to license his name for non-couture products. His face indicated his pleasure in seeing Chantal, and he eagerly approached her. Dany and Jean-Paul welcomed him but Chantal looked at him with impatience as if he were a plumber presenting a bill.

Andie watched they exchange words and the elderly man became increasingly unhappy, wincing and grimacing as she spoke. She was abrupt and Andie could see her mouth sneering as she spoke, her lovely hands pointing accusatorily at the old man. Dany, Jean-Paul and Ben - who was still at their table - seemed as if they were appalled but hiding it behind a veneer of *politesse*. Chantal turned away from them and marched off. Dany quickly asked the esteemed designer to join them and, deeply embarrassed, he gratefully sat down.

Andie vowed to get Ben to tell her what it was all about.

She and Max had worked out a clever arrangement of "April in Paris" segueing into "Besame Mucho" and they played it now. It was a sure-fire audience pleaser and provoked the usual response of delighted applause this night. As the last set was coming to a close, Andie saw Ben – Uncle Ben – take a seat at the bar near Eddie who was conferring with the bartender.

When Eddie noticed Ben, he brought him a Guinness, and the two of them looked at the stage, and Andie caught their attention. Eddie made a beckoning gesture and she nodded. When the last song ended, she leaned over to Max and indicated the two men at the bar and told him their presence was requested.

"This will be good," she said. "We can all pool information and find out who's who and what's going on."

"You think so?"

"Why not? We've been busy and they've been busy – I expect all kinds of revelations."

"Well, you're an incurable optimist. Even with all Fan's gossip, I don't feel I know any more than I did yesterday."

Andie shook her head in exasperation, "Why do you say that? You got a lot of motives from Fan."

"Correction - I got a lot of shady rumors from Fan. Who knows what's true?"

"I swear, Max. You are an incurable pessimist."

"If I were an incurable pessimist, I never would have married you."

"What does that mean?" she asked, slightly offended.

"Nothing at all. It was just a weak attempt at wit. Come on, let's go see what Uncle Ben has dug up."

They made their way slowly to the bar, receiving well wishes and congratulations from members of the audience. It was a time-consuming but welcome part of the job. Andie and Max had both experienced gigs where people in the audience talked all the way through the performance and basically ignored the entertainment onstage which only gave them a genuine gratitude and appreciation when they were applauded face to face after a good night.

"How are you doing, Uncle Ben?" Andie asked saucily when she finally sat down next to him.

"Uncle Ben is doing well, thank you very much," he answered with a smile. He liked Andie. She was fresh and unpredictable - what he thought of as a good American.

Eddie leaned over the bar, "I think we'll take the same table in the back to avoid distractions."

The foursome made their way to the banquette in the rear of Le Salon with Eddie bringing the drinks: Guinness for Max and white wine for Andie. He brought himself a full brandy snifter.

"So, what do we know?" he asked the other three. "Well, I'll start," he continued. "Montclair has identified the fingerprints and they pretty much don't tell us much more than we already know."

"Max learned a lot of gossip from Fan, of all people!" Andie exclaimed.

"Really? I thought Fan was so close-mouthed. I'm surprised he has any gossip at all. I would have thought he was above all that," Eddie said.

"You have no idea. He is a poisonous little snake. If I weren't investigating, I would have walked away when he started in on everyone. He had something nasty to tell me about each one of our little group," Max complained. "And I have no idea if any of it is true."

"Yes," Ben agreed, "That's the trouble with getting information second-hand. You always have to go to the one in question to verify what you've heard. And that's got its own set of difficulties – people deny or fabricate their own versions of the truth."

"How are we going to verify Mark Redmond – the executor of François's estate and a life long friend – was also his lover?"

Eddie spoke up, "Is that what Fan said? Interesting."

"How is that interesting?" Andie asked him.

"Because I think that may be true - not necessarily the affair, but the inclination, yes. I'm just surprised Fan knew this. That's what's interesting."

"Hmmm," Ben responded. "What else did he say?"

Max continued, "I'll be brief. Hassim was fired by François --- "

"and Marie-Claude lost her baby in a miscarriage when Hassim had to go back to Kashmir because François wouldn't let him stay with Marie-Claude, right?" Andie interrupted in a display of her hundred-words-a-minute facility.

"Right," Max nodded after a moment during which the group digested Andie's statement – after deciphering the word storm. "But that's what Fan says. Who knows if it's true?"

"Oh, I almost forgot," Andie said quickly, "Because there were complications, Marie-Claude was told she would never be able to carry a baby. I think it's quite a stretch to blame François for something like that, but I know it's sometimes a reflex when something terrible happens to assign blame. Sometimes terrible things happen for no reason."

"But maybe the combination of the lost job and lost baby sent Hassim over the edge," Eddie offered.

"It's possible," Ben responded. "What else, Max?"

"Let's see. Oh, Carter Philip is a scheming gold-digger, a lounge lizard," he said with a smile. "I don't think that's such a big secret, but Fan said there was some kind of scandal in the States with the last widow he was courting. I don't know the details, but apparently the authorities questioned him about the widow's death --- you know," he said suddenly, "I hate to spread these rumors, and that's all they are."

Ben stopped him with a wave of his hand, "No, this is not a rumor. There was a police investigation into her death; her children demanded it. But the attending doctor seemed quite sure it was a result of her heart congestion which he'd been treating, so the police dropped it. But he left town as soon as the will was read and he received his money. There was sufficient wealth that the children all inherited a lot of money, and they didn't pursue Carter since they wanted the scandal from the police inquiry to die down. Nonetheless, it's the kind of story that would quash any plans he had to catch another rich widow."

"Maybe he's here just because he's embarrassed," Andie suggested. She liked Carter. She could see behind his bright, white smile in his perfectly suntanned face. His eyes betrayed his loneliness. But he wasn't hurtful to anyone.

"Well," Max said, "Fan said François knew all the details and was going to warn Morgana."

"Morgana?" Eddie said, surprised.

"Right, Morgana. Anyway, you'd have to ask Carter," he said to Ben.

Ben nodded, "Anything else?"

"Mmm, oh yes, Danielle Dufault and Jean-Paul Toussaint had a ten-year-old son who was killed in a motorboat accident when François drove over him in Lake Como. The boy was visiting his godfather, François, and he died. And again, I feel I need to stress – this is according to Fan."

"How sad," Eddie looked down at his drink. "How very sad."

"There's something else," Ben looked around the table. "I learned more about Morgana. She has a story much like Carter's, as it turns out. She was born the daughter of a butcher in a poor section of London. But she was ambitious and ended up working in an office of Sir Charles Godfrey Standish's corporate real estate business. She made a good impression on him – she was driven as he once was. He was, oh, maybe thirty years older but he married her. They had a few good years, and then he died of a heart attack. The children from his first marriage asked for an autopsy, but the medical examiner found nothing that could be used as evidence, so …" his voice trailed off.

"Wow." Andie said quietly.

"Funny that the two of them were running from the same scandal," Max commented.

"Oh my Lord!" Eddie smacked his forehead and loudly proclaimed. "I am such an idiot. Now I remember, of course. I didn't connect Mogana Standish to Sir Charles Godfrey Standish. Sir Charles Standish was the great love –off and on – of our Celeste. I remember hearing stories. They were a beautiful couple – 'Sir Charles and C.C. were seen here; Sir Charles and C.C. were seen there' - but she wouldn't marry him. He asked her repeatedly. But she didn't want to get married. She said she needed to be independent. The last time she turned him down, he turned to Morgana and asked her. I guess he was getting lonely, I don't know; I mean, how do you go from filet mignon to hamburger?"

"Wow." Andie said quietly and took a sip of wine. "Wow."

"You have a real gift for insightful analysis," Max deadpanned in response.

"Well, there's so much to mull over now," Andie defended herself. "It seems everyone had a reason to want François or Morgana – or both! - dead. But I have to sort them out in my head first; you know, who was threatened by François? Who was threatened by Morgana? Although from what I overheard at the mourners' table, she was clearly baiting François's killer so that's no help – you'd have to consider everyone at that table, and we already are. And" she added shaking her head, "I can't imagine asking Dany about her dead child!"

"What makes you think you're going to be asking any questions of anybody?" Ben demanded. "I appreciate your helping me, but I can take it from here."

Eddie, Max and Andie all shook their heads with amused disbelief.

"Not to mention the others that we know nothing about – Fan, of course, his sister Bella, and Chantal. Oh, and Mme Chausson." Eddie stiffened when Andie came to the last name, as she knew he would. "I've waited patiently, Eddie, and I want to know now – what do you know about that woman – no, that man. I know it's a man, Eddie."

Eddie was stunned. "I hardly know what to say." He waited. He had to think.

Andie glanced over his shoulder as a figure entered the room.

"Well, speak of the devil -- Max, it's Chausson," and she pointed to the VP.

Ben, Eddie, Max and Andie stared as a stunning woman in a vintage St. Laurent "Le Smoking" - a perfectly fitted silk tuxedo - wearing a veiled black fedora walked towards the table.

"Love the suit – I know a woman who had one just like it – Morgana?" Andie waited for a response to the name, but got none. She added, "And I have a friend who would go nuts for it."

"Celeste? C.C.?" a man's voice asked her.

Before Andie could answer, Chausson took off his hat, shook out a full head of brunette hair which he proceeded to take off his head. His dark blond hair was a short, shaggy cut that made him suddenly appear quite masculine. What a difference a wig makes, Andie thought.

"Sasha?" she asked.

Eddie barked a short laugh while Chausson looked amused and then melancholy.

"No, no. I'm not Sasha," the sadness in his eyes evident. "I'm François."

"François?" Max and Andie chorused, stunned.

Quietly, Mark Redmond had also entered the room and was now approaching the table.

"Yes, he is François," Eddie said firmly. "And that's why his identity had to be a secret," he addressed Andie. "His life was in danger, and I promised to protect him."

"Wow," was all Andie could say.

"I have to agree with your husband; you really do have a way of summarizing a situation succinctly," Eddie laughed.

Ben asked François, "But I don't understand. Why now? Why are you telling all of us now? What has changed?"

Andie turned to him, "You knew? How could you let us go on believing she was Sasha?"

"It didn't really matter," Ben explained.

"What do you mean? Our investigation was predicated on finding François's killer. Of course it mattered." Andie was angry.

"Your investigation? That's the problem – it's not your investigation. It's my investigation," Ben reminded her. "Mine and Dash Montclair's!"

Andie ignored him and turned to François, "Why the masquerade?"

François replied, "It was my plan to discover who killed Sasha."

"Sasha?" Max asked.

"Yes. Sasha was the body in the jeep." Mark Redmond answered. "François asked me to help, and I identified Sasha as François and then arranged for the group of family and investors to come here for the burial and reading of the will."

"Wow," Andie again was speechless.

This time everyone at the table turned to her.

"Well, this takes a little time to digest," she said defensively. "After all, you've all been lying to us. With this information, Max and I can ask the right questions." She turned to Max, "We'll need to re-calibrate and make new approaches to our suspects."

She continued, looking sharply now at François. "I'm not sure I understand; you pretended to be a woman in order to spy on your friends at your funeral? I still don't know why."

François answered her calmly, "I was hoping to find out, to discover who was trying to kill me."

"You were trying to be a detective!" Andie exclaimed. "This is not something you just decide to do; you need skills to properly investigate – my God, François, you could have been killed. It's dangerous work, and I doubt you are fully prepared; you're certainly not trained in any investigative techniques."

"Pot," Ben nodded at Andie, "meet kettle," he gestured at François.

Andie scoffed, "Nonsense. Max and I are practically old pros at this point."

"The only detective at this table is me," Ben scolded both of them. "None of you has any business getting involved. I shouldn't have let you carry on in disguise for as long as I did, François; and Andie, please do not feel you have to participate any longer. I am grateful for your help, but it is no longer necessary. I am well on my way now. Will you promise me you won't interfere?" Ben asked Andie.

"Absolutely," Andie replied, bearing in mind it couldn't be interference if she was only continuing her own investigation. She couldn't interfere with herself, could she? Then she stood up and asked Max, "Are you ready to go home? I'm meeting the girls at the spa and I don't know how long they'll wait for me."

"Absolutely." Max nodded.

Ben looked up at her, "Are you two going to spend the night strategizing and plotting your next moves in spite of what I just said?" he said archly.

"Absolutely," Max and Andie answered in unison.

Eddie laughed and Ben shook his head with a big smile.

"Oh wait!" Andie suddenly remembered the scene with Chantal and the designer. "Ben - there was a scene with Chantal and that famous old designer – I can't remember his name – anyway, I saw it but couldn't hear it of course. What was that all about?"

"Glad you asked – it was very strange. The monsieur came up to her in a very friendly way to tell her he had just seen her parents. Well, her face froze and she said 'my parents?' as if she didn't have any. The old man ignored or failed to note her hostility and went on about how they looked wonderful and they all laughed and laughed about their past adventures. And then he mentioned they had a moment of sadness when they remembered Chantal's sister. He referred to a terrible thing that happened in a strange way."

Andie's eyebrows shot up, her eyes widened. "Go on."

Ben continued, "Chantal interrupted his recollections and told him she never sees her parents anymore. He had the temerity to question this in view of what had happened to the sister – he called it a tragedy."

"Wha--" Andie started to ask.

Ben waved her away with his hand, "And! And Chantal laughed - bitterly - and said 'those people are not my parents – that was never my family.' I remember the words because it was so strange. And then she left. Dany and Jean-Paul graciously asked the man to join them, and he did sit with us. He was very shocked and Dany changed the subject for his sake. As Uncle Ben, I had no reason to be curious about Chantal's family, but I'd like to find out what that was all about."

"No kidding," Andie said emphatically. "I'm going to find out – even if I have to ask Chantal herself."

Ben sighed. "I would ask you not to interfere, but in this case, I want to know what happened to her sister and why she's estranged from her family."

Max broke in, "Ben! Don't encourage her."

Andie said patiently, "I cannot believe asking someone a little about themselves could be dangerous. I mean, really. But if you like, I'll just ask Dany. I bet she knows the whole story."

Max looked relieved. "Thank you for that. Unless Dany has murderous skills and is a psycho serial killer, that will make me feel better."

"I think we would have known by now – she's been in the public eye for decades." Andie retorted as she stood up. "I've got a date with her right now, as a matter of fact, to soak in a tub."

It was Ben's turn to raise his eyebrows, "You're taking a bath together?"

"In a manner of speaking, yes." Andie laughed as she and Max made their farewells and left Le Salon.

When they entered their suite, Andie told Max in an impression of C.C., "Well, darling, I'm off to the spa for a jacuzzi soak with my new girlfriends. I'm tense and clenched and need to relax my body."

"'Tense and clenched', huh? That sounds great – what a line. We need to put it to music."

"Uh-huh. You do that. Get right on it. I'll be soaking in hot bubbles, gossiping with the girls," she laughed as she put on her big Hotel Rose terry-cloth robe. "When I get back, we're going to have to go over our plans with this new information. Knowing he's alive makes a difference."

"Only to us, though. The others all think he's dead. I don't think it makes a difference to them."

"Good point. Well, be that as it may, we do have a lot to think about."

She gave him a kiss on his forehead and left the suite for the spa. As she waited for the elevator, Andie thought about what Max said. Did it make any difference to the guilt or innocence of their suspects if Andie and Max knew François hadn't been killed? As far as the killer was concerned, the body was François's; as far as Ben, Andie and Max were concerned, it was Sasha's body. Either way, somebody was murdered, and one of these people was a murderer.

The gym and spa were open twenty-four hours a day to service guests arriving from different time zones all over the world. Andie often took jacuzzi soaks after a gig and the availability of this amenity was typical of the hotels in the Orchidea Group. They knew what you wanted and needed before it occurred to you. When they returned from the museum earlier that day, Dany, Marie-Claude and C.C. had suggested a late jacuzzi, and Andie responded with an enthusiastic "I'll be there!"

She exited the elevator and made her way to the spa with pleasant anticipation. She was in great need of a relaxing soak and thought her three new girlfriends would be perfect companions.

She entered the jacuzzi room to find C.C. and Dany in the water and Marie-Claude seated on the coping with only her feet in the water.

"Why aren't you soaking in the water?" Andie asked her while she took off her robe and lowered herself into the jacuzzi.

The three women turned to Andie with beaming faces.

Marie-Claude answered her with a big smile, "You were right."

"What was I right about? Which one of my crazy assumptions turned out to be true?"

Everyone chuckled and Dany answered, "She's pregnant."

"Oh! How wonderful!" Andie stood up to hug Marie-Claude. "I'm so happy for you, for you and Hassim; he must be over the moon!"

The three others looked nonplussed and C.C. asked "'Over the moon'?"

Andie answered, "Unbelievably happy."

Marie-Claude answered, "Yes, yes – Hassim is very happy. And he wants to keep me in bed for the next seven months."

"But how did you know, Andie?" Dany asked.

"I used to watch a soap opera, and the proverbial surprise pregnancy was a staple in daytime drama." Then she hastened to add, "I don't watch them anymore, of course," deliberately leaving out the explanation that she traveled too much nowadays to keep up with the storylines. Otherwise, she'd still be keeping up with her 'friends' in Pine Valley.

"Oh, my Lord – this feels so good," Andie couldn't keep her pleasure to herself.

"Isn't it? Nothing revives me like a jacuzzi, although it's also incredibly relaxing. Strange juxtaposition, I suppose," Dany agreed.

"I think it's because the body is unwinding coils of tension while your mind is freed to imagine and daydream."

"Well put, C.C."

The ladies were all very happy for Marie-Claude, and after the excitement of her news, they all settled in for a gossip session.

Andie led the group, "Tell me, what do you know about Bella? She is an enigma to me. I think she's attracted to Carter, but I can't tell. She's hard to read."

C.C.'s eyes brightened, "Oh, I know quite a bit about her. And it's not surprising she seems mysterious to you. She has a, well, let's just say she has an unusual personality."

Dany spoke up, "She couldn't take her eyes off you when you were dancing with Carter."

C.C. responded, "Oh, Carter – he's a funny duck, isn't he?"

Andie didn't want to discuss Carter; she knew he seemed suspicious to everyone but Bella, but Andie liked him. "He is a good dancer."

C.C. laughed, "Yes, I know, he's quite talented in that regard. I wonder if he has other talents we haven't seen," she said suggestively.

"C.C.! I'm surprised you would say something like that – you seem to be such a woman of the world."

"I am, I am. I guess I'm just gossiping – forgive me."

"Not to worry. I don't have any dish on Carter but he seems like a nice enough man," Andie smiled but didn't want to end the conversation. "What about Bella and Fan? You seem to know them well. What's the story?"

"Oh, I do know them well, and it's quite a story," she shook head and smiled. "You know, Bella said something the other day – she, Fan and François were all orphans when she was young. Of course, both François and Fan were of age when the Jardines were killed in an accident – plane crash – ghastly! Fan is seven years older than Bella and François was older than Fan. So, 'orphans' is a bit of an exaggeration. Anyway, what was I saying?"

"You were ---" Andie started, but C.C. picked right up where she left off.

"Fan was used to communicating through the family attorney for money and advice from the Desenfants, who were his and Bella's guardians after their parents died. When François's parents died, Fan was already of age so the guardianship was terminated. Well, one day Bella – who was all of fifteen and very inexperienced – came to Fan

175

and told him she thought she might be pregnant. To tell the truth, Andie, I'm surprised she even knew the signs of pregnancy – she was that sheltered."

"With no access to "All My Children", I suppose," Andie interjected.

C.C. gave her a look and continued, "Well, Bella tells Fan who more or less freaks out. He decides to call François because he is at a complete loss on how to proceed. Well! François also freaks out and tells Fan to fire the stableboy seducer – oh yes, Andie – a stableboy, how ridiculous is that?"

"From all accounts English stableboys must be real prizes – and supremely seductive!" Andie had to comment.

This time C.C. laughed at her comment, "It's true, isn't it? Anywaaaay ...where was I? Oh yes, François tells Fan to fire this Casanova, but Fan says he cannot so François says he'll fire him and pay him well to leave - permanently."

"Why couldn't Fan do it?"

"Darling, I have no idea. Perhaps Bella wasn't the only one the stableboy seduced."

"Oh, C.C.!" Dany exclaimed.

"Really?" Andie asked.

C.C. waved her hand, "I don't know but 'some have said'. Anyway, Bella can't find the stableboy, so she asks Fan where he is. Fan tells her François fired him and paid him to go far away. Well, the next thing you know, Bella becomes hysterical and miscarries! Fan takes her to hospital and from there she is sent to a sanitarium for a year. According to Fan, François sent her to the sanitarium. Can you imagine how she felt about her dear cousin François?"

"Wow," was all Andie managed. It had become her place-keeper while she thought of a response.

"I mean, first he sends away her true love," all four women rolled their eyes at C.C.'s description of the randy stableboy, "and causes her to lose her baby, but then he locks her up for a year in a looney bin. I mean, she's always been a little off, shall we say, but I don't see how a stay in a mental ward would help that."

"I've noticed she has a strange affect – I thought maybe she was autistic," Dany said.

"I don't know about that," C.C. responded. "Bella has powerful emotions, and I thought autistics were notably unemotional. But she is definitely an apple short of a bushel."

"C.C., do you think Bella is capable of killing someone? Do you think she may have sabotaged François's car?" Marie-Claude asked.

"Good heavens, Bella? Well, she grew up in the country and it's possible she learned something about driving - getting to the village and back. But I don't know. I agree she has a motive, though."

Andie was again surprised that C.C. went straight to 'motive'. "Oh?" She asked her, "So you think she could have done it?"

"Well, I suppose so. Anything's possible."

Andie flinched inwardly – do all Brits think anything's possible? Was it a strange English concept?

"And then," Andie continued, warming to a new theory, "Fan might have killed Morgana to protect her."

C.C. looked at her sharply, "Well," she drawled, "Fan is a funny bunny so you never know. He's almost unnaturally attached to Bella so I would think he would go to great lengths to protect her."

Andie forced herself not to look excited. She tried to appear blasé. She didn't want to stop the fountain of gossip coming out of C.C.'s mouth. Unfortunately, C.C. was done talking. Then, Andie remembered she wanted to ask C.C. about Chantal.

"I wanted to ask you about Chantal, C.C. What happened to her sister?"

C.C.'s face changed; her countenance fell, everything turned downward, "Ah, a tragedy. It was very sad, very sad … Chantal and her sister went to the pond to cool off on a hot summer day, and only Chantal returned." Her tone was flat, devoid of emotion.

"What happened?" Dany prodded her.

"No one knows. Chantal said her sister wanted to swim, and Chantal told her not to, and she did anyway and drowned." Her usual expressive voice returned as she recited the events.

"And?" Andie asked.

"Well, Chantal was the only witness, so everyone believed her." She shook her head. "But they all knew Chantal was jealous of Felice – that was her sister's name - and hated her. So ..." C.C. shrugged.

Dany, Andie and Marie-Claire shuddered.

"But who knows?" C.C. said, bringing the mood back up.

Don't say it, Andie thought.

C.C. continued, 'Anything's possible. Well, it's been lovely catching up, dearest dear," she began, "but I've got to go to bed now. It's hard to get my beauty sleep and stay up all night at the same time." She caught Andie's raised eyebrows and said, "Those days were when I was young – you don't need beauty sleep when you're young."

"C.C., you will always be young – that's your spirit," Dany exclaimed.

C.C. looked pensive a moment, "It's not always a good thing to be young when you're over sixty. I want to slow down, just like everybody else. And when you are old is the time to settle accounts, to bring balance to your life. It's the time to make amends and to avenge injustice ..." she stopped speaking, lost in thought.

Andie was silent. And amazed. C.C. sounded like a prophet from the Old Testament. C.C.! Andie couldn't imagine a more unlikely candidate for an avenger. C.C. was flip, light and gay – not judgmental and censorious. But here she was, talking about revenge and justice. Actually, Andie corrected herself, injustice. She was referring to injustice. As in murder.

C.C. stood up suddenly, splashing water and making small waves, "I must go now," she said over her shoulder to Andie as she stepped out of the pool and into her robe. "À demain, cherie." She blew Andie a kiss and walked away quickly.

"I should go, too," Marie-Claude said. "I guess I need to start thinking of my little passenger." She patted her stomach.

Dany and Andie laughed.

"Is the baby done for the night?" Dany asked.

"I imagine so. I'll have to start learning how to read the signs."

"I love the idea of a 'little passenger' - what a lovely way to think of a baby," Andie mused out loud.

Marie-Claude stood up and put on her robe, and Dany climbed out of the jacuzzi to join her.

"I am taking a cue from C.C. and heading for my beauty sleep."

"That's absurd, Dany. If anyone has no need for beauty sleep, it's you." Andie retorted. "Don't even try to tell me sleeping is responsible for this -" she gestured to Dany.

Dany smiled and said, "Maybe it is."

"If that were true, I'd spend all my days in bed."

Dany leaned over and kissed Andie on her head, "You are too sweet, Andie. I should hire you to follow me around so when I'm feeling old, I can turn to you and hear you assure me I look the same as I did forty years ago."

Marie-Claude looked at Andie and earnestly told her, "You are now my lucky charm. You knew before I did. Thank you."

Andie laughed, "I am very happy for you, Marie-Claude, but truly, I had nothing to do with it."

"Still …" Marie-Claude let her voice trail off.

"Now don't stay too long and get all wrinkled like a raisin in the sun." Dany cautioned.

"But I'm in the water, not the sun."

"You know what I mean. À demain, chérie," With a little wave of her hand, Dany turned around, and she and Marie-Claude left the spa.

Andie was happy and intrigued. What do you think about that? she wondered, both at the pregnancy news and the bizarre background story of Bella and Fan. She shook her head at this latest of an alarming number of surprises.

She closed her eyes again, enjoying the jacuzzi and the silence. So much to ponder.

Her eyes still closed, she was sort of half meditating, half day-dreaming when she heard she heard the spa door close. Her eyes opened quickly. Perhaps one of her friends had forgotten something and she had come back to retrieve it. She looked toward the entrance to the jacuzzi room expectantly, but no one appeared. She heard nothing else and assumed someone had simply left the spa later than her friends. Then, a troubling idea occurred to her: maybe someone had just entered the spa.

"Hello?" she called out. No response.

She put the thought out of her mind. She was just confused due to François's sudden appearance earlier that night. Such a shock, she thought. Talk about coming back from the dead. She shook her head. She had wasted so much time certain it was Sasha. And now what? And what about Chantal? Andie didn't want to be the one to tell her Sasha was dead. Chantal didn't seem to care much about François, but she would go crazy if she knew Sasha was dead.

Andie was getting less sleepy and more involved with her thoughts, all changed since the 'François reveal' and C.C.'s gossip. She had lost her meditative mood and was now actively analyzing the new information and how it impacted the investigation – Andie's and Max's investigation. She didn't think much of Ben's investigation – she was certain she and Max were better detectives.

She stretched her neck and tried to meditate again. It's bedtime, she scolded herself, time to relax. She gave out a loud sigh and rested her head against the pool coping. She opened her eyes for a second and saw a shadow across the jacuzzi in front of her. Was someone standing behind her?

She sat up straighter and before she could turn around, someone threw the terry cloth belt from a robe around her neck and pulled. She attempted to grab it in the front of her neck but it was already too tight, and she couldn't get her fingers under it. She thrashed and twisted her body in the water, but the belt didn't budge and only got tighter. She felt like a fish trying to escape a hook, jerking and throwing her body up and down and to the right and left. Nothing worked, and she began to feel suffocated, rapidly losing her breath. Please, God, she thought frantically, don't let me die in a jacuzzi! She couldn't breathe and darkness began to overtake her. She passed out.

"Spa service!" a voice called out. "Spa service!" The hotel maintained the spa all day and throughout the night; an attendant was coming in to make sure it was clean and otherwise inviting to any late-night guests. Andie's attacker ran out of the room.

Andie slowly regained consciousness, and the world went from black to gray. She rolled over from her back to her stomach as violent coughing racked her body.

"Madame? Madame!" A young Frenchwoman wearing a white uniform was leaning over Andie who was half in and half out of the water, gasping for breath.

"Madame! Qu'est-ce qu'il a fait? Ça va?" she asked Andie anxiously.

Andie nodded her head and waved a hand as she sat up. She attempted a smile but failed and burst into tears.

The attendant kneeled down to hold Andie, "Madame, shhhhhh, shhhh …" She spoke no English but recognized distress when she saw it, and she comforted Andie.

"Qu'est-ce qu'il a fait. Madame?" The attendant was concerned, but also very curious.

"Nada" Andie said without thinking. "Non - de rien, de rien. Ça va; merci." Andie gave the nice young woman a big smile as she helped her get to her feet. Andie felt fine now and only wanted to get back to Max.

She put on her robe and noticed the belt was missing. This brought fresh tears to her eyes; the idea that she was strangled with her own belt somehow upset her greatly, and this in turn made her laugh.

"J'ai besoin de mon mari," Andie said to the attendant between tears and laughter as she slid into her slippers and turned to go.

"Oui, oui! Allez-vous!" The excited young woman waved good-bye..

Andie hurried into the suite calling "Max! Max!"

He was in bed, reading, and looked up "What? What?" He had a broad smile that transformed into a frown at the sight of her face.

She burst into tears again, "Somebody just tried to kill me!"

"What? Who? Where?" He started to get up off the bed but Andie pushed him back down and fell on top of him.

"Oh, Max, I was so scared -"

"What happened? Where were you?"

"In the spa." Suddenly the tears stopped, replaced by a bright gleam, "Wait 'til you hear what I found out about Fan and Bella."

"Andie," Max sat them both up in the bed and said to her, "You have to tell me what happened."

She sighed. "Well, every time I realize someone wants me dead, I start to cry. It hurts to know someone dislikes you so much they want to kill you." She sniffed. "I was in the jacuzzi, alone - the girls had all left - "

Max started to interrupt her to ask what girls were these, but he restrained himself and nodded to her.

"I was meditating and thinking and suddenly somebody came from behind and threw the belt from the robe around my neck and started to strangle me by pulling me up out of the water by the belt – it was like being hanged. Although I've never been hanged, but ---"

Max was rapt and angry, "What happened?"

"Then a girl who maintains the spa at night came in, and I guess the strangler ran away before I was dead," with the last word, Andie started to cry again. "Who hates me so much?" she wailed.

"Andie, Andie, nobody hates you," Max smoothed her hair and rocked her in his arms.

"Someone does," she insisted crossly.

Max fought off the urge to chuckle, "Yes, but it's a murderer – who cares if a murderer hates you?"

Andie leaned back to look at him, "Max, do you hear yourself?"

With that facetious question, Andie seemed fully recovered to him now.

"We have to talk to Ben."

"Max - he told me to stay out of it, and I don't want to include him."

"Andie, this is an attempted murder – we're calling Ben."

She nodded but continued to look annoyed while Max spoke to Ben. They made a plan to meet in the morning for breakfast and a chance to go over it in detail.

Max turned to Andie after he hung up the phone, "He said he's very happy you survived the attempt, and he'll see us tomorrow morning. Come on," he said, patting the bed, "I've got a glass of wine and a movie with your name on it."

"The magic words!" She joined him on the big bed and the two of them snuggled into the pillows while the movie "*Death on the Nile*" began. As the Poirot mystery unfolded on the television, Andie and Max began to relax in each other's arms, enjoying the time and the comfort they shared being together.

Max yawned and said, "Weird day."

Andie murmured in response, "Ya think?"

CHAPTER SEVEN

Sasha Ivanov was the son of an alcoholic Russian immigrant tailor and a depressed and deeply pessimistic mother. His family fled the Revolution, but they were not White Russians. His mother, Olga, was the one who drove the emigration, not his father. She saw the violence and knew nobody was safe – both the monarchists and the revolutionaries in the streets were driven by desperation, paranoia, rage and blood lust. Sasha's parents were clinging to the middle class by their fingertips, and Olga knew there was no safety in moderation – hatred and revenge recognized no gray areas. Anyone who had something was a threat to those who had nothing. They had very little, but enough to escape to London where Sasha's father eked out a living picking up piecework from established tailors and seamstresses. As soon as his father got him a job with a haberdashery catering to the well-to-do, Sasha said good-bye to his family and his inglorious past.

He was a beautiful boy and he learned how to capitalize on his good looks early in life. He believed that was why the general manager of Foote & Sons hired him. He looked good greeting the upper crust and instinctively made them comfortable. His manager allowed him to buy clothes on credit, realizing he would be an excellent in-store model. Sasha had a great gift of sensitivity to others. He knew what to say and what to do to please a person. This made him an exceptional salesman. The smiles of satisfaction from both his customers and his employers gave him great confidence which informed his sense of self, and he began to aim much higher than his current position as a sales clerk in a high-end clothing shop.

One day, a young aristocrat oozing power and superiority came in to add to his wardrobe. He came in with a friend who called him Tony. Tony meandered around the room keeping an eye on Sasha.

"Isn't he beautiful?" Tony asked his friend Nicky.

"Oh yes. And he looks new – fresh and untarnished."

"Not for long," Tony replies with a laugh.

Sasha saw them laughing, and he knew he was the subject of the joke. He'd been aware of their stares and blushed with shame when they laughed at him.

Tony saw his red face and felt guilty.

"Would you mind helping me find a shirt?" he asked the clerk with an especially solicitous voice. "I'm a bit confused."

Sasha came to him warily, "How may I help?"

"I'm not sure if I want to invest in flannel this late in the season. Perhaps I should go to linen, or a soft cotton. What do you think?"

Sasha, still unsure if he was being mocked, answered tentatively, "It may depend on whether you'll be traveling in the near future. If you expect to be here in England, it may turn cold again." He felt it was a safe answer and not a cue for another joke at his expense.

Tony saw Sasha's discomfort and unease in his young, pretty face and felt a protective instinct towards him, "I'm going to rely on your good taste and judgement. As it happens, I won't be leaving London for at least a month. So I think I'll follow your advice and get one from this fabric," he pointed to a soft grey flannel, "and maybe one from this blue."

Nicky remarked sharply, "Just like your eyes. Your mother will love it." He saw that Tony was taken with the vulnerable clerk and didn't know if he approved.

As Sasha proceeded with the transaction, Tony realized that he was, in fact, taken with the young man whether Nicky approved or not.

"You have an account, of course, with your measurements," Sasha suggested.

"Yes," Tony answered agreeably, "Anthony Trembley ---"

"Lord Trembley," Nicky pointedly interrupted.

"Of course," Sasha responded, blushing again.

Tony loved the pink in his cheeks. Sasha had black hair and light blue eyes with a pale complexion that revealed his emotions too easily.

"Tell you what," Tony said. "I'll come back in for the fitting in a few days. Will you be here Thursday?"

"Yes," Sasha said quietly, hoping it made a difference to Lord Trembley whether he was here or not.

"Excellent. I'll see you this Thursday," Tony said with a reassuring smile.

Lord Trembley did come into the shop on Thursday – at the end of the working day. Sasha had waited all day to see him and was despondent when he had failed to appear. Then, just before closing, he appeared. Tony planned to take Sasha for drinks and by coming in as late as possible, he knew Sasha would be glad to accompany him after almost losing his connection with the aristocrat. Tony had experience with young, vulnerable innocents who had just arrived in the big city.

Sure enough, Sasha leapt at the chance to spend time with Lord Trembley – his first lord! Tony poured on the charm. It was easy to do because he was delighted with Sasha. What a beauty! Before they left the pub, they had arranged another date – this time at the latest musical comedy playing in the West End. Sasha couldn't believe his good fortune. It was like a dream, a Hollywood fantasy, and it was his life. Things would be different from now on. He decided quickly that his biography needed fine tuning and he would be a White Russian, an orphan, with no family in the world. His aristocratic relatives were all killed in the Revolution. When he related his sad story, he had no idea that Tony was amused by Sasha's presumption and was just playing along and pretending to believe the lies. Gradually the two men began an affair.

Sasha was a virgin when he met Tony, but he had always known he didn't feel particularly drawn to women or men. He responded to seduction, by either sex. Tony Trembley had had many affairs and was well-practiced in the art of seduction. It was almost too easy to make Sasha his lover.

Sasha was particularly delighted with Tony's gifts. He never smoked but when Tony gave him a gold lighter, he immediately took up the habit. Tony knew this, and he was very amused by it. Money meant nothing to him, and he was entertained by the lengths others would go to in pursuit of it. Sasha was like a young girl: flowers, candy, tokens of affection in gold or platinum – they all sent Sasha over the moon. He was in love with Tony, but Tony knew Sasha would never have looked at him twice if he weren't Lord Trembley. His wealth and his title were all part of his attraction for Sasha who continued to believe he was living a fantasy.

Sasha was staying at Tony's hotel, waiting for him excitedly one day in April. A courier had dropped off train tickets for Portofino, and Sasha thought it was a surprise from Tony. He had never been anywhere outside London and was thrilled to be going to the Riviera. He would need to shop, of course. Perhaps Tony would take him to Foote & Sons to outfit him for a sunny vacation.

When he heard the key in the front door of the suite, Sasha's heart started to beat faster. He told himself to play it casually. He could tell Tony was getting tired of his lack of sophistication. His naiveté could be a bore, he knew. But there was so much to learn!

"Hello?" Tony called out.

Sasha didn't answer him right away. He didn't want to seem eager.

"Maybe he's not here," another voice spoke.

"Oh please, where would he go without his master?" It was Nicky's voice this time, sharp and mean.

"Oh, Nicky, you can be such a prick," the third voice complained.

"No, he's right. Sasha is very dependent on me, clinging like a vine," Tony made a shivering motion with his shoulders. "It's just as well we're going south, otherwise it might be a lot rougher getting rid of him. As it is, he'll be gone by the time we return. Much more civilized."

Sasha was stunned – his heart felt like it stopped suddenly. It was as if someone had taken his breath away by punching him in the

188

stomach. Then he was burning, shaking with rage and sorrow. If he were alone, he would be sobbing and tearing his hair. He had never been betrayed before, and this was a monstrous act of disloyalty. He wished he could die instantly or at least disappear.

He remembered the servant's entrance and quickly rushed to the kitchen with its back door and staircase. He opened and closed the back door as quietly as he could and raced down the stairs to the street level exit. Tears filled his eyes as he hurried down the street with no destination in mind. He just wanted to get away from this hideous disgrace. How could he have been so stupid? So naïve? He looked back at his behavior with Tony and was deeply ashamed. All the while Tony was laughing at him behind his back, joking about him with his friends. Sasha kept crying and walking rapidly to get as far away as possible from this man who never cared for him but only used him for a joke. Never again, he vowed. Never again would he be the lover; from now on, he would be the loved. If he died trying, he would never again give in to love.

He couldn't return to Foote & Sons. He managed to get a job in a fine restaurant and, as usual, his boss decided he should be seen up front and had him assist the maître d' who needed no help and resented the beautiful young man. It was a difficult situation for Sasha, but he reasoned it was temporary until he decided what to do – or where to go – next.

He was turning over a table with a bus boy, folding the damask napkins, in the middle of a busy night, when he heard a familiar voice. He turned just as the man asked him "Sasha? It's Sasha, isn't it?"

He was a tall ginger haired Scot with a friendly long face.

"Have we met?" Sasha asked.

"Once, with Tony Trembley."

Sasha's face darkened and he looked with suspicion at the man. "I don't remember." He started to turn away when the man spoke again, "I'm sure you wouldn't. However, you have an extraordinary face, and I doubt many could forget you. I certainly couldn't."

Sasha smiled, "Really? To whom am I speaking?"

The Scot smiled in return, "Cam. My name is Cameron Andrews." He extended his hand to Sasha who shook it firmly.

"Well, it's nice to see you again. I'm working," he gestured to the annoyed maître d', "so I should return to my station."

"Of course. I'd love to see you again, though. Perhaps we might have lunch sometime?" Cam said, still smiling.

In an instant, Sasha understood that this time he knew what he was doing and wouldn't make the same mistakes. He also understood that he had found his destiny. He knew what he had of value, and he was going to make the most of it.

He answered Cam, "I would love to – Tony has my number." He turned away with a cynical smile. Once again, he was a White Russian.

Cam picked up where Tony had left off, installing Sasha in a small apartment and giving him an allowance. It was easy for Sasha to be happy with Cam in the short term. He didn't love Cam, but became fond of him. Cam was kind-hearted and not the snob Tony was. He came from an illustrious family in Scotland, had money and love for Sasha. They both knew it was a back-door romance, but the day came when Cam wanted to go out publicly with his beautiful boy.

"Sasha, my sister is getting married. I want to take you with me to the wedding."

Sasha was shocked. Meeting Cam's family? He didn't know whether to be pleased or terrified. "You are inviting me to your sister's wedding?"

Cam laughed. "I know, this is something we've never done, but we can come as old friends. Everyone there knows me, but they have no idea of my sexual inclination. They don't judge or criticize – they are family. If we act as friends do – with affection, but nothing physical - we can pass inspection."

He hastened to add, "I don't mean to hurt you, I hope I don't - I just want to include you more, but I also cannot expose myself. There's the family, you know. The family …" his voice trailed off.

Sasha was still thinking about it. "I suppose we can do it," he said slowly. "I would love to go, naturally, and if you think I can go, then I guess I will." He finished his sentence with a big smile. "I won't let you down, Cam. I promise."

It was a late spring wedding, and the weather was perfect: just warm enough not to be chilled under a wedgewood blue sky without a cloud in sight. Sasha was very nervous, but Cam calmed down as soon as his young nieces and nephews ran to greet him when he got out of the car. They fell upon him, laughing, and it was clear to Sasha that Cam was the favorite uncle. He wasn't surprised. Cam had a rare gift – a heart of gold.

"Sasha, come here – meet the Andrews rascals!"

Sasha smiled in response as the children jumped on Cam. They turned to Sasha and greeted him perfunctorily – he was a friend of Uncle Cam, so what? Sasha knew their indifference was the perfect juvenile response to an introduction to a grown-up, and he relaxed.

Trays of champagne were passed around and Sasha was careful not to drink too much. He kept being introduced to relative after relative, and he was trying to keep track as well as never losing awareness that he was playing the part of an old friend. As Cam had said, everyone he met was friendly and warm. They were thrilled to see Cam, and clearly, any friend of Cam ….

Apparently, Cam stayed away from the family seat for long periods of time. Sasha assumed it was to live his authentic life without fear. But he wondered if the Andrews family could really be entirely fooled? Cam was in his forties now, still unmarried. But perhaps they just accommodated each other: it isn't worth mentioning so don't mention it. And keep it away from here.

******

Chantal de Caqueray was standing on the terrace behind Thurell Hall, the family seat of the Andrews clan. On the far right was a small combo playing quiet jazz. People sat at small tables or wandered around the gardens just off the terrace. The slightly warm May weather enhanced the flowering lilacs and Korean spice viburnum making everyone feel languid and content. Chantal looked around the crowd for someone she knew. Her gaze paused on Sasha. What a beautiful boy, she thought. I must know him. She crossed the flagstone patio to his side.

Sasha became aware of a presence at his side. He turned to see a forty-ish woman with piercing thin green eyes. She had heavy eyebrows which flattered her striking eyes. She was voluptuous verging on stout, and when his gaze rose to her coiffure, Sasha could not imagine what would persuade any woman to wear her hair in a teased and lacquered bouffant that went out of style for good in the '60s. He looked down to escape the intensity of those green eyes and saw she was wearing stiletto heels with rhinestone covered leather straps wrapped around her calves like espadrilles. The hideous shoes only drew attention to the fact she had no ankles. Sasha shuddered mentally at her delusions. Then he realized that he was no different; he, too, was a victim of self-delusion; he sighed.

"Pardonne?" she responded to his sigh.

"Oh, nothing – de rien," he corrected himself and smiled at her.

"Chantal de Caqueray," she said and extended her arm to him.

He was startled by her directness and briefly wondered if he should kiss her hand.

"Sasha Ivanov", he shook her hand firmly.

"Are you a friend of the bride-to-be or the groom?" Chantal asked him but didn't care how he answered. She wanted this pretty boy.

"I'm an old friend of Heather's brother. And you?"

"I have known the Andrews family all my life. I had to make an appearance." She spoke a little sourly with an almost indiscernible French accent.

"But," she continued, flashing him a big smile which exposed her bright white veneers, "I have met you, and that is a wonderful thing, I think." Any bitterness was gone in her voice. And her eyes softened in the way a cat's eyes do just before an attack.

"Have you seen the gardens? It's early but there are already some lovely blooms. Come along," she said, turning away from him, gesturing with her hand to follow her.

Sasha thought, "why not?" He followed meekly, and by the time they returned to the party, she had persuaded him to leave Cam and England and join her on a trip to Rome and Florence. "And don't worry about your wardrobe," she said looking him up and down, "I have a tailor in Rome. He will take care of it."

Sasha was confused but seduced by the image of himself in Rome being fitted for a new wardrobe. Although she had terrible taste – if any at all – her clothes were expensive, and she had money. He wanted to travel, and with Chantal, he would travel in style. He cared for Cam, but he knew he had no future beyond the apartment in London. He didn't know what Chantal would bring to his life, but at least they didn't have to hide. And he could always return – both Chantal and Cam were in love with him.

The two of them found Cam with his mother. He watched them walk towards him with a smile both knowing and melancholy.

"Lovely party, Isabelle," Chantal murmured to Cam's mother and gave her air kisses. "Cam," she repeated the routine and then looked at Sasha.

Sasha had been looking away from Cam, and now he turned to him, "Cam ---"

"You haven't met my mother, Sasha," Cam interrupted. Sasha realized instantly he should have addressed her first and blushed at his social ineptitude.

"Isabelle," she said warmly to him, putting her hand out.

Sasha took it gratefully with both hands, "I'm so pleased to finally meet you. It's been a beautiful day, and your gardens are magnificent."

"Oh, thank you. I'm glad you got to see them. They are my life's work," she laughed at herself and Cam joined in.

"It's true – she loves her family, but only after her gardens."

"Oh, Cam," she gave him a hug and shushed him.

"Eh bien," Chantal spoke up. "We have to catch a plane so we must be going."

Cam flinched imperceptibly and nodded with a sad smile, "Well then, au revoir you two."

And that was that. Chantal had her beautiful boy.

*****

Sunday morning

Sunday morning, Marie-Claude ran her fingers through her sun-streaked blonde hair and looked at herself closely in the mirror. As happy as she was about the baby, she could see the tension in her face. It was going to be hard to forget what happened the last time she was this happy finding out she was pregnant. She was joyous then, each day more wonderful than the one before until she lost the baby - the saddest day of her life. When Hassim had to leave her to work with François, she had become sick with worry: she was anxious and nervous. She was convinced the fear and anxiety she felt contributed to the miscarriage. This time around, she vowed to avoid stress; she needed to calmly await her little miracle, her little passenger.

I will relax, she promised herself. When all this is over, we can finally go home. But when would that be? Day after day of the same nonsense. First François's death and now that horrid woman killed – Marie-Claude felt she was in a nightmare. These people, she thought, shaking her head. It was like being stuck on a lifeboat with strangers and no rescue ship in sight.

They weren't bad people, she reminded herself, and she was very fond of Dany and C.C. It was just, well, too many people. She was not a social person, she was shy, introverted. She wanted to be alone; she felt like she was acting a part every time she left her room. Even talking to Hassim was difficult, but at least he understood her reticence.

As if on cue, Hassim entered the bedroom and caught Marie-Claude's gaze in the mirror.

"I had a thought," he began. "I think we might go for a stroll in the Parc Monceau. One of the musicians, Max, told me how peaceful it was – and quiet – and I thought you might enjoy an afternoon out of the hotel. What do you think?"

"That might be nice," she considered. "It is becoming a bit claustrophobic in these rooms. Yes, I think that sounds like a nice way to spend the afternoon."

Hassim nodded happily. "Oh, and don't forget, we have that engagement party tonight."

A cloud passed over her face, "Oh, Hassim, I don't know. All those people …"

"I won't leave your side. And those people are so colorful and funny – *les fashionistas*."

She smiled, "Is that really a word? I thought it was made up."

"I believe you are correct, but it's an amusing group of celebrities. We can take a deck chair and watch them and be entertained. It will be fun."

"All right, if you don't leave me alone. I don't want to have to think of anything witty to say. They seem to wait for a faux pas and then broadcast it to the world."

Hassim smiled and shook his head, "Marie-Claude, surely you exaggerate, and besides, when did you start to care what other people were saying?"

She stood up abruptly and turned to him, "You are right. Let's go make the most of this day, and to hell what other people think. Let's go have breakfast."

"Le Jardin?"

"Where else?"

*****

The sun woke up Fan. It was shining in his face because he had forgotten to close the curtains when they returned last night. He reasoned it would be pointless to close them against the sun now that he was awake. All his fears and doubts from the past few days came to the forefront of his mind, this time not to be dismissed by sleep. Oh, Bella, he sighed.

He got out of bed and put his flannel robe over his cotton pajamas, splashed cold water on his face in his bathroom and thought that yes, he had much to discuss with his little sister.

"Bella," he knocked on her door and called quietly at first "Bella".

"Bella!" He raised his voice when she failed to answer. He opened her door slowly, as usual appalled by the mess in her bedroom. "Bella, wake up!"

She stirred and opened her eyes, unseeing and blind, the way she always woke up.

"Bella, please get up."

She shook the sleep out of her head and sat up. "What? Did something happen?"

Not for the first time, he marveled at her ability to be completely awake after her comatose sleepiness dispelled in an instant. And also not for the first time, he felt he preferred her in her unconscious sleep state – it was so much easier for him when she had no voice. Why was she always so contradictory?

"Wash your face," he commanded, "and meet me in the living room." He turned and left her.

Bella and Fan shared a large suite with separate bedrooms and bathrooms. Fan's half was spotless. His clothes were all either hung up carefully in the closet or carefully folded and placed in the chest of cedar lined drawers. He had his bed made daily, and at first glance, it appeared no one was staying in the room. Everything was put away where it belonged, out of sight. Even his robe was hanging on the closet hook. His clothes were private. For Fan, privacy was imperative; privacy was control.

His bathroom gleamed; the towels were always fresh and folded over the warming rack. He used shaving soap and a straight razor, toothpaste and brush and witch hazel. He had Caswell Massey soap and shampoo in the shower. He had an exact duplicate set of his bathroom essentials at home and kept his travel kit stocked and packed. His life was predicated on organization and order - control. He relied on his own predictability – he thrived on it. Change was chaos - not progress - in his world view and in his personal life.

He traveled with enough suits, shirts, sweaters and underwear to be able to forego hotel cleaners. And his limited personal hygiene made it easy to pack and go. If he traveled alone, he would be the most efficient and self-reliant man on the road. But he always traveled with Bella. She was his opposite in many ways; when it came to hotel stays, the comparison was very sharply defined: she was Oscar to his Felix.

Her bedroom was full of fluffy clouds of Liberty print fabrics occasionally broken up by piles of hats, scarves, underpants and brassieres which looked like small colorful tropical islands peeking out from the gauzy overcast of muslin and linen. The visual cacophony of her clothes pleased Bella. Spread out over every surface, the small pastel flower prints looked charming to her. And her lingerie and chapeaux delighted her. Her underclothes belied her staid exterior: they were silky, lacy and surprisingly sexy. She felt she was wearing a secret identity whenever she dressed. Nobody knew the real Bella, and it always brought a smile to her face when she thought about her hidden self.

Her bathroom was predictably messy and full of beauty aids she never used. She couldn't imagine wearing makeup in public, but she harbored a fantasy that someday she would paint her face and emerge from her cocoon so that everyone could see who she was – a woman of mystery, a beauty, a femme fatale. Not now, but soon she would become a butterfly. Not now, but soon.

In the meantime, she tended to her ablutions when she bathed; there were bath oils, bubble bath beads, herbal powders and lotions and serums for after bath. Most of the many bottles had been opened but not closed, and the fragrances piled up against and on top of each other into a powerful blend that overwhelmed Bella when she bathed, to her delight.

And wouldn't they all be surprised when she exposed herself – presenting the real Bella Roxanne Jardine! Especially Fan. Oh, that would be a priceless moment – the look on his face! Not now, but soon, she promised herself - not for the first time. But she believed that after years of patient waiting, that day was coming closer. She could feel it.

She heard a knock on her door, "Bella! Let's go. If you want to go to Le Jardin, we have to leave now."

"I'm coming," she called and very quickly came to the door. "Let's go," she smiled.

Fan and Bella settled into their chairs in Le Jardin. Neither of them was a bright bulb in the morning, but they were inoffensive and understood each other. No talking until the second cup of tea. Sometimes Bella ordered coffee, but she believed caffeine was dangerous so she tried to stick to tea.

"You know there's caffeine in tea, don't you?" Fan asked her once.

"Yes, but it doesn't feel like it; there's no jolt from tea, the caffeine creeps up on you."

This morning, both of them had tea with their breakfast. They drank and then ate very slowly. They both woke up like bears in the spring, slowly and deliberately. Not as dangerous as bears, perhaps, but definitely not sparkling or cheerful and definitely not ready for company.

By the end of the meal, they were conversing, planning the day.

"And don't forget," Fan spoke sharply to her, "we have that boat tonight. We must be at the dock exactly on time to catch the ship. I'm afraid you'll be late and we'll miss the boat."

Bella giggled at the pun. "Oh, I don't want to miss the boat – or I'll miss the boat!"

Fan shook his head. "Bella, are you paying attention? Do you comprehend the message? Don't make me wait for you. For once, be ready on time. Please."

Bella made a soothing sound, "Oh, Fansie, stop worrying about me. I'm fine and I'll be fine tonight. As a matter of fact, I'm going to be better than fine very soon," she teased.

He looked up from his plate, "What do you mean?" He was afraid to ask.

Bella smiled, "I told you not to worry and I meant it. Everything is going to be fine – me, you," she laughed again, "everybody!"

He shook his head, "Well, if you insist on playing coy, then never mind. Finish your eggs so we can go."

"I'm not ready yet. I want another glass of juice; would you order it for me?"

Fan sighed. In many ways he would be grateful to pass Bella on to another man – even a gold digger like Carter. The idea of living his own life and not just watching over his sister was like a beautiful fantasy, but it was also a bit threatening. What would he do with that freedom? What would it be like to be responsible for himself only?

More and more, he was willing to find out. How bad could it be? After all, taking care of Bella could be - and had been – awful, frightening and dangerous. Living by himself would never be as panic-driven as living with Bella had been.

He watched her eat slowly and realized she was stalling in the hope of seeing Carter walk in. What a teenager, he thought. A dangerous, unpredictable, passionate teenager. Would she ever grow up?

*****

Carter lay in bed, looking at the ceiling while his thoughts whirled in his brain. He needed money. He was almost broke, and he had no expectation of any future income. He was wrong – very wrong – to invest his meager life savings in a film! What was he thinking of?! He was trying to make an impression but he risked everything he had, and now that the filmmaker was dead – he may have lost everything. What a fool he'd been. How could he have missed the obvious result of François's death? He knew nothing of filmmaking. He had assumed that the process would move on, the documentary would be released and he'd get his money back plus his share of the box office receipts. How could he have been so stupid?

He felt no sadness at François's death – it was regrettable, but François meant nothing to him. He was not a friend – not that Carter had any friends – and his absence would have meant nothing if it hadn't affected his bottom line. He should have known; and like a line from a song he couldn't get out of his head, he kept repeating *I should have known, I should have known, I should have known.*

His only hope was Bella. She seemed captivated by him, but he knew she was still as attached to Fan as a barnacle to a sinking ship. He closed his eyes and frowned. He had to buck up and get back in the business of winning his prize – Bella. He couldn't imagine his future beyond this conquest – he had no future without her: he hadn't planned for one. He needed to focus.

Suddenly it occurred to him that Bella might not be the immediate goal. Perhaps he needed to shine his light on Fan. If he could seduce Fan, not literally, although … If Fan began to care for him, Carter might still make Bella his bride. He doubted Fan had ever had physical intimacy with anyone, and it was possible Carter would only have to charm him enough so that Fan would desire Carter's presence, would want him around, and marriage to Bella would accomplish that. And if it took a physical expression of romance, well, it wouldn't be the first time Carter had experienced male infatuation.

Carter had never been in love with anyone, and he didn't believe he was capable of truly caring about someone else. He had been raised to please, never to be pleased, and it only enhanced his ability to play hard to get, to raise his value in others' eyes. He grew up learning how to be an object of desire, and he had been an apt student. He began to feel better, more confident, more aware of his talents, his gifts. He could still pull it off. It was all about Fan now.

He sighed. He believed he could pull it off, but he was tired, very tired of the game he had been playing for as long as he could remember. He was exhausted, spent – an ironic word, he noted with a sad smile. He felt as if he had been at sea for too long, searching like a Columbus or a Magellan for a mythical land of riches. He had lost his compass, and he no longer had any sense of morality, much less a higher power to guide him. He was lost, and he wanted to rest, to stop exploring foreign shores and to finally return to a home port. He decided he would go home with the Jardines, one way or another. If he couldn't seduce Fan, well then, Fan would have to go. After all, people died all the time; look at François.

*****

Jean-Paul woke up before Dany and quietly got dressed. He knew she preferred waking up alone and taking her time to greet the new day. He was different: he was ready to go as soon as he got out of bed. When he was a young man, he might stay in bed all morning with a woman, but now things were different. He had changed. Oh yes, he smiled to himself, he had changed – he was old.

He was a philanderer when young and never missed a chance for a new affair; he loved all the girls he met when he was young. Even with Danielle he could not be faithful, and he loved her most of all. Young, handsome movie stars were never faithful - there was no reason for fidelity with so many pretty and willing girls available. It was a heady time for Jean-Paul, and he had no regrets. Fortunately, he was able to reunite with his one true love, Danielle, and she forgave him all his sins. Otherwise, he would have lived to the end of his days with regret.

He had survived the loss of their only child. It was devastating for them both at the time and undoubtedly played a part in their divorce. But although he thought about the boy at least once a day, and the pain of the memory stabbed his heart like a knife when he did, he had accepted it and made an effort to find something of joy remaining in life. He found Dany after he'd thought he lost her, and together they sought brief moments of happiness to light the melancholy shadow world they inhabited. Nobody understood the perpetual pain of loss they endured, and they found great comfort in knowing they were not alone, they had each other.

That he was impotent was only an ironic joke that they both found hilarious. Neither thought much about sex anymore so his loss of libido was amusing more than dismaying. In this asexual union, they were closer than they had ever been. Laughter returned to their lives as they re-discovered their shared view of the world they inhabited: rueful, humorous and compassionate. They helped each other mellow with age - although Danielle still had occasional moments when she succumbed to angry thoughts of vengeance.

She was shocked the first time the fury passed through her like lightning, an electrical charge she felt throughout her body. She felt out of control, and she believed whatever she did was defensible: if your feelings overwhelmed your reason, it was as correct as if your intellect overruled your emotions. They were two sides of the same coin and thus, equally valid. This seemed obvious to her, Danielle was French, born and raised in Paris, where the very air was *existencial*. Everyone is a *philosophe* in Paris – *c'est la raison d'être*, she thought wryly.

She slowly got out of bed, wrapped her quilted silk robe around her and walked over to the window. Sometimes she forgot which day it was; they were so much the same. Sunday, of course, there was no mail, so that one was easy. She retired from the world on Sundays and stayed home.

But today she made an exception for Marin, the daughter of one of her closest friends. Dany believed this would be Marin's first marriage. She was so young and pretty, and she was used to being indulged – well, eventually every man has something else to do. But she was unlikely to be having children for a few years, so, ah, who knows? she asked herself. Only saints and psychopaths are predictable.

"Jean-Paul?" she called out.

"Here I am, with a little breakfast," he entered the room with a tray. He brought coffee, croissants and *Le Monde*. "Simple, but effective." He put the tray on the small table by the windows and pulled out the chair.

"Mon chère," she said, smiling, and kissed him as she sat down. "This is all we need."

*****

Chantal woke up with a horrific headache. She did not drink much on a regular basis, and Grand Marnier was a very sugary drink which can cause massive hangovers. She grumbled to herself about switching to vodka. There was no question of not drinking. She had no other coping skills for this situation. She was rich! People didn't abandon her – she dumped them. She didn't mind paying anyone's way because she liked company. Once they began to bore her, she could send them home. But Sasha! He never bored her.

Sasha was the best toy she had ever acquired and the only one she lost. When she was growing up, she was quick to throw out the toys that had come to bore her over time. She tossed them with no regrets. And her indulgent parents never hesitated to replace them with something better. She treated acquaintances the same way. She never had friends - just classmates she tolerated out of necessity. Loners were bullied by other students, and she didn't want to bother with outbursts of hostility and antagonism, so she played the part of a joiner. It was easier to put on an accommodating, faux friendly face. She was her most complete self when she was alone.

Throughout her childhood, Chantal learned how to define her needs and wants and express them to her parents and other figures of authority she suffered. Nobody wanted to tell her 'no' or contradict her - it was always more trouble than it was worth. She would clam up and turn a completely blank face to teachers, heads of school and anyone else foolish enough to refuse her desires. Her stone face was more than uncanny, and the discomfiture of her opponent became greater than any principle involved in the matter. Rather than endure an apparently unending quiet rebellion from her, the teacher, head of school or parent simply brushed the offense aside and settled for Chantal's small pretense of acquiescence.

Right now, she needed a change of scenery. Paris was dreary without Sasha. Where was he? She couldn't stand being immobile. Day after day, just waiting for le Maître to read the will. After all, she didn't need any money from François's estate. She had all the money she could ever need. If it weren't for this absurd police investigation, she would just tell that lawyer to donate her bequest to charity.

She needed to go away somewhere. Perhaps the South Seas - Polynesia, Tahiti, Bali? A small smile played on her lips. Then she realized she couldn't go anywhere - she had to stay because of this nonsense about Morgana. That woman can annoy me from the grave! Is there no end to her interference? She shook her head, annoyed. Then it occurred to her that Sasha might still make it to the Hotel Rose. For that matter, he might already be here. She still couldn't understand what was going on with the singer from Le Salon Jazz and that strange man dressed like a woman. Any woman could see that was a man. And of course it was Sasha. Wasn't it? It had to be Sasha. Her head was throbbing now.

Then she remembered the spa downstairs. That's a wonderful solution. I can soak in the hot bubbles and relax my bones. Then a massage – oh, this is a heavenly idea. She took two aspirin and slipped into the hotel's roomy and soft terry cloth robe. *Splendide*, she thought. I'll be that much better tonight and with luck, tomorrow I'll be on my way. She left her room and took the elevator to the spa.

*****

Andie woke up with a sore throat. She was surprised because she expected bruising on her neck, but she hadn't realized how the inside of her throat would be affected.

"Damn, Max," she said angrily, "I'm really going to be annoyed if this affects my singing."

"What?" Max muttered and turned over to face her.

"I'm sorry, did I wake you? Go back to sleep, we'll talk later."

"Too late for that," he retorted sleepily as he sat up in bed. "Besides, Ben is probably just about to call us about breakfast."

"Oh ugh. I'd just as soon skip it. This is our day off and we're going to cruise the Seine tonight eating and listening to Aly. I think, as the victim, I should be able to dictate what we do today," she said in a haughty tone.

"Don't be ridiculous. Consider last night a dress rehearsal; the killer won't make the same mistake twice. You need protection."

"But Max, I've got you. Nobody cares more about my well-being than you do."

Max laughed a little and said, "That may or may not be true but that's not actually a defense if someone attacks you."

"Why wouldn't it be true?"

"Why wouldn't what be true?"

"Max! Pay attention."

"Andie, we're getting side-tracked. And I ---"

The ringing phone in the room cut him off.

Max quickly picked it up, "Hello?"

It was Ben, making sure they were awake. All Andie could hear was his end of the conversation. Bored, she got up and went to the bathroom to get ready for the day.

When she returned to the living room, Max left to take a quick shower after ordering room service. Andie made some coffee, and he and Andie were drinking coffee when first room service and then Ben showed up almost simultaneously.

"Perfect timing," Andie said.

"Your neck!" Ben exclaimed when he saw the dark purple bruises from the attack. "Good God, Andie. What have you done?"

"Well, that's uncalled for, Ben. I didn't do anything!" She retorted. Then she saw he had a bag from the patisserie. "What's in the bag?"

"A little something for the victim – I thought you told me you liked it."

He handed her the bag and she opened it to find her favorite French pastry, chausson aux pommes – apple turnovers.

"Oh, Ben! I love them, and these are warm. Perfect! You must have one," she gave one to him.

Ben took a bite, "You're right, this is delicious – what a treat. I'll have to remember – chausson aux pommes," he said it slowly to make it register in his memory.

Andie's head jerked up, startled, "You said chausson aux pommes, didn't you? I mean, I never really thought about the name for apple turnovers before - it was just a long French phrase for my favorite pastry – but chausson is a turnover! Mme. Chausson!"

Max laughed, "Yes! Oh, how funny. We certainly missed the joke."

"For Heaven's sake!" Ben chimed in. "What a bunch of dummies we are."

Andie nodded, "I know, and it was right in front of us the whole time. 'Turnover'! Good one, François."

They all laughed again.

"Not to be morbid, but we need to discuss your attack, Andie," Ben changed the subject. "Why you? What happened that made you a target?"

"Actually, I've been thinking about it, and I think I know what happened," Max said.

Andie and Ben looked expectantly at him, and he continued, "The only reason anyone connected to Morgana's death - or François's for that matter – would also come after Andie is if she poses a threat - of exposure. That's the only motive for killing her that I can think of, and I know what you did to give that impression," he turned to Andie. "The 'leetle gray cells'."

She jumped in, "Poirot! When I did my Poirot impression," she nodded vigorously, "of course."

Ben looked perplexed, "I don't recall any impersonations in your act – what Poirot?"

"It's not in the act," Max laughed, "that's not going to happen. It's something she does for me – a private joke, you might say."

"That he always enjoys, right?" Andie remarked.

"Toujours," Max leaned over to kiss her.

"I see. So how does this provide a motive for her assault?" Ben asked.

"She put on her Poirot voice and loudly proclaimed her intention to find out who killed Morgana in Le Jardin yesterday morning. Clearly, someone in the restaurant heard her and was threatened."

Ben looked at Andie, shaking his head, "I repeat: what have you done?!"

"Well, I don't think mimicking someone is dangerous – generally. So how could I be expected to anticipate that I might be provoking a murderer?"

Ben took a long look at her. "You know, I'm not entirely sure you weren't baiting a killer."

Max spoke up, "I really don't think that was her intention, Ben. But that brings me to my point, the reason I wanted to have breakfast with you. I want protection from the police for Andie until the killer is caught."

Ben leaned back, "Well, wait a minute now. I want her protected, but I know she's not going to take my advice."

"She's right here," Andie cut in.

Max said to Ben, "We have an obligation tonight on a cruise boat around the Seine. It's our only night off this week, and we've promised to attend a party. I want you and Montclair to be there too. We can't prevent the killer from trying again – tonight, tomorrow or two weeks from now." He paused for effect. "Wouldn't it be better to draw him – or her – out in a controlled space?"

"You mean use her as bait? After she's already been strangled, you want to invite another attempt?"

"She's smart and she can handle herself," Max argued.

"Still here," Andie said and raised her arm.

"All right. You make sense," Ben said reluctantly to Max. "I can get a crew, and I'll call Montclair immediately to fill him in."

He stood up and looked at the two of them. His face broke into a smile and he shook his head, "You kids, you two – I feel as if I've aged forty years since we met."

He shook Max's hand and paused, then gave Andie a strong hug and held her tightly for a moment.

"I cannot imagine having to face your father if something happens to you; I know just how he would feel."

"Ben, you and my father would like each other very much, but he wouldn't try and stop me, so don't worry about it."

Ben shook his head, said "Ciao," and he left them alone.

Andie and Max turned to each other and smiled at the prospect of a long day off work with a boat ride on the Seine at night.

"How magical it will be to hear the music go out over the water, with the lights sparkling on the waves and Aly Ocho's guitar ringing out? 'Oh how lovely' …" she sang the phrase from the English version of *Corcovado*. She had a habit of doing it whenever she saw something beautiful, from the Grand Canyon to a pair of Louboutin shoes. When Max pointed out that it made the phrase less meaningful if she overused it, she said "On the contrary, it means something is moving me to song. Besides, there are many lovely things in the world."

"What are you thinking for today?" Max changed the subject. "I would very much like to show you Parc Monceau. I think you'll like it. No, I'm sure you'll like it."

"All right. Sounds good," Andie replied.

"Really?"

"One thing I have learned over our wonderful time together is that you know me better than I know myself, and if you think I'll like it, the odds are I'll like it."

"That's sweet, albeit a little clinical. But it's nice to have your trust," he said as he kissed her forehead and handed her another black coffee.

"Hmm," Andie murmured - either for the kiss or the coffee, Max wasn't sure. "Yes," she continued warming to the subject – or the coffee, "I think it's because I am too subjective to know some things about myself that I wouldn't like. But you can see them and consider them, like in an equation."

"Again - clinical, plus maths – horrible," Max said, and Andie laughed.

They drank leisurely, enjoying the mood. Andie mused that working at night was like having a curfew: you had to be at the gig at the beginning of the night which was like having to be home at an early hour.

"In view of that, musicians must be the most stable and responsible people around at night. They're the only ones who are where they're supposed to be all night long. You might not know where Dad or Auntie June are at ten o'clock, but you know where Aly Balls is."

As they finished the coffee, Andie said, "I was thinking, if you were a victim of homicide, who would you want to solve the mystery of who did it?"

"Gosh, there are so many – Miss Marple has an excellent record. And you can't fool Dalgliesh. Too many people die while Jessica Fletcher is still pondering. Sam Spade always falls in love and if I've been killed, I don't want my detective wasting time on romance. I don't know. You?"

Andie took a sip of coffee, "I think I'd go with Sherlock. He's a classic. I like his intensity."

"Are you done with breakfast?"

"For now. But I might pick up something at the patisserie on the way to the park. Just in case."

Max shook his head, "Just in case we get lost in the park and have to forage for food, right?"

"Anything's ---"

"possible," he finished.

"Good Lord, now I'm saying it," she groaned.

*****

After he left Andie and Max, Ben met with Commissaire Montclair for coffee in Le Jardin.

"Ça va, Dash?" Ben knew Montclair was unhappy with the slow pace of the investigation and hoped to smooth over his complaints with a confident attitude, although he had no clue who the murderer was.

Montclair gave Ben a baleful stare. "Non - pas du tout."

"I understand your concerns, Dash, and I assure you I am also under great pressure to close this case. I cannot let these guests leave until I am sure we have the guilty party, and they are increasingly annoyed. Plus, the hotel is very concerned with publicity if I cannot keep it quiet and quick."

Montclair nodded.

"Do you have a plan? Do you have any ideas? Have you learned anything?" With each question, Montclair grew more agitated and accusatory.

Montclair had been commissaire long enough to recognize stalling for time. He had engaged in the same exercise himself with his superiors. He sighed, "I apologize, my friend. I know how these people can be – difficult. Very difficult. They make secrets of meaningless information just to put you off. For no reason! It only makes everybody look suspicious – it's like a wave is pulling you from the shore and you are trying to hold on to the sand to keep from being washed away."

Ben responded firmly, "I have plans, I have ideas and I've learned a lot. Unfortunately, I cannot tip my hand by focusing on any one individual. You know how that is, Dash."

Then he decided to jump right in with his request, "However, I am getting very close and with that in mind, I need your help tonight. I believe the killer will come after Andie – you remember, the singer – and I need you and some of your police to be there to apprehend the killer and save Andie. She escaped an attack last night, and it is certain the killer will return. She's going on a Seine River cruise this evening and I need a police presence on the boat."

Montclair looked stunned at first, "What are you saying? What are you doing – setting a trap? with that little singer as bait? You have been infected by those crazy people! Now, you are crazy. Mon Dieu!"

Ben had to laugh, then apologized for laughing when he saw Montclair's frown, "Excuse me, I know it's not funny. But if you help us, you can catch the killer tonight. You can put an end to this violence."

As Ben had hoped, Montclair understood and nodded slowly. Then he gave Ben a very serious look, "Somebody must be held responsible. It is up to me – and you! - to find justice for Morgana Standish."

Ben raised his eyebrows, "You sound like a cartoon superhero, Dash. Really? Where's your cape?"

For a moment, Montclair sat back - surprised, and then he began to laugh heartily, "Yes! I do sound like that! What is happening to me? These people all believe they are bigger than life, and it's beginning to affect me. *Mon dieu! Comme je suis fou! Idiot!*" He shook his head.

Ben shook his head in denial, "*Non! Non plus que moi.*"

Montclair smiled. "But I know you are crazy. Eh bien, your plan might work. I will come and bring some of my most trusted colleagues. They will not be in uniform so don't look for them; they will be there."

Ben hesitated but felt he should speak of the occasion, "It's an engagement party for a famous model and her rich fiancé. There will be, uh," he didn't know how to finish.

Montclair interrupted, "Mon ami, we are Parisians; we know how to dress."

He stood up to go and Ben followed his cue, "*Vraiment*, Dash. I should have realized or thought before I spoke. Thank you very much for your help – you are a good friend."

They shook hands and left the Hotel Rose together.

*****

Andie was already munching on the pain au chocolat when they entered the large, black iron gates.

"Oh," Andie said quietly and stopped chewing. "Oh how lovely ..." she sang slowly, quietly, and her voice trailed off.

On this occasion he was inclined to agree with her. "Isn't it?" he agreed.

They spent the afternoon in the park, and Andie enjoyed it as much as Max had hoped. He had a far better experience with her than with Fan. They strolled back to the hotel without a care, and when they entered their suite, Andie said, "I wanted to take a nap before our big night out, but I'm too excited. Do you want to play rummy?

"No. I'm going to lie down for a bit. Why don't you read your Dickens? That always knocks you out."

She laughed and agreed with him. She picked up her well-thumbed paperback and settled comfortably in the cushy armchair. She read for about fifteen minutes and then went to the bed and fell into a deep sleep.

Max woke up after twenty minutes and took his shower. He had to transcribe an arrangement Andie originally wrote for another singer and needed quiet time. Also, he knew Andie liked to nap longer and always told him when to wake her up.

He was just finishing the charts in which the Beatles' "*Norwegian Wood*" segued into "*All Blues*", the Miles Davis standard, when Andie came into the living room.

She leaned over and gave him a kiss on his forehead and asked, "How's it going?"

"All finished. We can play it tomorrow night. This was really a great idea you had."

Andie nodded in agreement, "It was so long ago when I wrote it - at school; it's so natural isn't it? I think the guys will love it too."

Andie showered and then dressed with extra care. When she dressed for the stage, there were priorities based on her performance: she had to be able to stand and sing for four sets – shoes had to be chosen with that in mind. But on a romantic night-time cruise with Max, she could indulge in fashion fantasy.

She briefly considered her stilettos – such beautiful shoes! - then quickly rejected them – it's a boat! – and looked for something special that wouldn't slip on the deck. It came to her in an instant – kitten heels, her silk palazzo pants, the spaghetti strapped tunic tied at the waist with a pashmina in case it got chilly – perfect. She added her collection of silver necklaces with charms and totems and wore small diamond posts.

Max whistled, and she blushed and said to him, "You look terrific." He wore his well-worn jeans with a light cashmere sweater in charcoal.

"Thanks. Should I bring a jacket in case you get cold?" he asked.

"How sweet of you to ask," Andie smiled. "No, I think I've got that covered."

They went downstairs then out to the sidewalk where Max hailed a taxi. The cab dropped them off at Port de la Bourdonnais at the foot of the Eiffel Tower. The evening was still warm with an occasional light breeze, and the sun was slowly setting in the west.

Andie couldn't help but feel excited: it was a lovely evening, they were going on a boat cruise on the Seine, they would be serenaded by Aly Ocho, and best of all, they were going to have a gourmet dinner. They walked up the gangplank and joined a growing crowd of very fashionably dressed passengers waiting along the deck for the arrival of the golden couple.

"That's right, I remember now. Aly said it was an engagement party for a top model from Scotland – Marin – to the very rich Brian Kerr, Sir Brian Kerr. That's why the fashions tonight are so wonderful."

"My thoughts exactly," Max said facetiously.

"It looks like a very happy crowd, doesn't it?"

"Or a very something."

Everyone seemed delighted to be there. Marin was very popular and had many friends. Somehow she had managed to exclude the usual extraneous crowd of extras – agents, publicists, managers, et al - that surround celebrities, and her husband-to-be came from a background sufficiently exclusive that there were no such things as wannabes or hangers-on – only fellow members of a dying - but still apparently potent - class.

A shiny white Jaquar drove on the dock and delivered the happy couple. Marin wore a skin-tight mini dress that looked as if black bandages had been wrapped around her torso. Her legs were longer than any Andie had ever seen, and her smile took over her face – it was infectious, and Andie had to smile back. Marin wore a crown of flowers in her long black hair which was worn in a loose updo.

Sir Brian Kerr held her hand, his suntanned face beaming. He was slightly taller than Marin, blonde and blue-eyed. He wore black perfectly tailored jacket and trousers over an open-necked black silk shirt. Andie thought the couple was impossibly good-looking - a match made in *Vogue*.

Walking backwards in front of them, taking their pictures, was Marin's best friend, Sonata, a very tall blonde model turned photographer. She wore a loose-fitting white man's tuxedo with a black lace camisole. She had a gardenia boutonniere and a very chic black fedora.

Everyone on the boat gave out cheers and applause as the beauties walked up the gangplank. The models – male and female - represented the best-looking young people from all over the world - each one better looking than the last.

Andie sighed, "These people are all too beautiful – I feel like we're in a commercial or a soap opera. Where do they come from? I never see people this good-looking in my daily life. Do they all live together somewhere? The land of handsome people? It looks like a room full of mannequins and androids!"

Max laughed and said diplomatically, "Well, you should know. You look like one of them."

She narrowed her eyes, "Why do you always know what to say? How do you do that?"

"I love my wife," he said smugly and threw his arm around her.

They went up the stairs to the top deck.

"Oh, this is nice," Max murmured as he leaned over and kissed Andie's head as they climbed.

"I'll say," she whispered back.

"Max! Andie!"

They turned and saw Aly waving at them.

They called and waved back and made their way to the stage. It was elevated and Aly reached down to clasp their hands.

"Glad you came," he said with a big smile. Everything on Aly was extra large, especially his smile.

"It's beautiful, Aly! Thanks for inviting us. I love it," Andie's excitement was genuine.

"Yes, thanks, man," Max agreed."

"We're going to hit in a couple minutes, but I'll meet you after the set." He turned to Andie, "Wait 'til you see the dinner! Fabulosos!" He kissed his fingertips and stood up.

The drummer got the band's attention and counted off "*A Day in the Life of a Fool*" which played as Andie and Max strolled the deck watching the sun set behind the silhouette of Notre Dame as the boat headed towards the Ile de France.

What made the Seine river cruises special and unique was that the entire trip, up the river and around the Île de la Cité and Île Saint Louis, cruised by the most important landmarks of French history – from the Place de la Concorde - an oxymoron, in Andie's opinion – where the seemingly endless hysteria and executions of the Revolution were carried out, to the heaven–bound spires of the cathedral of Notre Dame, exhilarating when seen from the river down below. The beauty of the old mansions and hotel particulairs on the shoreline and the majesty of the public edifices – Le Palais de Justice, L'Institut de France, the Louvre and the Musée D'Orsay told the history of France: literally, aesthetically and spiritually.

"You can feel the aspirations, the ideals and the efforts to live up to them – not to mention the involvement of the people. The

Enlightenment started here; imagine the conversations in the cafes – everybody had an opinion, just like you, Andie," he hugged her.

"Can you imagine? A city of hot heads like me?" she laughed. "Whenever I think of the French Revolution, it just seems so bloody to me. But I don't see the American or the Russian Revolutions that way. Why do you suppose that is?"

"Well, the Americans were fighting an enemy thousands of miles away; the French and Russians were essentially fighting each other."

The ship rounded a slight curve and the stunning Hôtel de Ville came into view. It was lit up and looked like a fairy castle against the deepening lavender twilight sky. "That's true. And I always think of the American War Between the States as very bloody. But here," she gestured towards the Hôtel, "the headquarters of the revolutionaries - and the Commune too! - it seems in Paris the streets really were running with blood."

"I know what you mean. These fellows took the idea of liberty and equality very seriously."

Andie laughed, "Ya think?"

They gazed at the shore and the people ambling along the river.

"You have to love them – they seem to live on a higher plane."

"The French?" Max was mildly aghast.

"Max, I've thought about this a lot, and I think the French have a cultural history that places philosophy and art at the apex of human endeavor. Not money, not power – but art."

"Andie, do you know what an 'apex' is?"

She giggled, "I'm not sure but it really sounds like the top, the peak, doesn't it? Or am I thinking of the mountain in Aspen called 'Ajax'?"

Max smiled, "Sometimes I think you're an *idiot savant* because you say such smart things and then follow it up with foolishness. You are one in a million," he leaned in to kiss her.

The evening cruise on the Seine was the most romantic place Andie and Max had been in a while, and they were showing the effects - of the night, the shore lights and their twinkling reflections in the water, the music and the fresh river air. "*La vie est belle,*" Andie sang quietly to Max. "*Très, très belle,*" she added in a whisper. They stood with their arms around each other leaning on the railing for some time.

*****

Andie could smell the dinner before it was announced, and she and Max were able to get a table for two on the top deck. Aly's band started to play a soft samba just as they started to eat.

"This could not be better," Max smiled after a sip of wine.

"Right?" she agreed and took a big bite of the candied lamb shoulder and caramelized onions.

Max laughed out loud, "I wasn't talking about the food – I should have realized what would grab your attention."

She nodded but didn't speak. She was enjoying the dinner too much to talk.

Inside the salon there were tables full of diners, but many people gathered at the bar or along the deck railings. These were the members of an industry that frowned on fat – a half inch increase in a waistline was a crisis better averted by defensive eating – which is to say little or none at all – as opposed to dieting after the fact. Sir Kerr's friends and family were not so inclined and they reveled in the food, not to mention the fine wines that accompanied each course. They reminded Andie of King Arthur's court - a lot of loud toasts and bellowing laughter.

C.C. held court at the bar in the stern of the boat along with several models from the 60s, veteran photographers and agents and the young women making their mark today, Marin's peers. She was dazzling in a bias-cut white charmeuse satin gown - a vintage Chanel from the thirties - that she accessorized with platinum bracelets with emeralds and a bobbed, wavy blonde wig. She wore bright yellow crocs on her feet. The conversation was light and lively as C.C.'s contemporaries reminisced with her, each story topping the next in improbability and hilarity. There was none of the usual melancholy, bittersweet memories found in reunions. These ladies had enjoyed their time in the sun and had moved on with grace and no regrets. They found their memories from thirty years ago vastly entertaining, although none of them seemed to identify with the characters in the stories. There appeared to be two different planets – *Then* and *Now* – separated by age and propriety, with the two feeding each other as they grew. To the young listeners, *Then* was infinitely preferable to *Now*.

******

Bella and Fan joined Carter and Chantal downstairs to eat. They spoke very little as they sampled the large menu. Soon they were forced to slow down and chat, sated for the time being. Bella and Fan were simply taking a pause; they loved to eat and they loved good food. They were expecting average cruise boat fare and were happily surprised by the gourmet quality of the food. Fan usually had to stop Bella from overeating, but tonight he thought if he kept her away from sugar and champagne, an excess of food might make her a little sleepy, certainly not nervous. When she was nervous, she made mistakes.

Carter felt a few people staring at him and knew it was because he looked like a 'mature' model. He had been approached by agents and briefly considered the occupation when he was twenty, but even then, he knew instinctively no wealthy woman would marry a male model. Rich men might marry a female model, but male models were often viewed as rent boys, and entering the profession did not look like a promising move. He had to admit, however, that he still liked being admired when he entered a room. Vanity, he thought with a chuckle. At least I know who and what I am, he reassured himself.

This was a rare insight in his circle of, well, not friends exactly, but acquaintances certainly. The people he was with could see each other with a social laser – through the outer camouflage and into the substance of identity. These people might miss the ambiguities, but not the vulnerabilities or the scars. Carter felt sometimes he was walking on a razor thin line between friend and nobody, and he might be relegated to the latter at any moment. But none of them seemed to shine that fierce light on themselves, and Carter knew that was his gift: he knew himself and he knew how to please others by knowing what he wanted.

He found he wanted Bella - he really cared for her - to his delight and dismay. He didn't want to lose. It was up to Fan, and Carter knew Fan despised him. He sighed. Be patient, he told himself. If you pull up the fishing pole too soon, the fish can wriggle off the hook. You must wait for the fish to bite down hard and take the bait.

******

Danielle and Jean-Paul had managed to evade discovery when they boarded the boat and were dining tête-à-tête upstairs on the opposite side of the ship from Andie and Max. They agreed to congratulate their young friends but wanted to spend some time alone if possible. The boat was seductively romantic – the music, the beautiful people, the lights that sparkled on the water, the fresh breezes – and they were feeling nostalgic and loving.

Danielle had long been one of the faces of St. Laurent, a fashion insider, and, as such, she had become close to Marin, developing maternal feelings for her. She remembered the heightened emotions and drama surrounding that first great love, especially when your pictures are on tabloids in newsstands all in Paris, London, Rome.

She would never forget walking down the street with Jean-Paul and seeing the cover of *O.K.* magazine with a full color photo of the two of them having an argument, their faces contorted with their mouths open - showing teeth - clearly saying terrible things to each other.

Dany sighed. It was horrible but very absurd – not to be taken seriously. She and Jean-Paul laughed about it now, and she wanted to tell Marin not to react to the cartoon world of celebrity, but she knew her words wouldn't be heard. Everyone follows their own path in love, and one may as well try to talk a cat into using a toilet as give advice to a young person in love. This thought made her think of her cat, Louis, who made his own rules and ignored - no, broke everyone else's.

She smiled and said, "I was just thinking of Louis Le Chat – he was something, non? A tyrant!"

Jean-Paul laughed, "Ah, Louis, the most beautiful cat in the world, as you insisted. I was a little jealous of Louis." He shook his head, "We were so thoughtless, non? So carefree and reckless. Taking a cat to hotels and on airplanes? How wonderful to be so irresponsible. I'm glad I had the chance to be so young and foolish."

Dany smiled and nodded, "Yes - and to survive, with no consequences. We were lucky. Happy idiots," she shook her head, laughing.

"We were fearless because we were so ignorant. Now, we know too much to dare. We have too much to risk – to lose," Jean-Paul took her hand and smiled.

"I won't let you lose me again, mon cher; I'll wear a bell around my neck," she smiled in return.

******

Andie and Max were upstairs, watching Aly and his band at the front of the boat, and Marie-Claude and Hassim were downstairs eating just underneath them. Although the music was not as bright for them as it was upstairs, it was just as seductive, perfectly capturing the happy celebration of two people in love. Marie-Claude looked out at the twinkling water and the beautifully lit famous Parisian landmark buildings on the shore.

She smiled at Hassim, "I'm glad you persuaded me to come tonight. It's so beautiful, the food is superb, the music is lovely – it's so romantic, Hassim! We need more of these occasions, don't we?" She reached out and held his hand.

Hassim beamed, "You are the reason it's so romantic, Marie. I wish you could see your face – you've never looked so lovely."

She blushed, "Well, you know why."

"I cannot believe our luck. The baby, Samia … we are blessed, truly."

"Samia would have loved this cruise, I'm sorry she didn't come."

Hassim shook his head, "No, she needs to stay in one place. I wanted to lock her up forever," he laughed, "but I settled for one night. I wanted to be alone with you, especially now to celebrate our new life." He took her hand and kissed it. "I don't know what the future holds, but I know I'm ready."

Marie-Claude smiled and nodded, "One thing I've learned from your adventure is that you will be a great father. You risked your life! You didn't know Ben was following you – you could have been killed if he hadn't been there." She looked frightened for a moment, then smiled again, "But one thing I know now, your instincts are those of a devoted parent. I – well, we ---" she looked down at her tiny passenger, "we couldn't be in better hands."

"I love you, Marie," he said.

"And I love you, Hassim. And I promise you, we will raise our child by the sea. I don't know where, but somewhere by the sea."

"You know my heart so well." Hassim had never felt so happy as he did now. He was afraid if he let himself accept the happiness, it might disappear again. Was he really going to be able to keep this feeling? Were the nightmares really all gone for good?

*****

Ben and Montclair and his men were trying to be everywhere on the boat. Montclair had brought four of his subordinates, the ones he respected and trusted the most. He knew they were cool in a crisis, and this would be of paramount importance on a crowded cruise boat. He assigned one of them to watch Andie, to shadow her wherever she went – stand outside the bathroom if necessary, Montclair told him. Ben had assured all of them that Max was a capable man and he could be counted on in an emergency, but Montclair wanted an officer for back-up. He reasoned Max wouldn't have a gun – why would he? - and the killer might. Ben, Montclair and his officers were all armed.

The others were stationed at different spots where they could get the best view of all the guests. The crowd was very big, however, and nobody could see what everybody was up to at any given time. Ben and Montclair focused on the principal characters in the 'François saga' since they believed the murderer was among them. Ben was downstairs, watching as discreetly as possible his main suspects: Bella, Fan, Carter and Chantal who were sharing a table. He was still suspicious of C.C., and Montclair was watching her. He, too, was not entirely persuaded of her innocence – she was too charming. He was guilty of the old "the least likely is the most likely" school of thought and realized that may be the only explanation for his doubts about C.C. He needed to keep an eye on her to make up his mind. And finally, he had to admit - at least to himself - that he enjoyed her *joie de vivre*, and watching her was entertaining. But because she had met him and they had spoken at length, he had to hide in the crowd. It was surprisingly easy.

The size of the crowd enabled both Ben and Montclair to remain unseen, or so they had to assume. The other three policemen had the advantage of being unrecognizable, and they promenaded around the boat, ready to back up either Ben or Montclair.

C.C. suddenly decided she wanted to dance. The band was playing "*A Sweet, Happy Life*", from the movie "Black Orpheus", and she couldn't sit still. She had seen Carter earlier in the middle of the boat and quickly went in search of him. She found him at a dinner table with Chantal, Bella and Fan. They were being served dessert, coffee and liqueurs.

"Carter! Carter, darling!" She rushed over to him with her arm extended. "Come, come, I want to dance." He stood up at her arrival and she grabbed his arm and pulled him towards the stairs. "It's upstairs - come, come …" her voice trailed over her shoulder.

Carter was delighted to go with C.C. Chantal was boring but dangerous, and he was glad to escape her clutches. He chuckled to himself, thinking of her white hands fluttering meaninglessly when she spoke. He thought sometimes he was being hypnotized by them, and he did get sleepy when she rattled on. But she could turn in a minute from one exaggerated mood to another. She was exhausting. And C.C. was great fun dancing – she had rhythm and was quite athletic - a great partner.

"Oh, look, Max," Andie said, "it's C.C. and Carter, dancing again. They're so good together."

Max turned his head to watch them. "They are a great dance team. Oh, and look over there -" he gestured to a couple of men standing against the rail on the other side of the small bandstand. "I do believe that's the VL."

"Where? Oh, I see. The VL is so anonymous when she's in her natural plumage. I wonder why François and Redmond are here. Do you suppose he's continuing his investigation? He really should leave that to those who know what they're doing." She shook her head.

"Like you?" Max asked with a grin.

"Not just me. You and Ben are also involved."

"Thanks, I guess. When Ben tells us not to get involved, why do I hear him so clearly but you don't pick up a word?"

"Selective deafness," Andie answered smugly. "I hear what I need to hear. After all, who's the one who overheard Morgana accusing someone of murdering François? I think my hearing is excellent."

"Look!" she interrupted herself. "C.C. has just seen him."

C.C.'s face went white and she stopped dancing, standing perfectly still. Carter looked confused but followed her gaze and he, too, went white. The two of them then looked at each other and fled the dance floor.

"Well, that's strange," Max observed.

"I wonder why they left and where they went. Why didn't they go to him and ask what happened? For Heaven's sake."

"I agree. What a bizarre reaction. If he were a friend of mine, I'd run to him with happiness to see he's alive. Don't you agree?"

Andie responded, "Yes - they look very suspicious to me."

"Well, everyone looks suspicious to you."

"Except you, Max. I confess I have never, ever thought you appeared suspicious. Truly."

"Did you know the word 'facetious' has every vowel in it in order?"

She thought for a minute and said triumphantly, "So does abstemiously."

Max rolled his eyes, "I told you that – and that word is completely foreign to you."

"Not when I have to lose a few pounds; that's how I eat when I'm over my weight – I cut out wine completely."

"I only hope to live long enough to see you dine abstemiously because that would mean you have actually gained weight – like the rest of us."

"Silly Max," she leaned over and kissed him.

Danielle and Jean-Paul had moved from their table to the bow of the boat to better hear the band. They stood by the railing, looking out over the water.

"Our city is so beautiful, n'est-ce pas?" Dany said as the boat passed the Tuileries with the Place de la Concorde just beyond it.

"Sometimes I cannot believe how lucky I am to be living here, with you," Jean-Paul beamed.

"We are very lucky. I never would have guessed when I was young how content I would be at this age. I'm not sure I ever thought about getting old," she added.

"After the accident," Jean-Paul started, "I never wanted to grow old."

Dany's face had darkened at the mention of the tragic loss of their son. "Nor did I." Then she turned to him with moist eyes, "But we survived, together."

Jean-Paul pulled her closer to him, "We are blessed, after all."

Dany returned his embrace and then turned to look at the band as Ally Ocho played an impossible glissando on his ringing guitar.

Suddenly the blood left her face, and she stiffened. "Jean-Paul! I see, I can't believe this, it's impossible – I see François."

He turned quickly, "Non, incroyable! Mais oui! C'est lui - François!"

The two of them were frozen, unable to move, stunned by the sight. "François - mon Dieu. François …" her voice trailed off in a whisper.

They looked at each other, and when they turned back, François had disappeared, again.

******

Bella, Fan and Chantal had also moved from their table to the deck. By the time they finished their spectacular banquet, they all felt compelled to take a walk around the boat. It was a lovely night, and because they had all overindulged in the cornucopia of food and wine that had proved irresistible, they needed to walk to aid digestion. They were subdued and sluggish from overeating, but comfortable and sated, companionable and enjoying their new-found familiarity.

"Good God!" Bella suddenly exclaimed. "I think I just saw François!"

"Oh, nonsense, Bella. You are over-imaginative, again."

"No! I know what I saw," Bella insisted. "I saw François!"

"You hardly know him, Bella. You saw someone who resembles him. He's dead." Bella started to object, and he repeated, "He's dead, Bella."

Chantal had stopped walking with them; she had glanced up when Bella claimed she saw François, and was struck dumb by the sight of the dead man.

Fan called back to her to rejoin them, "Chantal! Come along, Bella is just imagining things. François is not here, he cannot be here, he's dead."

Chantal approached them, gesticulating with her hands, hardly able to speak. She was making primal sounds, little bursts of wordless cries and moans. François had to be dead, he had to!

******

After they finished their meal, Andie and Max got up and walked over to the railing to watch the monuments the boat was passing. Suddenly Ben appeared on Max's right.

"Uncle Ben," Andie exclaimed. "How lovely to see you."

Ben rolled his eyes, "The pleasure is all mine."

They all leaned on the railing, enjoying the brisk fresh air blowing off the river.

"What a meal," Andie broke the silence. "Did you get a chance to eat?" she asked Ben.

He laughed, "No, I was too busy watching you eat. You can really put it away."

"Where?" Max retorted. "I can't see it."

Andie turned to him, "Someday it will all catch up with me, and I'll be huge."

"One hopes," he smiled at her.

Out of the corner of her eye, Andie saw small white birds, but when she turned her head, they were gone. Probably sea gulls, she thought. Seagulls come inland more than people realized and a boat with food would naturally attract them.

"I'm going downstairs to the Ladies Room; I'll be right back." She told the two men.

Ben started to follow her but Andie turned to him and said "Really? I'll be back in two shakes of a lamb's tail."

Ben stopped short and both he and Max echoed her, "Two shakes of a lamb's tail?" They chorused.

Andie just laughed and walked to the stairs.

As she started to descend she saw the white birds again, downstairs by the boat railing. Nonplussed, she shook her head and suddenly remembered the other white birds she'd seen, in the catacombs. She bent over and turned her head towards the railing and saw Chantal. Of course! Chantal. She was in front of them in the catacombs! Chantal - with the white gloves! She had to have waited for them to pass in order to make them think she'd been behind them. Why? Only one reason, Andie realized. She reached the bottom step, and slowly walked towards Chantal who had her back to Andie.

"It can't be" she was muttering just loud enough for Andie to hear. "He's dead, he has to be," she said softly.

She turned to Andie who was standing close to her. "I think I just saw François," she stammered, stunned, "It's impossible. He's dead … the jeep. He needs to be dead or Sasha won't come."

Her eyes were wide, the pupils enlarged so that her eyes were black.

Andie proceeded to speak cautiously, "No, he's not. He wasn't in the jeep – that was Sasha."

Chantal is jolted by this, "Nooooo, you're lying. That can't be...I..I..I saw him leave in the jeep...no. Tell me it isn't true! Sasha is here...somewhere...he has to be here!" She demanded desperately, her voice rising.

Exasperated, Andie replied, "Chantal, Sasha is dead!"

She lunged at Andie, her white gloved hands reaching out, "It's not true! You're lying! You bitch!" Her voice was loud and out of control.

Andie tried to push her back, but Chantal was getting increasingly hysterical and began to struggle with Andie against the rail. Andie had no leverage and realized Chantal was going to push her over the side. She fought back but Chantal had the advantage, and all Andie could do was hang on and pull her over the side with her.

The two women shouted as they fell through the air and landed in the water. Attracted by the loud argument, Max saw them and without a second's hesitation, he dove in after them in a beautiful swan dive worthy of an Olympic gold medal. Ben followed with a leap toward Chantal....Max swam furiously for Andie as a crew member threw two lifesavers into the water.

Andie surfaced, "Max! Max!" She called out, pushing her hair out of her eyes.

"I'm here," he answered as he surfaced next to her. He put his arm under hers and pulled her towards the lifesaver.

"Oh, Max – she went crazy, just crazy ---"

"I know, I know. Breathe – don't talk." He put her hands on the lifesaver and pushed it to the side of the boat.

They reached the boat and a ladder the crew had attached to the boat for them to re-board. When she was halfway up the stairs, Andie began to laugh uncontrollably. Max quickly climbed up behind her and managed to put his body around hers and hold her tightly.

"Shhh ..." he said soothingly, "It's all right. You're all right now."

She shuddered and started to weep, "Oh Max."

"Come on now. Let's get up the ladder. It's hard holding onto you and the ladder at the same time." She gave a short laugh and continued to climb up the ladder. She regained her presence of mind, and they both climbed back on board the boat.

When Ben jumped into the river to pull Chantal from a watery grave – or an escape – he was not as lucky as Max. Chantal resisted Ben's hands and tried to swim away. She was weighed down by her voluminous dress and her hands were too heavy from her gloves to adequately paddle, much less swim. Once he reached her, she thrashed and hit at him and threatened to pull him down under the water with her. Fortunately, one of Montclair's policemen had jumped in when Ben did, and he was able to assist in Chantal's apprehension. Nonetheless, getting her back on board the boat was no easy matter. Two other crew members and Montclair himself reached down to grab her arms while Ben and the policeman in the water attempted to push her up out of the water. Because she was fighting them all, ultimately the only way to handle her was with a large belt and winch: she was brought on board like a stubborn mule – literally.

Once on board again, Chantal was sputtering and cursing in French each time she caught her breath. An ambulance had been called and Ben, Montclair and the other policemen were able to confine her in the small captain's cabin near the stern on the lower deck.

"*Il faut d'un carcan! C'est absurde! Cette femme, elle est absurde!*" Montclair said vehemently to Ben.

"Yes!" Ben answered, stifling a smile, "but I don't think that straitjackets are standard issue on a cruise boat, although now that I think about it, maybe they should be."

They heard a growing siren sound coming towards the boat.

Montclair looked up at the heavens and said dramatically, "*Merci.*"

"Amen," Ben also looked up and marveled at the bright white round full moon. He laughed in relief and recognition of the insanity of Chantal's obsession.

"Maybe it's just the full moon, *mon ami.*" he said to Dash.

Montclair laughed out loud and put his arm around Ben's soaking wet shoulders, "*Peut-être, mon ami,* maybe."

*****

Andie wasn't hurt - nor was she the one experiencing a psychotic break – so she persuaded Max and Ben to let her go home. She wanted to shower and climb under the feather comforter with Max. Easily persuaded, Ben told her to go ahead and that he and Dash would come in the morning for her statement.

Max insisted she get a tetanus shot, at least, from the hotel doctor who lived at the hotel for the convenience of the guests.

"And maybe a shot for typhus? Cholera? What else can you get from a dirty river in the middle of a big city?"

"Max, calm down. I'll tell the doctor what happened, and he'll treat me accordingly, all right? The very first thing we do when we walk into the Rose is call the doctor, I promise."

Andie kept her promise to Max, and after the doctor's examination – and shots – she and Max made their way back to their hotel home.

"God, it's good to be here!" Andie exclaimed on her way to the bathroom.

Max started to respond but she already had the bath turned on and couldn't hear him.

The hot bath felt wonderful to Andie. She began to unwind and wept a little, but soon she felt lighter, especially when Max came in with a glass of wine and an offer to wash her back; then, all she felt was contentment.

She stepped into the big, fluffy robe Max held for her and then reached out for a hug. Max obliged, holding her tightly.

"Why am I always thanking God you didn't die?" he shook his head. "We must be doing this wrong."

They both laughed.

*****

Monday Morning

The next morning, all the members of last night's boat cruise who were in Francois' group met in the lounge. Ben and the Commissaire had requested their presence. They started gathering at 11:30 and were all present by noon.

Andie and Max rode down the elevator with C.C. who joked it was like an Agatha Christie climactic scene in reverse, "All the suspects - whom we know are innocent - gather together to be grilled by the detective. Why, do you think? The case is solved."

"I know he wanted our statements, but you weren't as involved in the action last night as we were, so I wonder why you were asked to be here."

"Maybe it has something to do with François. You saw him last night, didn't you?"

Andie heard a sharp intake of breath, but she couldn't tell if it was C.C. or Max – or both.

"Well," she continued, "maybe he's going to tell us how he's alive and what happened."

"I would love to know what's going on, this affair has just been so ghastly!" C.C. responded, as they entered the lounge.

Marie-Claude and Hassim were the last to arrive. Dany, C.C. and Andie all looked at her and then each other and smiled: as corny as it sounded, Andie thought Marie-Claude was glowing. She noticed Hassim was too, for that matter. She wondered if they knew about François - maybe that accounted for their happiness. Much less romantic, she thought, and hoped it was the baby.

When everyone was seated, Montclair walked in and joined Ben. They stood in front of the group, and Ben said, "There is someone else we want to join us this morning. Monsieur Redmond, please?"

The lawyer walked into the lounge, then he turned around and gestured to someone standing out of view.

Everyone in the room gasped when François entered the room. Marie-Claude jumped up from her seat and ran to embrace him, crying out his name, "François! François!" He took her in his arms as a thoroughly stunned Hassim walked slowly up to him. "François? *C'est toi?*" François opened his arms wide and Hassim joined the embrace with his wife.

Suddenly Marie-Claude pulled back from him, "Where were you? Why didn't you tell us? Why did you make us suffer?"

François hastened to soothe her, "I'm so sorry but I had to – I thought if I stayed dead, I could find out who killed me. I never wanted to make you suffer, Marie, non – *jamais!*"

He pulled her to him and held her head to his shoulder while she wept.

"François!" Dany rushed to him and embraced him. "It's so good to see you – tell us now, what happened?"

Andie was surprised and asked C.C., who was sitting next to her, "Why is Dany so happy to see him? I thought he killed her son."

C.C. looked surprised, "Where did you get that idea? Morgana was driving the boat – everyone knows that." She shook her head, "Really, Andie – you shouldn't listen to gossip – it's rarely accurate."

"But, well, what about you? I thought you held Morgana responsible for Sir Charles's death – is that true? You told us you wanted to correct an injustice – what was that about?"

C.C. looked shocked again, then started to laugh, "Did you think I killed her? Oh, Andie – you are one of a kind – no, no, I meant the painting, the Renoir in the Musée D'Orsay. Morgana wouldn't let him put his name on it because she was jealous of me. And I have arranged with the museum to put his name on it. Even after all this time, he must be honored for such an expression of love."

"I see," Andie was chagrined but happy to hear she was wrong about François. Maybe Max was right about Fan that the gossip was scurrilous and probably untrue. She wanted to ask about the others when François spoke.

233

"*Eh bien, maintenant j'en dit tous.* I will tell you everything. But first I must give my thanks to my angel – the little one who discovered the truth."

He walked over to the group. When he got close, Andie turned around to look for his 'angel'. She turned back to find him in front of her.

"Merci, Andie. You are kind and brave. And you were right, I should have left it to the professionals."

Ben coughed loudly; Andie blushed; Max rolled his eyes; and everyone else broke into applause.

"Now I've seen everything. *C'est absurde, complètement absurde.*" Montclair huffed while Ben shook his head.

"But what happened? Would someone please tell us what happened?" Fan said to Ben and Montclair with a touch of annoyance in his voice.

François looked at Ben who nodded and started to speak.

"François invited all of you to celebrate the finish of his film. He was also celebrating his new love, but nobody knew about it – that was a secret. He planned on leaving Mumbai after the banquet with his lover, he was coming here to Paris to edit his film. But someone wanted him to die, and rigged the brakes on the jeep so the car couldn't be stopped and would fly off the cliff – which it did. But there were two people in the jeep - François and his lover. Nobody saw the second person in the car so everyone assumed the body was François's. But François was thrown clear – his was not the body in the jeep. It was his lover's." Here Ben paused for effect, to make sure everyone understood what had happened on that night.

He continued, "As soon as he regained his senses, François hurried to the nearest phone booth to call Mark, his trusted friend and adviser. He had driven his jeep all over the world and it was very clear to him that the car had been sabotaged. He wanted to find out who wanted to kill him, and, what was most important to him, he wanted to find out who did kill his lover."

"How?" Carter asked. "How could he find out? Did he have a plan? Really François, you were playing with fire," he spoke impatiently with concern.

"Not really," François spoke up. "All I knew was I had to keep my own survival a secret. I didn't want to be attacked again by an unknown assailant. How could I protect myself if I didn't know who wanted me dead?"

"In any case," Ben continued. "He directed Mark Redmond to corral the suspects here at the Orchidea Rose by telling them there were bequests for them all if they came to the hotel for a few days. You know the rest."

The group all protested – loudly - that they did not know the rest and would he please continue.

Ben threw his hands up, "All right, all right, So, it turns out that Morgana knew the jeep had been tampered with because she saw someone run away from the car just before François came outside to leave. She had been smoking a cigarillo outside, thinking of her late husband and pondering her future when she saw a furtive figure leave the garage. It was dark and she couldn't make out a face, but she thought the figure moved like a woman. Naturally what she saw had no significance until the accident. Then, she was sure he had been killed – on purpose, not accidentally. And you all heard what she said in the lounge – dangerously – that she knew one of them was a murderer, and it got her killed."

"I knew it," Max said.

"I knew it," Andie corrected him.

Carter was walking by their table, heading for Bella, when Andie pulled his arm. He stopped with a smile, "Yes?"

"Carter," Andie began. "I need to ask you something. Was François going to reveal your past to Morgana? Did he tell you that?"

Carter smiled, "Oh, no. He told me he would not tell anyone. He was very kind and told me he had taken a liking to me. He only warned me that word had spread to Europe and that I should be careful. No," he assured Andie, "François was acting with the best of intentions – and I owe him."

He moved on to join Bella at her table.

Andie was relieved but annoyed. She leaned over to whisper to Max, "You were right about Fan – it seems everything he told you was a nasty lie."

"I'm not at all surprised – and he took such pleasure in recounting the rumors." Max shuddered.

"I wonder about the others – like Marie-Claude and Hassim. And Bella! They all seem so happy to see he's alive." Andie was frustrated.

She was close enough to Marie-Claude to be frank with her and ascertain the truth about the miscarriage. Hassim had walked over to the table with coffee and tea, and Andie approached him there.

"Hassim, pardon me for being so blunt, but I need to know – did François fire you?"

"Fire me? What do you mean?" Hassim was not offended, but he was confused. "We finished the film together."

"Yes, I know. I mean, well, I was told he fired you from the next project. And," she dove into the other part of the gossip, "that he insisted you accompany him to Kashmir and that's why Marie-Claude had the miscarriage." She had spoken the last part very quickly so as not to linger on the unpleasant image.

To her relief, Hassim laughed out loud. "Oh, that's absurd! No, no, no. I have been hired for a lot more money for one film, then I will rejoin François for his next project. How funny. And as for the miscarriage," his face darkened momentarily, "that was just a stroke of bad luck, I suppose. We will never know why it happened, but it was no one's fault, not at all." They the joy returned to his eyes, "And it only makes this baby even more wonderful – you understand?"

"I do, I do. I'm so happy for you both." Andie couldn't help but gush, she was so relieved to erase another black mark from François's name.

Andie hurried back to Max to tell him another rumor had been quashed.

"So Fan lied about all the others," Andie said triumphantly. "I wonder if C.C. knows the truth about Bella's unfortunate incarceration in the booby hatch. I have a feeling François was innocent of that too."

Max cleared his throat, "I'm not sure you want to pursue that, Andie. Everyone is happy, why ruin it?"

"It just seems to me that Bella should know the truth. François is her cousin, one of the few people left in her family – I don't want him under a cloud in her eyes."

"What if you're wrong about this? Maybe he did commit her; why bring it up now?"

"What about her future? She needs to know what Fan is capable of," she insisted.

"I suppose." Max agreed.

"You know Carter wants to marry her – and she should be allowed to answer for herself. I have an idea."

"God help us," Max said, raising his eyes to heaven.

Andie laughed and turned to find Fan. He was alone, getting a refill of coffee. Andie hurried to his side before he walked away.

"Fan?" she asked him.

"Yes?" he responded as he turned to see who was speaking.

Once again, Andie dove right in, "I understand you committed Bella to the sanitarium but you told her it was François who did it. Did you ever tell her the truth?"

Fan's eyes widened alarmingly and he sputtered, "What are you saying? How ... what ... who, who said that? Who told you that?" His anger was growing and Andie felt unsure for an instant, but she persevered.

"Bella deserves to know the truth. She deserves to be treated with respect."

"You know nothing about it. Nothing!"

"I know she is a young woman who has the right to a future with a man who loves her. I am going to tell her if you won't. She has rights!" As she spoke the words, Andie realized she sounded a little ridiculous and over-the-top, but Fan was not someone who appreciated subtlety.

"All right," he raised his hands as if to push her away. "All right. But I have to protect her – what if she makes a mistake? What if she marries a gold-digger?" He gestured to Carter.

"Who cares? It's her business, not yours. She has already undergone the trauma of losing her first love and a baby – she survived, and she'll survive again if another man breaks her heart. She is much stronger than you realize. Let her go."

Fan looked dubious, but Andie wasn't finished.

"I will let you tell her the truth in your own time, but if you don't, I will know and I will show up at your door and tell her. I'll know. As a matter of fact, I'll tell C.C. and ask her to find out if you tell Bella the truth. C.C. will ask Bella herself – do you understand?" Andie felt very powerful as she spoke, recognizing her options as she said the words.

Fan realized Andie would follow through on her threat and his entire body slumped as he promised Andie he would tell Bella the truth and treat her as an adult.

"I only wanted to protect her. She's not entirely stable," he explained lamely. "I'm all she has, and she needs --- "

"She has all she needs, Fan. You're a good brother, but you go overboard. Do you understand?"

Fan nodded. He was tired of keeping an eye on Bella. The constant baby-sitting/body-guarding was exhausting. He was more than ready to move on with his own life. He was surprised to find it was easy to acquiesce to Andie's demands. He wanted the release. With this in mind, he abruptly reached out to Andie and hugged her, to her surprise.

"Why Fan," she began.

"Excuse me for my impertinence," he blushed, "but you have told me something I realize I wanted to hear. When I free Bella, I will be freeing myself. I owe you thanks, Andie. *Merci*." he finished in French for no particular reason.

"*De rien*," she answered, confused that they were now speaking French, but relieved at the way their prickly conversation finished.

Equally contented, they walked back to the others who were still peppering Ben and the Commissaire with questions.

"But why did Chantal want to kill him?" Bella asked.

The rest of them nodded in agreement, looking at Ben expectantly; Bella added, "And what will happen to Chantal now?"

Ben and Montclair looked at each other.

Montclair shrugged, "*Pourquoi pas?* Why not? I will tell you what the doctor told me. *Cette femme* – this woman - is mentally unbalanced – she is a psychopath. Sasha told her he was leaving her and going to Bali with a friend. In truth, he was leaving her for François. But she didn't know this – this was not her motive. She believed Sasha was leaving for Bali, but she didn't know the truth. So she thought of a way to bring Sasha back to Paris – and her." He shook his head.

Ben took up the tale, "She killed François because she knew Sasha would come back to Paris for the funeral. She could see him then and persuade him to return to her."

"That's incredible!" Carter declared.

"*Incroyable!*" Jean-Paul exclaimed.

"Vraiment," Dany said quietly.

"That's crazy," Bella said gleefully.

"Pot, kettle," Andie whispered to Max.

"You mean to tell me that Chantal killed François just to see Sasha at the funeral? You can't be serious – that's just too much. I mean, some people," C.C. shook her head with annoyance, "Really." She drew out the last word and it sounded like 'rilllllllllllley' to Andie. C.C. never disappointed her.

"That's the way a psychopath sees things – without our sensibilities. Chantal didn't feel emotions like we do, she cannot feel remorse – she's nuts all right," Andie laughed with her last words.

Max agreed, "Ultimately, we can't figure out a psychopath because a lot of what they say and do is irrational to us – but not to them. They see a logic where we don't, so they can be very hard to read."

"They're like sharks," Bella said to the surprise of everyone, who were startled by her insight. Every once in a while, Bella said something very smart. Her intellect was obscured by her fuzzy social skills.

Ben was the first to respond, "That's very astute, Bella. And accurate."

"You nailed it," Carter said to her. He was sitting next to her and the proximity made her blush with pleasure.

"A shark? *Non, non, pardonez-moi* – sharks kill to eat, not to meet other sharks," Montclair protested.

Andie thought this was hilarious and started to laugh at the image of a shark trying to get a date; her laughter was infectious and in short order, Dany, Marie-Claude, Bella and C.C. joined in. Then Carter started to laugh; François, Max, Fan and Ben followed and finally the commissaire himself gave a robust snorting laugh.

Just then, Samia entered the lounge and said, "What's everybody laughing about?"

"Joie de vivre, ma petite, joie de vivre" Marie Claude responded.

The mood in the room became celebratory with the deepening realization François had returned – he was alive and well. One by one, his friends came to him to embrace him, chat with him a bit – revel in his vibrant presence.

Dany asked him about Sasha, "I am surprised you had an affair with him. I don't want to hurt you, François, but he was ---"

"A gigolo," François finished the sentence. "I know, Dany, but one afternoon, we were on the terrace at Chantal's Portofino villa, and we started talking. As we talked, Sasha began to open up with me. He told me where he was from and how he got to that terrace, and I was moved. He spoke the truth; he dropped his tough shell. So we became friends, and when our paths crossed, we became closer friends. I found I wanted to protect him…at first. But then, over time, I fell in love with him. He was simple inside, and I am simple inside – we are simpatico, do you know what I mean?" He had turned to Marie-Claude with the last question.

With tears in her eyes, Marie-Claude nodded. "I know exactly what you mean."

Dany told him, "I'm happy for you and sad for you at the same time, François. You found love and then – poof," she waved her hand sideways, "it's gone. I'm so sad for you."

"Ah," he shrugged, and his eyes turned melancholic, "at least I know what love is now. I never knew before Sasha. Even if I never find it again, I will feel it whenever I think of him, and I will be content."

"Oh, how lovely …" Andie sang softly to Max who nodded in agreement.

*****

CODA

Later that afternoon, Andie, Max and Eddie were coming back from the local patisserie, bringing 'just in case' sweets home with them. Max had told Eddie the story of Andie's bringing a pain au chocolat to the park just in case she got hungry.

Eddie replied, "Actually, I like that idea. She's right, you know; I can become hungry without any warning, and I never have any food with me. I like that plan."

"You like it because you're in a patisserie," Andie jibed. "I doubt it would sound as promising if we were in a butcher's shop."

Eddie laughed, "What difference does it make? As long as I am in this patisserie, I'm bringing a couple pommes aux chausson back with me."

"Good choice - my favorite, too."

As they approached the hotel, they saw Dany and Jean-Paul walk to a limousine. All François's guests were departing today. Dany saw them and waved. Jean-Paul turned and he waved too.

"They're going to Honfluer. She urged me to join them, but I thought maybe another time. Jean-Paul seemed exceptionally intoxicated with her. That would be a fun trip, don't you think?"

Eddie said, "It's gorgeous there. You should take her up on that invitation some time."

C.C. was the next to exit the hotel. She saw Andie and called out, "Annnnnndeeeeee" Darling!" She ran up to them and hugged Andie, then Max and Eddie.

"I cannot leave without saying good-bye to my newest little girlfriend. You promised you'd call from Sussex, remember. *Au revoir, mes chères – je vous aime*!" She twirled around and ran back to her limo which took off immediately, C.C. leaning out the window and waving madly.

"We must have her visit us at my parents' - they will be delighted to see her again." Max said to Andie.

Eddie sighed, "She is one in a million. I always knew I'd never get married, but if she would marry me – I'd snatch her up before she had a chance to change her mind."

Max and Andie chuckled.

Marie-Claude, Hassim and Samia came out of the hotel. They stood on the sidewalk waiting for their car as Andie, Max and Eddie reached them.

Marie-Claude pulled Andie aside and kissed her on both cheeks in a firm embrace. "I will never forget you – you told me I was pregnant before I knew myself!"

"Well, not really - I asked," Andie demurred.

"That's an unimportant detail – you knew, that's why you asked. I will always think of you."

"Not when you're going through the painful part of birth, I hope."

Marie-Claude laughed, "You are a funny girl. You must visit us when we build our new house. We're taking Samia to her mother and father in Marseille, and then Hassim and I are going to find a property for our home by the sea."

"Where are you looking?" Eddie asked.

Hassim answered, "In Sète, do you know it? It's near Montpelier, also in Arles. It's on the other coast where the rich people don't go."

They all chuckled and Marie-Claude said, "Hassim needs to smell the salt air of the sea. And I need Hassim," she laughed as she said it and Hassim put his arm around her shoulder and pulled her to him.

"Are we going? Or what?" Samia called from the open door of the car.

They all laughed and said their good-byes.

After their limo pulled away, Andie started to open the hotel's front door when Fan was exiting.

"Oh, so sorry," Fan exclaimed. "I didn't see you – the sun was in my eyes. I apologize," he said earnestly.

Andie was pleasantly surprised at his friendly tone. "Oh, it's nothing Fan." She backed out to let him exit. Bella bustled out after him. When she saw Andie, she broke into a big smile. She was wearing bright red lipstick.

"I'm so glad I get to say good-bye to you. You were such fun!" She put her arms around Andie and gave her a bear hug, almost knocking her over.

Andie laughed, "And I enjoyed my time with you, Bella. And I love the lipstick shade you're wearing."

Bella gave her a big smile in return, and started to walk away with Fan. Then Bella turned around as the hotel door opened and brightly called out, "Are you coming?"

"Yes, dear. I was settling the bill."

"Carter!" Andie couldn't keep the surprise out of her voice.

"Come along, brother," Fan reached an arm out to Carter with a big smile. "We don't want to miss the boat." When Bella heard this, she laughed and Fan joined in.

Carter took a second or two to shake Andie's, Max's and Eddie's hands. Then he hurried off to join his new family, laughing with happiness.

Andie watched them drive away and sighed, "I just love happy endings."

Fin

ABOUT THE AUTHORS

Julie Stewart and Laurie Stewart are sisters who grew up in Los Angeles, forming a band and pursuing a career in the music business. Julie moved to Paris and Laurie to Nashville where they each continued music composition and performance. Over the ensuing decades, they each performed in Europe, and Julie carved out a career performing in Asia as well. Upon retirement, they teamed up again to write mystery books combining music and murder. Currently, Julie lives in Brazil, and Laurie lives in Upstate New York. They have completed four of their Andie and Max series of mystery books, and are presently working on the fifth installment.

Made in the USA
Monee, IL
21 December 2024

063eeeee-851b-42a7-b0fc-6c46dccc2df8R01